The Iron Vault

*A case of Sherlock Holmes
and
Professor Moriarty*

by

Stephen Lees

This book is the sequel to *The Iron Mausoleum* by
Stephen Lees ISBN Number 978-0-9571629-0-7

This paperback edition published in 2012 by SPEL
prodev@globalnet.co.uk

Copyright © Stephen Lees 2012
ISBN 978-0-9571629-1-4

A CIP catalogue record of this book is available from the British
Library.

Book and Cover design by SPEL

Typeset in Garamond

Printed and bound by CPI Antony Rowe, Chippenham and
Eastbourne, England

Stephen Lees has asserted his rights under the Copyright Design &
Patents Act 1988 to be identified as the author of this work.

The author acknowledges the kind permission obtained from the
Administrator of the Conan Doyle Copyrights to use some characters by
name, in addition to the permission from the Bloomsbury Publisher A
& C Black to reproduce some images from '*Visions of Architecture*' ISBN
978-1-4081-2881-7 by the same author.

Contents

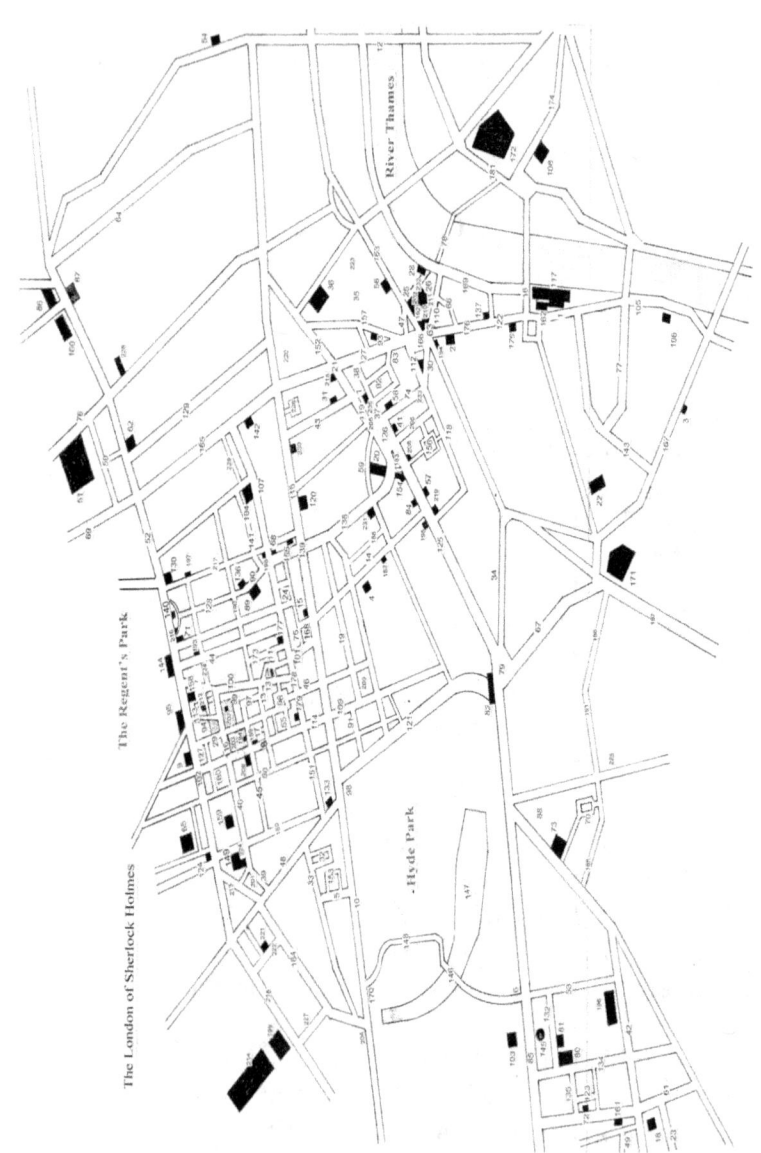

The London of Sherlock Holmes

The Regent's Park

River Thames

Hyde Park

Index of Place Names

156 St. James's Square
157 St. Martin's Lane
158 St. Marylebone Church
159 St. Mary's Church
160 St. Pancras Hotel
161 St. Stephen's Church
162 St. Stephen's Hall
163 Strand
164 Sussex Gardens
165 Tottenham Court Road
166 Trafalgar Square
167 Vauxhall Bridge Road
168 Vere Street
169 Victoria Embankment
170 Victoria Gate
171 Victoria Railway Station
172 Waterloo Railway Station
173 Welbeck Street
174 Westminster Bridge Road
175 Westminster Bridge Road Underground Station
176 Whitehall
177 Wigmore Hall
178 Wigmore Street
179 Wigmore Street Post Office at No.132
180 York Place
181 York Road

Names of places and streets appearing in The Iron Vault

182 Agnew's Gallery
183 Air Street
184 Barley Mow Public House
185 Beauchamp Place
186 Belgrave Place
187 Buckingham Palace Road
188 Burlington Street
189 Camden House
190 Cavendish Street
191 Chesham Place
192 Craven Passage
193 2 Devonshire Place.

Prologue

A ship of the White Star Line, believed to be the '*Titanic*', has been sunk in mid-Atlantic for a variety of reasons, chief amongst which is the concealment of forged artwork *en route* to a lucrative art exhibition at the World Columbian Exposition in Chicago.

Holmes has explained to Sir James Walter of the British Admiralty the role Moriarty played in the deliberate sinking of the so-called '*Titanic*'. Sir James implores Holmes to take up the case against Moriarty and bring him to justice for the part he played in the death of over 1,500 souls during that fateful sinking, and to recover the reputation of the British merchant marine.

Scotland Yard, too, is keen to exact justice on Moriarty, not a simple matter since Moriarty neither resides in England or within the Empire. Pinkerton agents in the United States are also anxious to interview him, as are the Jesuits.

There is also the question of the missing works of art, of great value, believed to have gone down with the '*Titanic*'. By inquiring into this mystery, Holmes and Watson are drawn into direct conflict with Robber Barons, Bankers, Rail Road Giants and Steel Titans in a rarefied world where art, finance and industrial power clash.

These encounters take place as the pair travel to the World's Columbian Exposition in Chicago, where they re-encounter the Oklahoma heiress, Katherine. Whilst there Holmes formulates a theory more startling in its implication than the deliberate sinking of the *'Titanic'* ship!

*This book is dedicated to the
Members of the Colony Room Club
without whom it would have been
completed earlier.*

221b Baker Street

Chapter 1

The Unexpected Visitor

It was neither warm nor cold, but typical of a late autumnal afternoon in London. Holmes had been out since early morning, for what purpose I could not say, since we have become distant since the dreadful affair of the sinking of the ill-fated RMS *'Titanic'*, or whatever the boat was called, with the loss of over fifteen hundred souls. Holmes has taken the failure to prevent this calamity very personally indeed, despite my attempts to disabuse him of this unwarranted admonishment. He has instead reverted back to his 7% solution and I feel disappointed at his relapse and blame myself for my inability to intervene more vigorously.

The afternoon wore on producing feelings of listlessness and inertia, making me unable to decide where to settle in our drawing room at 221b Baker Street or indeed, with what reading matter to occupy my mind. It was, therefore, with half-hearted interest that I began to read an article in the *Daily Telegraph* that caught my attention. It described a new musical work called the *'Planets Suite'* by a fellow called Gustav Holst, that is to be premiered at the St James' Hall in the Portland Road near Regent's Circus. In this work the composer explores the known universe, in particular the planets and their musical association with ancient classical gods. For example, the article informed me, Venus is the Bringer of

Peace, Mars of War, Uranus is the Magician, and so on and so forth. This fact about Uranus, for some unfathomable reason, lodged itself in my mind and I drifted off into a reverie.

It was, therefore, with pleasant anticipation that I welcomed, as I came to, what was a commotion on the staircase leading to our rooms on the first floor. Before I could rise from my armchair to draw back the *portière* door curtain and open the drawing room door onto the landing, it was flung open. A moment later, like a Man-of-War in full sail during a gale, in stepped Sir James Walter from the Admiralty with inordinate enthusiasm and delight, quite unlike his previous character and bearing. I responded in similar manner and we greeted each other as though long lost friends. Indeed, our previous encounters, brought about by the most *outré* of events, might possibly make us share a common experience of friendship that would last throughout the remainder of our lives. Who could not have been touched or moved by those events of a few months past?

"Watson, Doctor Watson how very good to see you again after – oh nearly a year now!"

"Sir James, I am equally delighted to see you. Please let me take your hat and coat and pray do sit down!"

"Shall I bring some cucumber sandwiches or would you prefer my fish-based 'Bloater Delights', Sir James?" inquired Mrs Hudson, our resident housekeeper. "After all," she continued, "you did not refuse them last time you were here!"

Sir James attempted to mumble a response to her, but his previous experience of Mrs Hudson's 'Bloater Delights' seared through his mind causing him momentary paralysis due to his panic.

"Thank you, Mrs Hudson, I can take it from here."

I tried to close the door of our drawing room on her, but

2

somehow her somewhat indelicate foot barred my doing so.

"Doctor Watson, Sir James specifically asked to see Sherlock Holmes, not you!"

"Yes, yes, yes, Mrs Hudson. Thank you."

This time, my not inconsiderable pressure upon the door, despite my thigh injury, a legacy of the third Sudanese Fiasco whilst serving as surgeon in the army, proved successful and, turning around to Sir James, I asked if he would like a drink in place of Mrs Hudson's 'Bloater Delights'?

"You know my feelings about drink, Watson – consider the consequences. Imagine the damage to your brain, the cost and the elation, only to be followed by the despondency and confusion. The rash promises made whilst under its influence, the bravado and the idiotic behaviour. What drives a man to this destructive habit? However, if the option is either those 'Bloater Delights' or alcohol, then I will risk permanent brain damage by joining you in what looks like a recklessly large whisky and a dash of aërated water?"

"Sir James, trouble at the Admiralty?"

"Well rather, but I would prefer to wait until Holmes is present before commencing my *interesting narrative*, as you say Doctor."

"Holmes has gone out and it may be some time before he returns, if indeed he does return," I ventured.

"I am assured by his wire that he will be joining us here in these very rooms this late afternoon."

"You know Doctor Watson, I still have difficulty quite believing the sequence of events that led to the sinking of the *'Titanic'*, sorry, *'Olympic'*. It is indicative of the incredibility of those astonishing facts, unbelievable as they are, and which the public still refer to after eleven months as the sinking of the *'Titanic'* and not the *'Olympic'!"

"It is a very difficult concept to grasp that such a heinous crime, with its attendant callous disregard for human life, could be perpetrated all for the sake of Professor Moriarty's personal emolument."

"I suppose if we examine the facts in sequence we can begin to discern a rationale to explain clearly a fact that did occur, however dreadful. Consider: the north Atlantic immigration trade route between Europe and America is a lucrative business attracting the White Star Line owned by Mr JP Morgan, the wealthy American merchant banker. The White Star Line commissioned three massive ocean liners the *'Olympic'*, *'Titanic'* and *'Majestic'*, each capable of carrying twenty-two hundred persons, to serve this trade," I said.

"The first of these three ships," offered Sir James, "the *'Olympic'* is launched but, from the beginning, she is a failure, progressing from one collision to another because of the difficulty in manoeuvring and steering her due to her size and draft. She becomes a wreck and a liability, incapable of generating the profits she was designed to."

"I agree with and well-remember the words of Katherine from Eureka Springs, near the Oklahoma Territory, when she visited us here. She realised that something was wrong with the RMS *'Olympic'* ship that conveyed her to England. Now, what was it exactly that did she say?" I mused, getting up and referring to Holmes's green-covered commonplace notebook wherein he recorded all his clients' relevant statements.

"Ah, here it is: 'Apart from the fact the ship could not even get out of New York harbour without crashing into other ships, I was amazed it got through the Atlantic Ocean during the equinoctial gales without sinking! The ship had a pronounced list and its basic metal structure was warped, out of alignment, bent, and the boat creaked like mad. It was literally falling apart, with me in it! Throughout the journey things did not work. Taps failed to deliver water. The ship seemed to be powerless, at times almost drifting in the water.

4

The crew acted as if they did not give a damn, and it was common talk among them that the ship was useful only as an 'Iron Mausoleum'. On that '*Olympic*' boat, the over-riding sentiment was that of riding a wreck on its last voyage to the scrap yard.'

"The '*Olympic*' was effectively a floating wreck!" I concluded.

"Well yes, Watson, far from making a profit, the '*Olympic*' was costing the White Star Line vast amounts in lost revenue and in the cost of repairs. How Mr JP Morgan must have wished he could just lose the damaged vessel. What was it he reputedly said to one of his directors? 'Sink it in the middle of the Atlantic!' That basic wish must have filtered back to Professor Moriarty and with some plausibility. Remember, ships have been sunk at sea deliberately since time immemorial," replied Sir James.

"I recall that the fiancé of Katherine from Eureka Springs, who worked for the JP Morgan Bank, was done away with because he knew something of the conspiracy. So was your Cadogan Smith who worked at the Admiralty Building here in London," I responded.

We both paused to consider the incredibility of these facts, still shocking even after several months had elapsed, whilst I replenished our drinks.

"The second ship to be launched was the '*Titanic*'," Sir James continued, "and it was present in the Thompson Graving Dock being fitted out at the very same time as the damaged '*Olympic*' was also there to be repaired. Professor Moriarty with his intellectual prowess, aided by the colossal wealth of Morgan, took advantage of that situation. Both ships were identical in construction and shape and were often mistaken for one another, even by their owners. It was a simple matter to exchange the bronze name-plates, plus a few other minor details, and substitute one ship with the other."

"What sailed out from Liverpool into the bleak Atlantic

Ocean on that fateful day was the *'Olympic'* disguised as the *'Titanic'*!" I interposed.

"Moriarty had previously gone through the motions of arranging an exhibition of English and European paintings to be exhibited at the World's Columbian Exposition, to be held in Chicago, under the guise of promoting this art to wealthy Americans. He had no intention of sending the original paintings to America, but instead, with the help of an artist named Lyon, gathered around him a group of forgers led by an Arthur Staunton, to make faked copies of the original paintings.

"Moriarty kept the originals and the fake paintings were placed, with great publicity, on board the *'Olympic'* masquerading as the *'Titanic'*. The fake paintings were to go to America, accompanied by the artists who had created the genuine works and who, upon arrival in Chicago, were to promote and sell them. It was also imperative that those paintings did not reach the exhibition at the World's Exposition, where the fact they were fakes would be discovered and revealed by experts or by the very artists responsible for the originals. Likewise, the faked paintings could never be returned to their owners because of the risk of their being detected as counterfeits, so they had to be seen to be loaded onto the *'Titanic'*. Therefore the *'Olympic'*, disguised as the *'Titanic'*, had to be seen, in full public gaze, to sink without trace! Indeed, Moriarty ensured that the artists on board accompanying their *faked* paintings did not make it into the lifeboats, and so they perished in the freezing waters of the north Atlantic," I said.

"It is astounding, is it not, that Moriarty went to these inordinate lengths and killed all those artists in order that his secret would be preserved, by persuading the public that the original paintings were lost forever in the cargo hold of the stricken *'Titanic'*," commented Sir James.

"Yes, Sir James," I said, "but are we not forgetting the

secret hoard of art we discovered in Harley Street after Lyon was done in, as Holmes and I conjectured, because he had deceived Moriarty."

"How did he manage to do that?" asked Sir James.

"Quite simply, Moriarty thought he possessed the original paintings, either for his personal enjoyment or, to be forwarded on to a third person or buyer. In fact, however, the deceitful Lyon secretly had a second set of fakes made up by another group of forgers led by John Clay, which he substituted for those earmarked for Moriarty. Clearly Moriarty found out about his substituted collection of fakes and revenged himself upon Lyon, who had betrayed him. We are, after all Sir James, talking about a substantial number of works of art here and their market value."

"Worth sinking a ship for?"

"Well yes, at least so it would seem to Moriarty and his cohorts."

"Yes! Think of it. This is where Moriarty's genius came into its own. He has, with Morgan's connivance, achieved the sinking of the damaged ship '*Olympic*', which we know was masquerading as the '*Titanic*'. Sunk a vast collection of faked artwork, which now lies beyond examination at the bottom of the Atlantic. Drowned the artists who created that art work, and, in so doing, as collateral to that act, brought about the disintegration of the Colony Room Club in Soho. For now its members are dispersed to the four zephyrs, including those that ride the gales that blast their way to heaven!" I replied.

"But," said Sir James, "he has failed to acquire the original paintings that are hidden, as you say, in Harley Street; how is that?"

"Ah, you will have to ask Holmes that question. As far as I know, it was Lyon who, with his venal mind, saw a flawed opportunity to enrich himself at Moriarty's expense, but paid the price for that failed adventure. It is, however, a betting certainty that Moriarty knows not of the whereabouts of that cache of paintings, for all his trouble."

"However, Watson, we have to apprehend this Moriarty, and I am informed that he has abandoned his house at Well Road, Hampstead and repaired to Meiringen near the Reichenbach Falls, in Switzerland, a favourite retreat of his. I was speaking with the Commissioner at Scotland Yard yesterday and he does not forget. I believe he is in regular contact with the Pinkerton Agency in America, and they are very anxious to apprehend Moriarty. So are we, preferably before the Pinkerton agents do; after all, he is a British subject and must be prosecuted here in England for his heinous crimes. Hence my wish to consult your friend Sherlock Holmes and exact justice on this Moriarty!" So said Sir James delivering his intention upon the subject.

"You know Sir James we were always curious about your living at Hans Place in Knightsbridge, do tell me..."

However, that question was to remain unfinished, for at that very instant we heard, or rather felt, our main door onto Baker Street, the one with 221b impressed upon it, slam, as was Holmes' wont to do when returning to these chambers. This was his way of alerting Mrs Hudson as to his immediate needs, be they for breakfast in the afternoon or a four-course meal with full-bodied red Burgundy wine for breakfast, or just the latest newspaper to be obtained. I heard him thank Mrs Hudson as he made his way to our drawing room door. Sir James stood up in anticipation and deep trepidation.

Chapter 2

The Re-Statement of the Case

Holmes opened the door and entered our drawing room carefully drawing back the *portière* door curtain to keep out the draft and the conversation in.

"I see you have managed to persuade Sir James to indulge in your life-destroying habit, Watson! Have I not advised you repeatedly to consider the consequences? Imagine the damage to your brain, the cost and the elation, only to be followed by the despondency and confusion. The rash promises made whilst under its influence, the bravado and your idiotic behaviour?"

"What?" I spluttered

"However," continued Holmes, "it would be pointless in my tolerating both of you in your present state. Accordingly, I shall join you in order that your ramblings might make some kind of sense to me. There is, however, another reason I shall have this whisky, thank you Watson, which is because the mere fact Sir James is here tells me something untoward has happened. What has made Sir James leave the confines of the Admiralty to join us here at Baker Street? I suspect strongly, that it is not for our conviviality: I surmise, therefore, that it has to do with Moriarty?"

When we had all settled down with our drinks and cigars, Sir James started in.

"Mr Holmes," he said, "you are indeed perceptive with regard to Moriarty, and the British Government is grateful for your sterling work in unravelling the mystery of Cadogan West's death, together with that of the subsequent terrifying events surrounding the sinking of the '*Titanic*', sorry '*Olympic*'. However, Parliament is clamouring for this Moriarty to be brought to justice, preferably in an British court of law."

"Well surely that is a matter for the Home Secretary and Scotland Yard, is it not? Hardly a matter for the Admiralty?" remarked Holmes.

"I agree, but the First Lord of the Treasury,* in conjunction with your brother Mycroft, the Permanent Secretary to the Cabinet and *de facto* head of the Government, has insisted that I continue to act for them in this matter of appealing to you. The facts of the case, as you know and as Doctor Watson and I discussed just prior to your return, are these. Moriarty essentially has used his extensive criminal organisation to execute an outrageous crime. That atrocity resulting in the loss of fifteen hundred souls was due to the deliberate sinking of a capital boat of the line. Not only has he brought the British merchant marine into disrepute, but also the nation's cultural establishments, now tainted with the fraud that was perpetrated on works of art for which they were responsible. He has poisoned an Admiralty clerk at Charing Cross and a crook in Harley Street, to say nothing of what he has done to the Jesuit College of St George. Moriarty must be stopped and apprehended, and you are the only person in England equal to the challenge, Mr Holmes," pleaded Sir James.

Holmes looked impassive, an expression alas more natural to his facial features of late, due to the inner turmoil in his mind.

"I still say it is a matter for Scotland Yard as they too have access to the resources of the British Government. I have no more power or authority to go up to Moriarty and arrest him than Mrs Hudson our housekeeper has."

And with that remark Holmes got up, bade Sir James good bye and walked out of our drawing room to retire to his own chamber.

Sir James looked at me for some support, which I was unable to lend. At length, and with an air of resignation, Sir James gathered up his coat, top hat and cane and, having thanked me for my hospitality, descended the staircase to Baker Street with an air of dejection.

I looked out of our bay window and watched Sir James clamber into his Barouche carriage, drawn by a four-in-hand driven by a liveried coachman, and clatter off down a busy Baker Street. I then raised my eyes to the ominous and deeply reddening skies.

Later Holmes reëntered our drawing room and I said without hesitation and with deliberate aspersion in my voice.

"Why will you not take the case on? It might snap you out of this lethargy that has affected you these last few months past. And what of that remark by Sir James stating that you are the only man in England, acting in concert with the British Government, to create an organisation powerful enough to deal with Moriarty's criminal organisation and his terrifying, murderous acts? What also is to become of the cache of art we discovered in that false mezzanine floor in the house on the junction of Harley Street and the Marylebone Road?"

"What of it?"

"I beg your pardon Holmes, but what do you mean, 'what of it?'"

"You will recall Watson, that we, or rather I, was retained by Sir James to unravel the mystery regarding the death of Cadogan West, whose body was found in a railway carriage at Charing Cross Station. There was never an instruction or request implied or implicit to hunt for stolen works of art. Our discovering that art work was purely fortuitous, nothing more."

"But Holmes, you cannot just ignore its existence. That art work has been amassed by means of fraud, larceny and a well-organised criminal conspiracy. Presumably some innocent party is bereft of their ownership in those paintings."

"As usual, Watson, you see and hear all that I do, but fail to pick up the singular points from the first-hand statements of the various witnesses we have talked with. Typically, your failing to appreciate the implication of what the Principal of St George's Jesuit College had to say when we met with him in the Diogenes Club. Instead of paying attention to his narrative, you spent your time scribbling incoherent notes as a basis for your emotional and defective account to be published later as a definitive interpretation of actual facts, contained as they are in your 'stories'!"

"Now listen hear Holmes, let me remind you of a time not so long..."

"Watson, if you had paid attention, you would have realised that yes, Moriarty has perpetrated a fraud upon various bodies and individuals in taking their art work, and then claiming it was lost forever when the ill-fated 'Titanic' sank. However, in the case of the Jesuits, he deliberately returned fakes to the College, knowing what the repercussions would be. What did the Principal say?" said Holmes, referring to his green commonplace book wherein he wrote down relevant notes and statements. "Ah, here we are the Principal said the following:

"'...later that evening, I returned to the gallery with a powerful lamp fuelled by acetylene gas, and examined the damaged painting that had been returned by Moriarty. It was not the damage that had caught my attention earlier in the day, but something else and, to my horror my suspicion was confirmed. That particular painting is at least thirty-five years old. Yet when I put my fingers onto the damaged area on the canvass I expected the paint finish to be dry and brittle, instead it was still damp and, as I ran my finger along the short gash, wet paint was deposited on it. The painting was wet, Holmes, wet! I went to the next painting and discovered that by pushing gently onto an area of thick daubs of paint, it gave way, forming a little round indentation. The paint should be dry and hard as adamantine chain, not spongy and soft.

"Needless to say, Mr Holmes, I spent the entire evening examining those paintings within my reach, and each one of them was fake! Our collection is no more than a collection of canvas and oil paint, more fit for the furnaces that heat the College than for display. The paintings are not insured. What is now a matter of desperation is the fact that the paintings are often used, as collateral to secure bank loans should funds be required. The College is potentially bankrupt and I am powerless to prevent this calamity, since I can neither conceal the fraud nor expose it!"

"I have given up my soul on this matter and will not get involved. Good evening, Watson."

I sat back in my chair, cigar in one hand and whisky in the other, thinking how this state of inaction had now been with us for nearly a year. The encounter and attendant rudeness I had just endured were not the exception but rather the rule and becoming progressively intolerable. Holmes was in a chronic state of depression and in a continual and insufferable brown study from which there seemed no escape. Even the most trivial of mysteries could not engage his undoubtedly superior and incisive intellect. I knew from my days of serving with the British army as a surgeon that this state of mind is at best corrosive of the spirit and at worst lethal to life. Whilst dwelling on these thoughts I became aware that, even though it was only mid-evening, there was a omnipresent stillness inside our rooms and also outside. I decided to retire to my room, draw the curtains and read Aesop's fable *The Nightingale and the Rose*.**

Whilst pondering this short story, I wondered whether it might be worthwhile getting that Sigmund Freud, the eminent psychoanalyst and commentator on hysteria, to examine Holmes, who was clearly a walking combination of various phobias and complexes. I recall his continued horror of the word, figure or sound of 'five' as a direct result of his failing to protect his client's life in the outlandish case of the 'Five Orange Pips'. Without being Freud, even I was able to determine that a terrible re-action would come upon him where failure involving a death was an integral result of any of his cases.

That is it! I determined, whether Holmes agrees or not, to prevail upon Freud to visit us here in our rooms. Compensation will be plentiful enough for his time, especially since Sir James and the British Treasury would be picking up the bill for his fees. About time the Admiralty paid Holmes for his mental torment. After all, I reasoned, if Freud could deal successfully with the composer Gustav Mahler, and return him to normality by relieving him of his chronic condition, there might be a chance, albeit slender, that he could do the same for Holmes. I then fell into a fitful sleep, but not before realising I had spilled my whisky onto the pillow.

The following morning I entered our breakfast room and pulled impatiently on our bell rope to summon my coffee and rashers of Harrod's bacon. From experience, I did not expect to see Holmes there as he had got into the habit of not rising until at least late morning. I had, during my ablutions, reminded myself sternly that I would seek Freud's assistance in dealing with Holmes' malaise and depression. Indeed, I thought, irrespective of Freud's falling in with my plan, it would be worthwhile persuading him, with the aid of my army service revolver to his head, to treat Holmes, just to reverse the state of Holmes' insufferable attitude towards Mrs

Hudson, her housemaids and, not least, towards me. I then realised to my horror that being insufferable was not the unique domain of Holmes. An oppressive fog had descended upon the Metropolis yet again, heralded by the stillness already evident yesterday evening. My spirits sank to a level almost probably lower than that of Holmes'.

* Prime Minister
** No, it was by Oscar Wilde.

Chapter 3

The Release from the Shadow

I knew from common knowledge that Professor Sigmund Freud resided in the Doctors' Quarter located not far from Baker Street in the Cavendish Square district of Marylebone, the Borough in which Holmes and I reside. A search in my Medical Almanac informed me that indeed Freud lives at No. 2 Devonshire Place. I resolved to go around there immediately after breakfast, when I had steeled myself to enter that clammy and acrid fog.

Descending our staircase to street level, I felt the claustrophobic effects of the fog affecting me immediately and merely opening the door onto Baker Street reënforced this feeling. I stepped out onto the shiny York flagstones, on which the fog had condensed, making them slippery. Turning left from the corner of Dorset Street, I headed north to Crawford Street, where I decided to chance crossing over Baker Street. Before doing so I stopped and listened for any audible sound of a vehicle coming toward me. I detected none, so started to walk across the road. Then suddenly, a green tender lamp came thundering towards me, causing me to momentarily panic as I stepped backwards to safety. The lamp heralded a huge pantechnicon carrying furniture that went lumbering by and, as it did so, caused the fog to swirl around into vortices. Presently I did gain the eastern aspect of Baker Street despite the thick fog.

Gathering my wits from that near encounter with the furniture wagon not only made me nervous but served to remind me of the perils that fog can afford. I looked up to make sure that I was on the southern side of Paddington Street. This was so, and I continued past Sherlock Mews and over Chilton Street and, a few feet later, came to a wall topped with cast iron railings, behind which I knew to be Marylebone burial grounds. I seemed to recall then that the fog of last year was denser in these grounds than elsewhere. In particular, the concentration of the fog had the effect of deadening sound and inducing feelings of isolation with attendant claustrophobia. Both sensations were now combining rapidly, making me more anxious almost by the minute. As a doctor, I knew such feelings were an irrational re-action caused by the effects of fog, and told myself so.

I remembered this spot last year and the feeling of near panic that had gripped my heart, even in the presence of Holmes, who was impervious to such emotion. No wonder people lose their tenuous grip on reality and considered for a moment whether I too might consult Freud about this condition. I gripped one of the railings to steady myself and, in doing so, looked behind it into the gloomy precinct of the Marylebone burial grounds, complete with Mausoleum. By degrees I could just make out a monument or headstone and realised that this was, of course, the old churchyard for the St Marylebone Church. An eerie silence pervaded the stillness of the fog that partially shrouded the tombs, no wonder the yellow fog was stilled and heavier, with a pungent acridity.

I continued, walking nervously, but with care along the pavement next to the railings for reference if nothing more. Without concentrating properly, I instinctively crossed Paddington Street and turned left into Luxborough Street and then into Nottingham Street. I knew then that I had made a

Marylebone Mausoleum

wrong turning and was unsure as to my bearings. I walked along the north side of Nottingham Street and stopped to get a bearing. I looked up at an odd looking house, No. 7a. For some reason this low, three-story house connected to larger buildings looked like an afterthought in its construction. Despite its peculiar leaded mansard attic roof, punctuated by three arched windows, it still had a premonitory look about it, as though shielding a secret.

The fact that I could hear forced laughter emanating from within the house, but seemingly more manic than jovial, made me feel extremely nervous. Feeling uncomfortable in the vicinity of that house, I continued groping my way along the pavement. Several minutes later, having negotiated my way out of Nottingham Street with relief and regained my bearings, I arrived intact at Marylebone High Street and turned right. Though the street's name indicates its role in the Borough it appeared almost empty with only a few brave souls scuttling by, their hunched shoulders giving an impression of grim deformity. Continuing my quest, I turned left into West Devonshire Street and headed east for two or three blocks, past the Public House* with no name and onward to my destination at Devonshire Place.

No. 2 Devonshire Place is typical of those Georgian town houses of which the majority of the streets in Marylebone are made. Flat-fronted and often with a metal-railed balcony addressing the *piano nobile* of the first floor, they represent the epitome of respectability and solidity in all the matters one associates with stability and affluence. I suppose these visible characteristics of the buildings would be an essential requirement for a practitioner, such as Freud, in establishing his consulting rooms. Especially when he might have to deal, on an all too regular basis, with the hysterical, the confirmed hypochondriac and indeed the generally mentally deranged.

Undeterred by these personality traits, possibly applicable to me, I approached Freud's black-painted, cruciform-panelled, double-leaf front door, which was completed by a highly polished brass knocker and matching handle. I pulled at the adjacent bell wire and a faint tinkle announced my presence. Presently the hall light shone through the semicircular glass window above the door, upon which was inscribed the name of the house, as being 'Conan... Suddenly, the door was opened and a button pageboy beckoned me into the hallway and then led the way up a broad red-carpeted staircase to the *piano nobile* in which Professor Freud held his clinic, consulting on nervous diseases.

I was shown into the study of the great psychoanalyst and commentator on the new fashion of hysteria.

"Lie down on that *chaise-longue* and make yourself comfortable," he instructed, whilst referring to a sheaf of papers with his back to me.

"Well I am not long risen from my bed and do not really feel tired," I replied.

"Please do as I have advised, it is part of your way forward. Please now, how bad are you feeling?"

Somewhat taken aback by this over-familiarity and intrusive line of inquiry into *my* personal life, I was at a loss to reply, but could only conclude that this was perhaps how one greets a person in Vienna, since it is from that great city that Sigmund Freud emanates.

"Not bad actually," I said, with some degree of aspersion in my reply.

"Really? When now did you begin to dislike your father?" continued Freud

"I am not certain as to the correct form of answer, or from whence the dislike came, but he passed away some fifteen years ago."

"Interesting. When did you begin to harbour feelings of revenge towards your mother?"

"I beg your pardon, whom do you think you are addressing?" I replied, with all the feelings of outrage at my command to summon, whilst rising reluctantly from the comfortable *chaise-longue*.

"You really must learn to control your emotional outbursts and consider the situation from the perspective of other persons and not your own selfish ego-centric view," replied Freud.

"Now look here, I came here to elicit your help, not to be insulted!"

"People that come here invariably wish me to help them, otherwise their journey would be futile. Is your journey futile, or are you willing to be positive? Professor Freud inquired.

"Well," I replied, "feelings of inadequacy often attend my thoughts but inevitably I rise above them."

"You do surprise me, for I thought you were a manic-depressive with what I term a 'Bi-Polar Syndrome', causing you to experience extreme mood swings, ranging from the respectful and attentive to the downright rude and aggressive."

Bi-Polar? This could very well have described Holmes' condition: mood swings, rude and aggressive, I thought.

"I am not perfect, but would hardly describe myself in that way…"

"I am describing you in that way, it is what I am paid to do," interrupted Freud, finally turning around to face me.

"You! Who are you?"

"My name is Doctor John Watson of Baker Street and I have come to ask you to consult with a colleague of mine."

Freud waved me into a comfortable armchair facing his desk into which I sank quite literally, as I could barely see over the top of his desk.

"Doctor Wilson, I think you have made a mistake. I was expecting a psychotic patient of mine, a new patient, a woman called Rayment who suffers increasingly from Bi-Polar Syndrome"

I noted, but resisted the urge to re-act to the incorrect pronunciation of my surname, and also disregarded Freud's blatant attempt to impute failure in me for *his* mistake. Was I not shown into his study by the button pageboy and had I not merely complied with Freud's request to make myself comfortable on the *chaise-longue* whilst answering his inquiries, I asked myself? I now began to harbour thoughts that, like Moriarty, Freud too suffers from monomania, given his propensity for denial, total denial, for his failure – or was I confusing this personality trait with Bi-Polar Syndrome?

"If the patient you are expecting is a psychotic woman, then why did you fail to detect in my voice that I am clearly a man?"

"Because the neurotic woman Rayment, in her feeble endeavours to dominate, acts and speaks like a man, which is symptomatic of her chronic state of Bi-Polar Syndrome.

Not allowing Freud any more opportunities for insults at my expense, I started in.

"Now look here, as I have said before, my name is Doctor John Wilson, sorry I mean Watson, and I am a colleague of Sherlock Holmes, the famous consulting detective. You might possibly have heard of him?"

"Consulting what?" Freud asked.

"He is a consulting detective and will, upon request by a client, investigate singular circumstances and offer solutions to those who are in desperate search of an answer."

I knew this definition to be meaningless even whilst speaking it. Instead, I reverted to an old stand-by.

"Does the name Sherlock Holmes mean nothing to you?" I demanded.

"No, Doctor, it does not. Now as I have intimated before, a psychotic patient of mine, a woman called Rayment, is expected and takes priority over your friend's offer to do detective work for me, since I am not in need of his services as I have no one who needs detecting. Good day Doctor."

And with that Parthian shot, Freud returned to his sheaf of papers whilst pulling at the bell rope for the pageboy to escort me off the premises.

Once again I found myself in Devonshire Place and wished to God I had brought my service revolver with me and coerced that arrogant Freud to attend at gunpoint Holmes' predicament. Ludicrous, I eventually reasoned, but still had to deal with Holmes' mental condition, including his reluctance to take up the case. Whilst pondering this dilemma I saw the green tender lamp of a Hackney carriage approaching me from out of the fog.

"221b Baker Street!"

"Oh, whereabouts is that, Guv?"

"Are you telling me you do not know where 221b Baker Street is?"

"Well, in this fog, from 'ere I do not."

"Oh, very well then," I said, "whip up your horse and have it face West in that direction, down West Devonshire Street, turn left into Marylebone High Street and sharp right into Paddington Street."

To my surprise, the cab driver complied and we clattered along these streets. I then told the driver to turn left into Kendrick Place and continue until we reached the Barley Mow Public House on the corner of Dorset Street, then turn right. We then cantered up to the junction with Baker Street, immediately next to Camden House, from which the murderous Colonel Moran, with an air rifle, tried to shoot Holmes as he sat in our drawing room opposite, on the north-western side of the junction above a Bank

"Cor Guv, I thought 221b Baker Street was farther up Baker Street, almost opposite the Regent's Park!"

"Everybody makes that basic mistake. But, no my good man, 221b Baker Street is here, as you can see by the street number on our door."

"It looks like a Bank, what with that red-brick work and Portland stone dressing, not to mention the fancy detailed semi-circular stone pediment to the front door Guv."

"Very observant of you in recognising it as being a bank, the National Provincial Bank in fact, but the upper floors, including mine on the first floor, are residential chambers."

"Well I am blessed, Guv, you learn something everyday and that will be five shillings," he said holding out his grubby hand.

"Five shillings!" I exclaimed. "And what of the geography lesson I have just taught you?"

"Makes no difference to me. I would have got you here all the same even if it meant going around the back doubles."

"Yes, but it would have taken you longer, without knowing the direct and *correct* route," I emphasised.

Weary of this conversation, I handed the carriage driver

five shillings in as much small change as I could count confidently without inadvertently over-paying him. I then began walking away, hoping the fog would shroud me in its embrace, leaving the cab driver unsure as to his gain or loss!

Before going home across the road, I went into a Book-maker's agent hard by to collect some winnings due to me from a race held yesterday at Epsom.

On my arrival home, I was vaguely aware of voices coming down from our rooms on the first floor. I recognised Mrs Hudson's as being the dominant one in what sounded like an argument. I became curious as I opened the drawing room door from the landing and saw Mrs Hudson berating Holmes who looked flushed with anger.

"You cannot just hang around here feeling sorry for yourself and acting like a prima donna. Watson does that well enough," she said, oblivious to my presence – I hoped.

"There has been a great heinous and horrendous crime perpetrated on society, resulting in mass murder and God knows what else we are not privy to. Sir James is right, absolutely right, in asking for your help. Holmes, given those talents you are for ever boasting about… …synthesising the solution via deductive reasoning as opposed to inductive reasoning… …systematic reasoning… …whatever remains must be the truth… and analysing the solution retrogressively from consequences to principles…whatever that means …do you not think that you should act?"

Holmes simply looked impassively at the woman admonishing him.

"Well, why do you not apply those party tricks of yours and snap out of this over-indulgent idiocy, Holmes, and try to restore reassurance to a society that is being sorely tried and which yearns for answers and security from that degenerate maniac, Moriarty.

I considered intervening to protect Holmes from Mrs

Hudson's onslaught on his shattered constitution, but felt that to do so would be futile and so thought better of it. Besides, she might well easily divert her attack from Holmes onto me. She looked at me, not in the least bit surprised at my being here!

"There are widows, widowers, orphans and frightened people, all of whom want justice and an end to this madness and uncertainty wrought by a maniac on the loose. You, Holmes, have those God-given powers to think and to apply solutions to finding answers. Should you need my help, you only have to ask me. Do not act the proud misogynist I know you to be. I can forgive you for that but not for inaction where I *know* you ought to be active. Am I right, Doctor?"

"Er, yes," I agreed hesitantly.

This berating went on for some time and, with our combined efforts, I in the role of the soft, affectionate adversary and Hudson in the role of the opposite, we began to break down Holmes' resolve. Whether it was Holmes' realising his responsibility to society, or his repressed but deep fear of Mrs Hudson, I could not tell, but suspect it was the latter. By now even the housemaids had appeared, without invitation, in our drawing room, as had indeed Billy our pageboy, all of whom contributed to a moral pressure on Holmes to act.

By degrees a change came over his facial expression that reflected his inner turmoil.

"No buts, Holmes, just do it," boomed out Mrs Hudson, who by now, I think, had become so exasperated with Holmes' intransigence, that she was looking around the room for a broomstick or other weapon to deploy on him. I think Holmes realised this and a smirk began to play around his lips. I knew then that we had got him back from the brink of the precipice and, in so doing, released him from the grip of the shadow of the '*Titanic*'.

We had!

Later, I made the mistake of telling Mrs Hudson of my experience at Freud's, and her reply was as refreshing as it was blunt.

"Well Doctor, what do you expect from a person who spends all of his time in the company of blabbering lunatics? It can only be expected that a man who deals exclusively with the hyper-loquacious mental wreck is perforce going to have a somewhat warped view of humanity in general, and a jaded view of you in particular, in his endeavour to conceal his own innate inadequacies!"

* The Public House is called '1888', the year in which Gustav Mahler composed his D minor Symphony – called "The Titan" - an ancient classical god from whom the *'Titanic'* boat derived its name.

Chapter 4

The Sealed Chamber

Later in the day, when the excitement had dissipated, Billy the pageboy heralded the arrival of Stanley Hopkins, the Scotland Yard inspector who had been active in the earlier case when we had arrested Peterson, the Admiralty commissionaire, for his involvement in the death of Cadogan West.

"Good of you to come, Inspector. You of course remember my good friend and colleague Doctor Watson."

"I do indeed," said the Inspector shaking our hands, "I got your telegram and hurried around here at my earliest. Am I to understand that we are going for that Moriarty? Better late than never is what I say! Oh well, just a small whisky. Thank you."

"Inspector, we have to bring you into our confidence and explain some facts that were not expressed at our last meeting in this room some eleven months ago. They concern a house in Harley Street, a very singular house in Harley Street. You might remember a fellow, an artist called Lyon, who was done away with in his rooms there, almost certainly by a henchman of Moriarty's.

"I do remember the case being reported by the local police inspector as one of natural death," said Hopkins.

Holmes continued: "It was a revenge murder, designed to

keep Moriarty's henchmen and members of his criminal gang very much in check, and to impose strict obedience with no deviation as to loyalty. I believe that Lyon was done in because he had secreted the original paintings somehow during the process of copying the originals, and had created not one fake, but two of each. One copy to be shipped, surrounded by publicity, on the '*Titanic*' to New York, and hence onward to the World's Columbian Exposition in Chicago, and the second to Moriarty. The paintings, of course, never reached New York nor indeed did the artists accompanying their works of art."

"We believe that Lyon replaced the originals with fakes that *he* had commissioned unbeknownst to Moriarty, who was given fake paintings, whilst Lyon kept the originals for himself. I found them in his house in Harley Street, hidden in a false mezzanine floor," I said triumphantly, with the aura of someone with something of importance to impart.

I noticed that Hopkins was slightly put out by this omission of evidence, but also that he could see an opportunity for his being credited as the official who would discover this hidden hoard of art treasure.

"I propose, Hopkins, that we obtain warrants to visit the house and secure the art work."

"That is easily done. I will telegraph Scotland Yard with the request."

"Please do so, and have them bring along a substantial and securely covered pantechnicon to Harley Street in order to remove the art to a safe place," said Holmes.

In the meantime, I pulled at the bell rope to summon the pageboy to deliver Hopkins' telegraph to the Sub-Telegraph Office in Wigmore Street, in addition to the one Holmes had scribbled to Sir James at the Admiralty.

"In the intervening time, Hopkins," Holmes said, "let us do justice to that York ham on the sideboard and avail ourselves of Watson's carving skill, while I open these excellent bottles of full-bodied Beaune red Burgundy wine."

We did indeed do justice to the York ham and even more so to the bottles of wine, with which we acquitted ourselves with some pride. Later, having donned our overcoats, we headed out to visit the house in Harley Street. Our walk along the Marylebone Road was uneventful, as it seemed most of the citizens of the Metropolis had elected to stay indoors to avoid the suffocating effects of this particularly acrid fog. It had descended upon us with a vengeance and, in so doing, exacerbated the condition of those with symptoms of respiratory problems. Alongside us in the carriageway continued the ghostly procession of green carriage lanterns lumbering towards us as red lanterns retreated away from us, into the vortices of swirling fog. Eventually we reached No. 2 Harley Street on the junction of the Marylebone Road and, whilst Holmes knocked on the front door, I stood back to look at the building and remind myself of its peculiarity.

The ground floor had two entrances, both comprising tall oak double doors set in frames of stone with intricately decorated corbels supporting entablatures above each one. The design of the doorframes was based on ancient Greek in style. They had peculiar design details on them, especially on the upper sections; above each door the relief panels were of a later fashion and not consistent with the overall style of the building. In between these doors was a large stone-framed window reveal, forming a shallow arch on top of which was inserted, for decoration only, a prominent *voussoir* block forming a keystone. Into this shallow, elliptical, arched reveal was inserted a glazed panel, at least twelve feet in height and seven in width, immediately above a basement area opening in the footpath surrounded by a simple, cross-braced, patterned metal fence.

The building was of indeterminate architectural design, but

reflected a combination of pseudo-Classical Greek and Roman motifs and Renaissance styles. It was clearly designed to reflect the success of the wealthy patron, who had caused the structure to be created, resembling more a prosperous merchant's house than an artist's dwelling.

Even now, however, the building did not look quite right so, in order to gain a better view of it, I stepped back into the carriageway in Harley Street. I did this at considerable risk to my person, for traffic was still extant and lumbering along only feet away.

I reëxamined the building's façades to remind myself of the architectural detail that had first caught my attention. Immediately above the ground-floor window frame arch where the keystone is fitted was a protuberance of stone resembling a balcony three feet high and jutting out by one foot. This regular undecorated projection girdled the building, creating an overhanging plinth upon which the rest of the upper building looked as if it had been constructed.

At last the front door opened revealing Mrs Bernstone, the housekeeper at No. 2 Harley Street, who was, if anything, looking younger than when last I saw her. Then she had appeared almost frail and haggard, probably due to the unexpected death of her master, Lyon. Now, she looked genuinely pleased to see me, though not Holmes, for whom she still maintained a mild but effective form of antagonism.

"Doctor Watson, what a nice surprise, and I see you are still with that detecting fellow, whatever. How are your patients, is he one of them?"

I explained the nature of our visit as being a police matter, and that we would need access to Lyon's rooms to remove some trifling evidence, but that she was not to be concerned or bothered, as it was just a routine matter for the police.

"I will get the keys for you. No one has been there since they took his body away about eleven months ago. I do not care to go into those rooms so I keep them locked. In any case, it is probably stuffy and dusty up there, but you can open a window if you care to.

Hopkins and I followed the brass candelabra Holmes was holding aloft as we ascended the stairs to Lyon's chamber on the *piano nobile* of the first floor. A feeling of incipient foreboding that one associates with being in the presence of death swept over me, as it usually does. I knew that Lyon's corpse had been removed a year ago to the Middlesex Hospital near-by, but still half-expected him to be waiting for us in the chair in which he died.

"Lend a hand here Watson; the door to Lyon's chamber appears jammed."

In my attempt to push against it with my shoulder, weakened from a stray bullet received at the murderous battle of Maiwand, I distinctly heard something crack, but remain uncertain as to whether it was the door giving way or a bone in my shoulder. Accordingly, I yielded and made way for Hopkins to endeavour to damage his shoulder. At length he succeeded in forcing open the door to the sealed chamber, and immediately a rush of stale almost putrid air assailed our nostrils. The blast of air had the effect of disturbing the layers of dust that had accumulated over the year into a choking cloud. With handkerchiefs covering the lower part of our faces, we all instinctively made for the windows. Drawing back two heavy velvet drapes, I gained the windows and, after some difficulty, succeeded in opening two sets overlooking Harley Street.

It was dingy and subdued, of course, but the poor light did not stop Holmes finding and availing himself of a wax taper from a sheath below the gas mantel and lighting two large town gas-jet *appliqués* in the form of angels holding forth firebrands in front of them. These coal-gas jets gave out their weak blue light sufficiently to provide enough illumination for us to see clearly the extent of the dusty interior of Lyon's chambers, including the large drawing room. To say nothing had changed since we were last standing in this room would, I suppose, be the literal truth, because nothing could have happened during the intervening eleven or so months. There was still though, that pervasive feeling of horror I associate with the death of Lyon. I remember his being poisoned through the skin of the fingers as he read a letter sent to him by Moriarty, written on paper from the Penrice paper mills in Highgate, that had been drenched in strychnine, and especially the subsequent look of terror upon his face.

The rooms were sparsely furnished, but the items lying around were of the highest quality, including furniture by Biedermeier which, I think, enjoyed a European vogue for a while. Notwithstanding that, and even in the dim light, I could discern quality, though not in the loose carpets that covered the timber floorboards. Certainly the paintings on the walls were not what I would have expected of someone like Lyons. They were of middle-range quality, not at all appropriate for a man whose taste ran to acquiring Biedermeier furniture. The paintings were more suited, I thought, to adorn the walls of our housekeeper Mrs Hudson's quarters in Baker Street.

In one corner I saw a tall, elegant chest of drawers, with a fold-down writing shelf, made of a honey-coloured wood inlaid with intricately shaped marble and red veneers impressed into its various surfaces. Ranged around the room were Biedermeier sofas covered in fine striped silks and plain watermarked silk-covered chairs with armrests. Lyon was very particular about his comfort, I thought.

Holmes looked neither at the furniture nor the paintings on the wall, but busied himself examining the floor. Placed against a wall near a front window was a fairly substantial item of furniture in the form of an ornate Biedermeier sideboard. As I approached it I saw that it too was made of golden coloured wood, but with distinctive fluted Corinthian columns made of black ebony, with ornate gilded Capitals attached to its four corners. How did they, I wondered, get this large item of furniture from the street, up those stairs we just climbed, and into this room?

"Just a few more inches and we will have cleared the trapdoor in the floor. You see, Hopkins, that Lyon covered this trapdoor with a rug upon which he positioned this heavy Biedermeier furniture, on castors for ease of movement. It was our observant Watson here who noticed the scratches and grooves caused by their regular movement on the floor," said Holmes to Hopkins.

"Here, let me help you; I remember that this trap door was quite heavy the last time we hauled it back," I remarked to Holmes. Once it was open, Holmes leapt into the void bearing the candelabra in his hand, to Hopkins' great surprise.

"After you, Inspector. Be careful, as the ceiling is only a few feet high," I warned, handing him a lit candle, then followed him in, bearing my own illumination.

We all three of us were making our own foray and stopping to look at this small but highly valuable collection.

"Well it is still here intact, which surprises me," I said.

"On the contrary, I expected nothing less," remarked Holmes.

"Impressive, but not worth dying for," said Hopkins, who was I could see weighing up the promotion he could expect to earn from the 'discovery' of this cache of art.

"Look at this Old Master here, Holmes; see how the light from my taper plays on the iridescence of the patina. Astounding! I will say that Lyon, irrespective of his venal and thief-like traits, cannot be faulted for his taste in art. Indeed, I would go so far to say it ought to be applauded. See here, *'The End of a Reign'* by Delville, and here, the *'Island of the Dead'* by Arnold Böcklin. Over there are Aubrey Beardsley's *'The*

Rheingold' and Gabriel Rosetti's '*Astarte Syriaca*'?' I exclaimed, barely able to contain my emotions at being surrounded by so much beautiful art. I could well understand Lyon's desire to own these fabulous paintings, including the one I was holding called '*Landscape with Psyche and the Palace of Amor*' by Claude Lorrain.

"Watson, Watson! You are forgetting yourself, we are here on a mission not on an outing to a picture gallery," admonished Holmes.

"Inspector, we have to get these paintings up and out of this vault and I suggest we form a chain and hand them to each other. First we shall stack them upright below the trapdoor and thence we can offer them up into the drawing room above."

As we carried out this task in total silence, I stared at each painting in turn, gazing momentarily into their inner depths for clues as to why they radiated such beauty. One in particular, Thomas Cole's '*The Course of Empire*' held me in such fascination that I was most reluctant to relinquish it to Hopkins who held out his hands to receive it. These moments, brief as they were, gave me a fleeting sense of… stewardship. Hopkins merely methodically stacked them as though they were crates of turnips.

"The police pantechnicon has arrived," I said, looking out of the window down to the street.

"Good. Now Inspector, get your constables to reverse the pantechnicon right up hard against the street door to block out any view of what we are loading into the wagon. I do not want this art hoard becoming public knowledge through your officers talking about it to others. We may need this art to bargain with or use as leverage before the end to our quest is in sight," said Holmes.

It was only after having spent several minutes transporting the art down the stairs and into the police pantechnicon that we had completed the exercise, after which Hopkins locked the doors of the wagon with a stout padlock, the key of which he handed to Holmes.

"I and my constables will drive this van straight to the Naval Provost's yard at the Admiralty, Mr Holmes, and you can be certain that no one, but no one, will gain access to its contents."

And with that announcement the van, with royal ciphers to its side panels, accompanied by the police constables went clattering off into the fog, becoming invisible within seconds, showing only its rear red tender light, seemingly suspended above the carriageway.

"There you are, Mrs Bernstone, the keys to Lyon's rooms. We have concluded our business and shall not disturb you any further. Thank you for your help and, my dear, do look after yourself," I advised.

"Oh, you are so kind, Sir!" she replied, dropping a shallow curtsey to me, and then disappeared through the front door of the house, candelabra in one hand and keys in the other.

"Holmes, now that you are recovered, do you feel equal to the task of witnessing the first performance of the '*Planets Suite*' by Gustav Holst and in particular his musical interpretation of Uranus?"

I had found myself referring to Uranus again, but for no particular reason.

"Yes, where is this work to be premiered?"

"At the St James' Concert Hall in the Portland Road. You know the place; when we were there the last time, the management suggested our presence would be more appropriate and therefore more appreciated in The George Public House near by in Mortimer Street than in the Dress Circle of their august music auditorium!"

"Of course, I do now vaguely recollect our experience on that particularly wet Thursday afternoon. Was it over a minor altercation about the interpretation of Frederic Chopin's

Etude in B flat major?"

"Rather. It was our searching around the Dress Circle seats looking for 'The Lost Chord'!"

The concert, given by the London Philharmonic Society Orchestra and conducted by the renowned Hans Richter, opened with excerpts from Richard Wagner's opera '*Das Liebesverbot*'. * This work, in comparison with his more famous operas, is a seemingly frivolous piece and not at all what one expects from the master of the Leitmotif, but nonetheless enjoyable. The major work, the '*Planets Suite*', which was the reason for our attendance, was a resounding success. I revelled in the work's luxuriant treatment of the thematic material, especially in the section addressing Jupiter, where huge orchestral forces were marshalled and deployed to great effect. This treatment was made all the more effective in comparison with the pensive feelings of regret extant in the section devoted to Neptune. On the whole, I thought Holst's Opus 32 innovative, particularly in reference to Uranus. Again I keep thinking about Uranus for reasons I cannot fathom.

Given our previous experience at this Hall, we availed ourselves only of a modest drink at the crush bar in order to revive our spirits. We then groped our way up the Portland Road, still shrouded in the fog that showed no signs of dissipating, in order to take dinner at Gatti's Restaurant. The Dining Rooms were quite full with the usual cacophony and din, as silver cutlery struck Crown Derby porcelain. At length a waiter showed us to a table secreted in an alcove where the noise was slightly reduced.

"A bottle of your best Bordeaux and one of Burgundy – the Volnay Beaune please – and I will start with the Oyster Creams followed by Fillet of Beef with Madeira Sauce, and finish with a generous slice of Almond Cheesecake."

I waited with anticipation what Holmes would choose from the *carte* given his propensity for selecting the least appetising food on any menu. He did not disappoint and waded in accordingly.

"A bottle of House Claret, Potted Shrimps served with hot dry toast followed by Mr Gay's recipe for Boiled Knuckle of Veal with Spinach. For dessert I shall have the Stewed Prunes and Custard, followed by a slab of Dutch Edam cheese to match Watson's Cheesecake."

Our dinner was enjoyable, if, in the case of Holmes' choice, peculiar.

"One thing is for certain Watson, there is more to this case than just Moriarty and some theft of art work. I feel the presence of an *eminence grise* in the background that troubles me," confided Holmes.

We discussed our progress in the case and its parameters, also speculating on how we could reasonably expect it to develop. After we had finished our brandy and cigars we left the infinitely preferable and comfortable confines of the restaurant and stepped out into the fog that felt even more clammy, producing a sticky sensation upon our faces. We waited for a passing cab, but none appeared. After several minutes had elapsed, Holmes suggested we make our way up the Portland Road in the direction of the Metropolitan Railway Station of the same name. I fell in eagerly with his plan. On reaching the Station's booking hall we approached the ticket window, but no servant of the Railway was present to dispense tickets to us. After two or three minutes I was determined to attract the attention of someone by whatever means. I therefore with a penny coin tapped on the window, expecting no response.

I could scarcely believe my eyes when a rather surly looking individual, dressed in his black velveteen uniform with red piping, appeared at the window, clearly put out by my summons as I had disturbed his reading of a newspaper out of sight.

"Yes, whatever," he uttered

"Do tell me, do you sell railway tickets from this window or are we supposed to purchase them elsewhere?" I said facetiously to this imbecile.

"Yes we do. What do you want?"

"Oh! You do surprise me. Two single tickets to Baker Street," I said, pushing several coins through the opening in the window counter, and collected the tickets. The servant then, with a further display of his innate ill manners, moved out of view to resume his perusal of the newspaper. Our descent to the westbound platform was well timed, because almost immediately a train of the Metropolitan Railway came trundling down the permanent way, pushing aside the extant fog in front of it.

On our return back to Baker Street there was a letter marked 'Urgent' delivered earlier by the District Messenger. It was from Sir James, informing Holmes that the carriage had been impounded in a special stable where access could only be via him or the Naval Provost. He concluded by expressing his gratitude to Holmes for resuming his work on the case.

* The Ban on Love.

Chapter 5

The Visit to Oceanic House

The next morning, on entering our breakfast room, I noticed that Holmes was absorbed with a sheaf of papers, all bearing the Admiralty cipher of Dolphins, Rope and Anchor. I busied myself scouring *The Times* for any newsworthy items. I could find none and so, with a sigh of resignation at so early a time in the morning, looked to Holmes for something meaningful. He did not disappoint.

"Watson, when we have breakfasted do you feel equal to the task of visiting the Oceanic House in Pall Mall?"

"Oceanic House?" I inquired.

"Yes," continued Holmes, "Oceanic House is the Head Quarters of the White Star Line, or at least the British Head Office. It is in there that we need to meet with Mr Bruce Ismay, Chairman of that Line. Sir James has sent these papers to me to aid us in our quest.

Holmes donned his Inverness and I my army great coat that had kept me warm through those dread-filled freezing nights in the Khyber Pass during the fateful Afghan Campaign, which had brought me nothing but misery and further wounds. Descending the staircase to our front door, we emerged into the still fog-bound Baker Street.

"There are some rather intriguing, to say nothing of *outré*, features to this case, Watson," Holmes suddenly offered whilst we were treading carefully down Baker Street. In particular, why Charles Peace was anxious for us to visit Lyon after Moriarty had done away with him; what was the point?"

"The man was dead, what could we do and I have always thought that it was a futile visit other than that we discovered the hidden art work?"

"Possibly Watson, but here is a Hansom cab," said Holmes as he leapt out into the carriageway, forcing the horse to stop abruptly. "Oceanic House in Pall Mall."

We climbed in and headed down Baker Street and into Orchard Place, which led us over Oxford Street into North Audley Street and fashionable Mayfair. Passing Lees Place on our right, we made a left turn into Grosvenor Square and Brook Street, then right into Bond Street. Travelling down this street lined with expensive shops, I thought about Agnew's Gallery located farther down at No. 43. It was from that gallery, I remembered, that the famous painting of the Duchess of Devonshire by Gainsborough was stolen in a daring daylight raid. We passed the gallery and I noticed the frontage appeared to have been modified by the installation of the necessary precautions to prevent a repetition of that outrage.

Our driver reined our horse left to the southern end of Burlington Street, past the Arcade that leads down to Piccadilly and then we travelled onward to the Regent's Street. As we were about to enter the Regent's Street our horse stopped at the junction momentarily due to the vicissitudes of traffic. I took this opportunity to look up at the familiar façade of Vigo House. We had good reason to remember this building and the bizarre practices that took place in the circular domed structure on its roof! Although I have always considered the edifice to be basically Neo-Classic in style, it is the way the entablature progresses upward from the roofline architrave that suggests to me repressed monumentalism.

Vigo House

At length, a gap in the procession of carriages of every type, caused by the dignified, if slow, progress of a hearse pulled by black-plumed horses, enabled us to join this ribbon of traffic lumbering along like ghosts in the fog. We continued over Piccadilly and down the Lower Regent's Street, turning left adjacent to the Crimea Memorial located at Waterloo Place. At length, having traversed Pall Mall in the company of omnibuses covered in gaudy advertising posters extolling their spurious claims and dubious testimonials, pantechnicon and prolific dray wagons, we arrived at our destination. In so doing, I could just barely make out Oceanic House in the fog, home of the White Star Line, situated right next to my favourite Bookmaker's agent.

We presented ourselves to the concierge who immediately misunderstood the nature of our visit. He insisted on informing us quite clearly that Mr Ismay was the Chairman of the company and did not involve himself in actually selling steamboat tickets.

"Our visit involves the *'Titanic',*" I said in my attempt to resolve this nonsensical situation.

The concierge looked at us as if we were lunatics.

"We are hardly in a position to sell you tickets for the *'Titanic'* and obviously you are not informed, because if you were, you would know that the *'Titanic'* sank several months ago."

It was only after Holmes had described clearly to the concierge the precise purpose of our visit, even referring to the papers received from the Admiralty about the appointment with Ismay, that the concierge relented and asked us to wait. Eventually a clerk appeared and we were shown up to the Chairman's office and formally introduced to that gentleman.

"I know who you are Mr Holmes," said Ismay, "and of course your reputation precedes you!"

Holmes gave a shallow bow in acknowledgement of this generous, if unexpected, verbal accolade.

"You are that busy-body, that nosy Parker, that interfering investigator who considers that he has a right to incommode any one for the flimsiest of reason. Well Holmes, I have survived two inquiries, one in America and the other in London, about the loss of the *'Titanic'*, and have been exonerated by both!"

"Those inquiries are not the only things you have survived; you managed to survive the sinking of the *'Titanic'* too, by clambering into a life boat ahead of your passengers," I interjected, absolutely flabbergasted by Ismay's confident outburst.

"And who the devil are you, Sir?"

"I will tell you who the devil I am," I replied, thrusting out my chest, "I am a Britisher who is disgusted by you and your cowardly behaviour on the deck of that stricken ship. You Sir, yes you Sir, in your capacity as chairman, you are responsible for the loss of over fifteen hundred souls, including those of children!"

Holmes laid his hand on my arm. Ismay's countenance all of a sudden assumed the ashen look of a man about to collapse, but I made no movement toward him, irrespective of the Hippocratic Oath to which I agreed as a doctor. What I had said had visibly disturbed him and probably conjured up into a real presence those spectres that must perforce haunt his dreams.

It was certainly not my intention to deliver my soul's feelings on this subject to Ismay, but something in his character made me need to admonish him.

Ismay then resumed his chair and beckoned us both to take a seat in front of his desk.

"Gentlemen," he said, "I am not certain that I can be of any assistance to you for I am about to resign as Managing Director of the White Star Line. The board feels that my continued association with the White Star Line can in the long run only be disruptive and injurious to its business."

For the first time Holmes spoke, asking Ismay to outline the sequence of events leading up to the loss of the ill-fated 'Titanic'.

Ismay thought for a moment, then, with the determination of someone who has concluded something in his mind, started in.

"You may not know, Sir, but the White Star Line, owner of the 'Titanic', was subsumed into the International Mercantile & Marine combine. This organisation was deliberately set up to bring order to competing shipping companies and control prices, thus guaranteeing a profit. A fellow called JP Morgan, who is, essentially, a New York banker, runs it. It became clearer to me as Managing Director of the White Star Line that the acquisition of our Line, by Morgan, was not thought out properly and that perhaps he might have over-reached himself.

"The new International Mercantile & Marine combine started life rather precariously and was heading for failure when Morgan asked me to assume the position of the President of the International Mercantile & Marine combine and Managing Director of the White Star Line. I accepted these positions and we began returning a decent profit."

"What can you tell me about the inter-changeability of the '*Titanic*' and the '*Olympic*' ships respectively?" asked Holmes.

"Very little. I am a business man not a marine engineer. However, both boats were identical in many respects as they were created from the same set of blue prints."

"You mentioned that the International Mercantile & Marine combine started out in a precarious situation. Just how unsound were the financial fortunes of Morgan's shipping combine?" asked Holmes.

"Very precarious, largely due to the fact that the '*Olympic*', the first of three 'Wonder Ships' as we called them, a rather fanciful term admittedly, was continuously colliding with other ships, including a Royal Navy vessel. Consequently, rather than making a profit from the lucrative north-Atlantic trade to the United States and Canada, she was often holed up in the Thompson Graving Dock under-going repairs. At one time I actually wrote to Morgan expressing my concern that the '*Olympic*' 'will be the death of us, for she is capable of sinking not only herself, but indeed International Mercantile & Marine combine, together with the White Star Line'. His reply to me was as terse as it was bitter, and I half expected him to get the first boat, any boat, out of New York to

London. He does, alas, have a reputation for being rather, as it were, emotional in certain matters, a bit like a bull in a Chinese shop."

Whether it was Ismay's last sentence or the information he imparted, but Holmes got up and collected his hat and coat, as did I, knowing that this interview was over, thankfully and made my way toward the door.

"And for your information, my good Doctor," said Ismay, "both inquiries did clear me. Each investigation concluded that, had I not taken a place in one of the lifeboats which still had spaces left, a further futile loss of life would have occurred."

Such arrogance, I thought, and refused his outstretched hand, though I noticed Holmes took it.

I considered momentarily the anguish and mental torment that must be searing through Ismay's mind. My emotional outburst against him, I knew, had unnerved him to the extent that his countenance quivered in front of me, but I could not forgive him. My instinct was to be supportive to him in his predicament, but his arrogance prevented my giving any such relief.

I felt weakened by my experience, but was certainly glad to be out of his office that struck me as being somehow less preferable than the acrid and clammy fog into which we now made our way.

"We have made some headway, Watson, if we did but know it, and I know precisely what we need to do now."

"I found his conversation rather stilted and guarded, and not in any way useful or indeed informative," I replied.

"The trick here, Watson, is to make the other person think that the information they are imparting is of supreme indifference to you. Consequently, to gain your attention, they will impress upon their narrative far more information than they initially intended. Bruce Ismay is precisely the type of individual to fall into such a trap and, as such, must be listened to closely, taking into consideration all the details."

Holmes surprised me then with an abrupt, "Do tell me Watson, how would you feel about journeying to New York and the New World?"

Instantly, I thought of Katherine from Eureka Springs, but also realised this would be no vacation. Rather, the mention of New York suggested that the game was now afoot and we must perforce venture further afield.

"I should very much like to accompany you to the New World!" I said without hesitation and with total conviction in my voice.

"Good, well let us now take luncheon in that excellent Carvery at the Charing Cross Hotel," suggested Holmes.

"Delighted to, but let us first refresh ourselves in the near-by Northumberland Public House in the Northumberland Avenue at the junction of Northumberland Street and Craven Passage, which leads underneath Charing Cross Station and thence up to the Hotel. First however, I have a small task to attend to, so I will see you there. Yes, a large whisky with a dash, only a dash mind, of aërated water for me."

And, with that cheering instruction, I darted off through the banks of fog in the direction of my Bookmaker's agent, there to place a wager on a favourite horse called *Desborough* running at Ascot at tolerable odds. Shortly afterwards, I headed off in what I thought was the direction of the Charing Cross Hotel on the other side of Trafalgar Square. Walking along the southern aspect of the Square, past Drummond's Bank wherein I held an account until they terminated its use, I gained the Northumberland Avenue, which is dominated by the imposing Grand Hotel.

Feeling considerably lighter, I approached the Public House and, looking up at its name painted on the overhanging sign board, realised that it was not called the Northumberland but another, which I could not make out through the swirling fog. Still, Holmes, with his deductive reasoning, would have surmised that this was the Public House I had suggested. Whilst there are bars on the ground floor it is the first-floor bar for which this establishment is renowned. Ascending the stairs into the bar, resplendent in all its luxuriant fittings and opulence, I was greeted by two carved white Carrara marble Nymphs on the stair's head plinths. Each held in their hands a white opaque-glazed, illuminated globe lantern.

The most striking aspect of this opulent luxury were two smooth, gold-painted columns tapering to lavish Corinthian capitals, seemingly holding up the ornate stucco ceiling with its intricate raised and gilded tracery designs. Echoing these pillars were a pair of grooved mahogany pilasters set flush against the wall. In between them, the walls were lined with red silk wallpaper ornamented with gold filigree. Set into the architrave were highly varnished panels depicting even more complex designs. Some of the recesses were sufficiently deep as to take highly decorated porcelain vases. With the exception of four ceiling-mounted lights, ostentatious wall-mounted acetylene gas fuelled globe lanterns and candelabra provided most of the illumination.

The bar, combining Queen Anne and Baroque styles with brass fittings and ornaments, was constructed of highly polished carved elm, supporting a counter of white Perlino Bianco marble. The back bar, set in front of a mirrored wall, displayed decorated bronze stands on which were fixed curved glass globes containing various liqueurs. In between them and dominating the ensemble was an enormous brass till of such intricate and ornate design as to be almost a work of art rather than a cash depository.

Complementing the general style throughout were incorporated rich velvet drapes of red, framing engraved windows and decorative glazed panel openings in the internal timber partition walls. The ceilings were of painted and gilded moulded plaster looking down on elaborately patterned carpets upon which were positioned several ubiquitous indoor palm trees. The effect was one of an opulent, sumptuous, if meretricious, establishment of the 'Gin Palace' variety, patronised by the wealthier classes.

After a considerable period had elapsed we eventually abandoned this ornate Saloon Bar and made our way down Craven Passage, one of the vaulted arches upon which Charing Cross Station is built, and passed the boisterous, red-plush Hungerford Music Hall also built into the arches. Climbing a steep set of steps rising from Villiers Street, we emerged into the rear of the Hotel. Walking up the broad red-carpeted staircase to the first floor *piano nobile* on which the restaurant is located, I recalled being here with Holmes when he met with that unpleasant fellow John Clay, who twice succeeded in causing me to spill my whisky onto my lap.

We made our way along the elevated glazed corridor running over Villiers Street to the Restaurant. Having been shown our table I ordered immediately, because by now my hunger was as keen as my appetite eager.

"Potted Cheese and Pickled Onions. The Stuffed shoulder of Lamb with Onion Sauce, Shallots and Cauliflower looks good and, to follow, I shall have the Boodle's Orange Fool. Now what to drink? Ah yes, I shall enjoy a bottle of your best chilled Chablis."

Holmes countered with, "'The London Particular'* to start, followed by the Boiled Chicken with Cucumber Sauce and Turnips."

Normally Holmes and I are fed from the same menu of food prepared by Mrs Hudson, our housekeeper at Baker Street. However, I never cease to wonder at Holmes' choice of food when left to his own inclinations, as in a restaurant or commercial Dining Room.

He continued. "Bread and Butter Pudding and a bottle of Imperial Tokay."

"Do you deliberately go out of your way to choose the most unappetising food available on the menu?" I asked of him.

"Watson, unlike you I am not a slave to my stomach. Eating to me is but a function, a time of acquiring energy, not enjoyment in taste. I would no sooner praise the fact of going to bed to sleep when tired or extol the virtues of bathing when necessary!"

After we had consumed our brandy and cigars we quitted the Charing Cross Hotel and stood in the Strand.

"Carriage!" I shouted, as a Phaeton carriage came gliding out of the banks of fog. "221b Baker Street."

* Pea soup

Chapter 6

The Race Against Time

Upon our arrival at Baker Street, Mrs Hudson came rushing out to us.

"Mr Holmes, where have you been? You have visitor who has been waiting for you since ten o'clock. He says, it is vitally important!"

"They all do," remarked Holmes.

Indeed, that our visitor had been waiting for some time was obvious by the number of cigarettes he had smoked in his anxiety to speak with Holmes. The person responsible for the state of our ashtray was, surprisingly, no less than Sir James Walter from the Admiralty.

"Thank God, Holmes, that you are back! I thought the news of such import that I would entrust no one but myself in conveying it directly to you. We have just received word that Moriarty is in England! In fact, at a country house called Fonthill Abbey! He is on English soil and we shall have him Mr Holmes, we shall have him!"

"Trains to Fonthill run out of Paddington on the Great Western Railway," I offered, referring to my trusty Bradshaw's Railway Guide.

"For God's sake Watson, make sure you read that Railway Guide properly to be certain that we get the right train, as there can be no margin for error here," interjected Holmes.

He then disappeared into his bedroom leaving me to gather a few necessary items, including my service revolver, which I slipped into the inside pocket of my coat. Much to the chagrin, evident upon Sir James' face, that I should resort to such a weapon, not least in carrying it about my person.

"We are dealing with a particularly vituperative individual, Sir James," I responded to his look of disdain.

Upon Holmes' return to our parlour, Sir James said, "I shall wire ahead to the local constabulary and have an inspector and constables meet you at Fonthill Station to assist your entering Fonthill Abbey and arresting the murderous Moriarty."

Sir James seemed genuinely pleased at the prospect of our capturing Moriarty and seemed hardly able to contain his corpulent self. I think he was on the verge, had he been in such a position, of offering his services too and accompanying us on our quest. Moments later we were in Baker Street and clambering into Sir James' Barouche, drawn by a four-in-hand, whereupon he said to his liveried coachman.

"Drive like the Furies to Paddington Station, for we have but minutes to board the train to Fonthill!"

The driver took him at his word and, abandoning all caution and concern whipped up his team of four horses. Our carriage then charged headlong into the blinding fog along Baker Street, turned left into Crawford Street, headed west over Gloucester Place and onward to the junction of Seymour Place. I remember this junction as the one that is dominated by Seymour Buildings and despite the fog, recognise clearly the ornate architectural details to building's façade. These included several elaborate terracotta mouldings of the bearded heads of the Greek god Titan with drain pipes protruding from their mouths. What a curious architectural detail, I pondered, designed to remove rainwater from the flat fenced roof of this Victorian apartment building. Nor was the connection lost on me between these Titan heads and our continuing quest to resolve the mystery surrounding the events leading to the sinking of the ill-fated *Titanic*!

Our driver then veered right into a small street, named for the Greek theoretician, Homer. That street lead to what I recognised as being the Old Marylebone Road that gave access to the bustling Edgware Road.

Whether it was the spectre of our four galloping horses or premonition, the traffic stopped instinctively to allow us to progress into Sussex Gardens and onward to Paddington unhindered. Once in this road we turned right into Sale Place, rattling by The Royal Exchange Public House from which laughter and jollity could be heard faintly, and onwards into Praed Street where Paddington Station is located. Racing down this street with only minutes to spare, our horses seemed to understand the urgency of our mission and charged even harder into the fog in our race against time. I could just make out the Great Western Hotel, looming up as a white cliff and informing me that we were entering the Station. We did and, as the horses turned right, our carriage made a sickening sideways motion as it skidded round the corner, leaving me in full expectation that we were going to turn over. We then clattered down the ramp toward the Station's platforms.

"Which platform gents?" Came the inquiry from Sir James' liveried coachman.

"Platform Eight!"

With that last command the driver of the Barouche whipped his horses into a full gallop along the platform, missing by inches railway servants and members of the public who were gathered there. Divine Providence must have been on our side!

Our train had actually started progressing along the edge of the platform as we opened a carriage door and clambered on board. This was much to the annoyance of another railway servant upon the platform who was yelling at us to desist.

I looked back to see that a constable had run after our carriage driver and was remonstrating with him. With Sir James being present, I thought, the constable would be wiser to abandon, on this occasion, his enthusiasm for the enforcement of the law.

Once we had made ourselves comfortable on the buttoned seats in an empty First Class carriage, I whipped out my gun and, with a pencil and handkerchief, began to clean it, checking too that the mechanisms were functioning properly. Holmes looked askance at me.

"Do we want this thing jamming up or failing to deliver a bullet into Moriarty, were he to attempt to make a run for it, fail to cooperate or indeed become awkward?" I invited.

Our train by now had cleared the confines of Paddington Station having passed through the adjacent Bishop's Road Metropolitan Station and was gaining speed. It whistled through the Royal Oak Metropolitan Railway Station and then began swaying gently from side to side as it gained momentum. The swaying turned to a rocking motion as it increased velocity, and a screech was heard from the locomotive whistle as it blasted its way through Westbourne Park Metropolitan Railway Station. It then settled in on the main permanent way of the railway track of the Great Western Railway heading towards the western skies.

Our train steamed down the track and through stations, allowing only fleeting impressions of buildings and people. We had, I noticed gratefully, also cleared the oppressive fog of London. Eventually our train pulled into Fonthill Station, where the fading daylight before dusk created an ominous red sky. We stepped from the train carriage onto the platform and were immediately met by a burly looking individual wearing a Prince-of-Wales check suit and a brown Derby hat who came up to me and said.

"Mr Sherlock Holmes, a pleasure to meet you Sir. My name

is Inspector Athelney Jones. I received Sir James' wire and, as instructed, have some stout constables standing by with me to deal with this Professor Moriarty. I know very little about the case, so perhaps you can advise me of the details as we drive to Fonthill Abbey."

I coughed and indicated Holmes.

"Inspector, he is Holmes, I am Doctor John Watson."

We followed the Inspector into a Clarence carriage, surprising for the rural area in which we found ourselves. The constables followed us in a more robust police wagon. We clattered through the little village of Fonthill whilst Holmes briefed the Inspector as to the quarry in our sights. We had not travelled far before I saw it. Rising up into the sky at least two miles' distant was a tower, a colossal stone tower, the type of which one does not expect to see in the countryside. It looked monstrous, as if it ought not to be standing there, but rather in ruins, a heap of rubble. Clearly the Inspector saw in my face the incongruity of the vision that I beheld.

"Doctor Watson, let me tell you about the place we are going to enter with or without permission. That building, Fonthill Abbey, is a Gothick fantasy and is disliked by the locals who consider it an abomination and a blight on their locality. From the very early beginnings, when a wealthy but eccentric author, a Mr William Beckford, bought the original Abbey he has, to the annoyance of all, extended the building to create that Gothick pile. His idea took on the form of a full-size replica of Salisbury Cathedral, but with the style and dimensions of the building exaggerated to terrifying proportions in order to create his residential Gothick fantasy."

"Yes, I have read of this wealthy eccentric, but thought the reports in the *Daily Telegraph* to be more exaggeration than fact."

"Well I cannot say I am aware of the *Daily Telegraph's* version of events. What I can say is that Beckford, from all accounts,

Fonthill Abbey

was a member of a group of rather privileged and wealthy individuals whose mission was to *'Gothicise'* anything in sight. This included the original Fonthill Abbey, which was a medieval ruin before Beckford converted it into the monstrosity you see rising before us. Their aim was to take an existing Georgian country house and romanticise it by applying Gothick motifs and architectural details, such as battlements, towers and four-leaf or quatrefoil windows, and turn the building into a romantic Gothick fantasy, as you shall see at Fonthill."

"I am intrigued, Inspector, at the prospect of arriving at Fonthill."

"As you can see, Doctor," continued the inspector, "that

stone wall we are approaching is twelve feet high and extends for eight miles, enclosing the Abbey grounds!"

The inspector had under-played the spectre of this building. I for one certainly did not know such structures existed in England. It resembled a fairy-tale castle, the type of which had been built by King Ludwig of Bavaria. The imposing presence of Fonthill Abbey on that Autumnal evening was, to say the least, disconcerting, and yet at the same time exhilarating. The huge structure was a fusion of architectural motifs; complete with crocketted pinnacles crenellated gable ends, steeply pitched roofs, and detailed tracery on the exterior wall surfaces. An octagonal Gothick tower, rising at least three hundred feet into the reddening evening sky, dominated the building and vicinity.

As we approached a small Gothick gatehouse, one of the constables vaulted the gate and entered it. Moments later he emerged with a dazed woman whose duty, he informed the Inspector is to look after the gate.

"Constable, open the gate and remain with her until we return," instructed Inspector Jones.

As we drove through the gate, penetrating the twelve-foot-high perimeter wall, I was conscious of the height of the wall as being somehow abnormal. The memory of this observation lodged firmly in my mind. Clearly Moriarty intends no one to invade his domain and disrupt his privacy, and to this end he will defend to the utmost his preference. We experienced his fortress mentality when some months ago we called upon him at his house in Well Road, Hampstead, in London.

Our two carriages clattered up the driveway lined with elm trees, and the awesome spectacle of the Fonthill Abbey came into view. The sheer size of this Gothick fantasy defied description, except in monumental terms. Inspector Athelney Jones and two constables moved towards the front portal and banged on the huge timber doors, which were studded with raised bolts to reënforce the impression of strength. In the meantime, the rest of us stood back trying to take in the enormity of the building whilst we waited. At length, the double doors opened to reveal the butler, who was made all the more diminutive and insignificant by the huge doorposts that flanked him. I observed Holmes, who in turn looked expectantly but somewhat resignedly at this butler, a man who displayed all the symptoms of a thyroid condition to complement his somewhat intrinsic and very evident surly countenance.

Despite this, the opened doors revealed a huge Hall measuring about eight hundred feet, the ceiling of which was at least a hundred-and-twenty feet high. The Inspector had not exaggerated; the whole building was constructed to the dimensions of a full-sized Cathedral! Having gained the threshold of the door, the butler, a morose-looking person, ventured no question as to who we might be, but simply looked at us with a blank expression upon his face.

Athelney Jones wasted no time and started in.

"Who are you?"

"Pardon?"

"You heard me," said Jones.

"I am Stephens, the head butler."

"Stephens, a likely name," responded Jones. "Are you sure?"

Stephens, I noted, did not even bother to respond to Jones, but still looked vacantly at the Inspector in preparation for the next onslaught that was not long in being delivered.

"The purpose of our visit," said Jones whilst waving a search warrant in the air, "is to arrest your master, a certain Professor Moriarty, for the following reasons specified and confirmed in this document. Where is he? I demand to see him now."

Stephens, who appeared shocked at the revelation that his

master was in some way a mentally deranged criminal and responsible for the sinking of the '*Titanic*', took some time to gather his imbecile wits and respond.

"The Professor could be anywhere in the Abbey, and this moment I do not know of his precise whereabouts," answered Stephens, whilst beckoning us to step through the doors and into the Hall.

"Well, we shall have to find him, will we not Stephens. Now lead the way," retorted the Inspector.

The Great Western Hall in which we were standing was literally the size of a Cathedral along the lines of which it was obviously designed. Complete with a timber hammer-beam roof looking down on a flight of stone steps at least twenty-five feet wide, which in turn rose up to about twenty feet in height and addressed an elongated arched opening some ninety-odd feet in height. It was this staircase that Stephens now ascended, with us following him through the archway into what I assumed must be the first floor *piano nobile*, upon which were several book-lined corridors beneath ornate fan-vaulted stone ceilings. Stephens took us along one such corridor to a large oaken door fashioned in the mediaeval style. He knocked upon its highly varnished surface and then slowly opened the door in order for us to peer into the room. The Purple Gothick Room, as it was called, had a white stucco fan-vaulted ceiling and was lightly furnished. It was also devoid of Moriarty, as Athelney Jones was quick to point out to Stephens.

A further walk brought us to another oaken door. Without much ado or ceremony, Jones opened it into a dark room that somehow exuded a ghostly and monstrous aspect to its appointment. In the centre was a long table with a heavy purple velvet cloth draped over it. Ranged around this purple velvet-covered plinth were six tall brass candlesticks about seven feet in height with candles actually burning in them. It was with a sharp intake of breath that I realised we had stumbled into a funereal preparation parlour and the miasma I had recognised was in fact the stench of a deceased corpse that must have occupied this room within the last two hours or so!

This residence was assuming all the appearance and attributes of something quite disturbing, although I could not discern why or indeed precisely what it was that concerned me.

"What is going on here Stephens? Has there been a dead body in this room? Was its death natural and recorded at the Vestry and with the Coroner? I shall be looking into all of this, Stephens, and there had better be nothing untoward or you will be for it."

Stephens just looked impassively at the police inspector and motioned us to follow him down yet another corridor. This book-lined tunnel terminated in a door upon which were inscribed letters informing us that it led to St Anthony's Altar. Not surprisingly we were confused as we could not, without great difficulty, conceive of finding Moriarty praying at the altar of St Anthony, or to any other Saint for that matter. Stephens knocked on the door, but no answer was heard, and when we at length stepped in to the chamber, it turned out to be another large drawing room, with no ecclesiastical connotations whatsoever. Needless to say, Moriarty was not in evidence.

Stephens, who clearly knew his way around, led us down one corridor after another, and we eventually reached St Michael's Gallery. Our searches for Moriarty were becoming futile, but despite this we progressed further, into the St Edward's Gallery, still without success, and finally into the Crimson Room, with a dwindling hope of locating him.

I was realising gradually that the way in which many of the apartments of Fonthill Abbey were described was by using the romanticised ecclesiastical terminology suggested by its name, and had nothing at all to do with religious usage. Indeed, the butler Stephens, with a silly grin upon his face, had described to us these areas of the Abbey as though using ordinary commonplace names in an off-hand, almost nonchalant, manner. Throughout, the building seemed to me to be no more than a concentration of romantic Gothick metaphors and a suitable home for a mentally deranged Moriarty.

Moving through this building represented nothing less than a series of surreal experiences and emotions.

Presently Stephens knocked on yet another door and opened it and pulled back the *portière,* door curtain. This time I stepped into a room and immediately wished that I had not done so. It was sparsely furnished save for the detailed raised Gothick designs of the tracery on the walls, interspersed with red and blue drapes which half concealed the shelves of books behind them all subject to an inordinately ornate fan-vaulted ceiling. A high-backed Gothick-styled chair was positioned in the middle of the room facing an Oriel window framed in stone with mauve curtains looking out onto the deeply reddening sky above an increasingly dark countryside.

My heart began to pound as never before as I approached the back of the chair to ascertain if, indeed, it was occupied. Even with Holmes, the Inspector, and his constables just feet away, the presentiment of horror and concentrated evil was all-pervasive in this room. Had a ghost walked out from one wall and into another, it would have come as no surprise to me. At length, I looked to the front of the chair. It was empty, save for the fact that, resting there on the rose-coloured silk seat covering, were sheets of a musical score. I picked them up. Moriarty had been reading the piano transcription of Richard Strauss' opera, *'Die Frau Ohne Schatten'** Then I noticed that the acrid smell of a cigar was still strong in this room. Someone had been sitting there, in the chair, and had only left only recently!

I re-joined the group and we marched off down a hallway and into a long Gallery that, Stephens informed us, is named for St Edward. The furnishings comprised a red carpet running the length of the Gallery below a plasterwork ceiling decorated with yet more intricate raised Gothick designs. The walls were lined with books of which a University library would have been proud. Several fireplaces were set into the walls and above one hung a picture of St Edward. From this Gallery, we progressed on in our search for Moriarty and entered yet another Gallery, this time dedicated to St Michael. Again, it was carpeted along its length, but this time in purple, with red drapes hanging from the walls. The immediate difference in this Gallery was the ornate ceiling that comprised a very intricate and finely fashioned fan vaulting of quite stupendous appearance.

As our group made its way through the labyrinth of corridors and halls, a feeling of profound unease, almost foreboding, began to envelop me. It may have just been the overwhelming beauty of the architecture, gigantic and surreal as it was, but I detected something sinister at large in the building. We knew that Moriarty was nowhere near above reproach, hence our presence here at this instant. And in the building there was nothing in particular to point out as being wrong, defective or malignant. Somehow though, it took little imagination to appreciate that this would have been the perfect place to plan the sinking of the 'Titanic' and the deliberate loss of over fifteen hundred souls.

"Look here Stephens," said Athelney Jones, "we have come here to arrest a dangerous criminal, not to join a guided tour of a country house. Now, where is he? If I do not get results from you soon, Stephens, you shall be arrested and charged with wasting police time, in addition to aiding and abetting a known fugitive. Do I make myself understood, Stephens?"

Stephens looked resigned and merely pointed the way down

yet another hallway called the Sanctuary, so he reliably informed us. Again we found ourselves following this truculent flunky down yet another corridor that in turn lead into the aptly named Oratory, which did make sense of that room. However, despite knocking on several doors leading to such exotic areas of the building as the Yellow Breakfast Room, the Crimson Drawing Room and even the outlandishly named Funereal Chapel, we did not locate Moriarty.

The various names assigned to different parts of the building, albeit of fantastical proportions, were at variance and almost incongruous with its actual use as a residence, rather than a Cathedral. The whole structure was built to a monumental scale, expressing all the indications of megalomania of terrifying proportions, but which could appeal to the rampant, if fertile, imagination.

Despite this dichotomy, we had still not managed to find, let alone apprehend, Moriarty, and this was of concern not only to the Inspector but also to Holmes and therefore to me.

Instinctively we moved away from Stephens to avoid his overhearing us whilst continuing our discussions.

"This rather complicates events, Inspector. Moriarty, or indeed a legion of Moriartys, could be concealed in this rambling building for months. We have neither the time nor men at our disposal to search this place thoroughly in the vain hope that we find our quarry," said Holmes.

"We may have to accept the fact that Moriarty has eluded us. As we approached the front of this building he could well have been making good his escape from us through any number of doors to the rear," replied the Inspector.

"Well we at least know that he is in England and not Europe," I ventured.

"Why England?" asked Holmes. "Does he intend another outrage?"

With that chilling prospect in our thoughts, we reëntered

our carriages for our forlorn respective journeys home.

"Stephens, get in that police wagon. You are coming with me, for I have not quite finished with you yet."

To which instruction Stephens nodded, as though dazed, yet with indifference, as if he were merely carrying out his normal duties as butler.

"So what are we to do now, Holmes? One thing is for certain, Sir James will be deeply disappointed at your failure to apprehend Moriarty, and he does not come across as a person who tolerates poor results lightly, and… what is this? Is not that the constable we left at the Gatehouse to stand guard? Yes, I believe it is," I said, leaping down from the carriage followed by Holmes and joined by Inspector Jones.

"Report, constable," said Inspector Athelney Jones.

The constable complied. Apparently, not twenty minutes after we had gone up to the Abbey, a Brougham carriage, carrying luggage of portmanteaux and bearing three men in top hats and capes, was driven furiously down the drive towards him and the open gate. He had attempted to stop them by standing in the middle of the drive with his hand held out. Whether they could not see him in the twilight beneath the canopy of these trees he could not be certain, but he was sure that if he had not jumped out of the way he would have been run down and crushed under foot.

We all of us instantly pronounced Moriarty's name!

"He is making for the Continent! Watson, do you have your trusty Bradshaw's Railway Guide about your person?" asked Holmes.

"Of course."

"Good! Find out what train Moriarty will have to catch to quit these shores in a hurry, and from which station he would have to depart.

"Salisbury Station, about 16 miles east of here, and he has a head start," responded the Inspector.

"Knowing Moriarty, he will almost certainly engage a Special Train to take him without hindrance or delay all the way to Folkestone," said Holmes looking extremely agitated at the prospect of Moriarty slipping once more through his fingers to freedom.

"There is another way. We can drive to the railway lines about four miles south of here and stop and board any train going towards Reading, where you can board any of the London-bound crack expresses going into Paddington Station."

Athelney Jones had barely finished these words before we were all in our respective carriages rattling off south to intercept any train. I confirmed this information with my trusty Bradshaw's Railway Guide.

Our drive was a hair-raising one, not dissimilar to the dash to Paddington Station earlier in the day, except this was more perilous because it was night and we were on small, confined country lanes, with only very weak light from our Clarence carriage lanterns to illuminate the way ahead. In a surprisingly short time we stopped at a fence on top of a steep embankment, at the base of which ran the permanent way of a railway.

Inspector Jones was clearly the master of the situation and gave out instructions accordingly.

"You two constables, one of you run down the track for a couple of hundred yards, and the other to three hundred. Use your whistles to alert any train going east and coming towards us. That way the train driver will have time to stop here. Use your 'Bull's Eye' lanterns and anything else to get the driver's attention, including fire. I want whatever train that comes along stopped."

We all of us clambered and part slid down the embankment, stumbling onto the railway tracks, and waited as the two constables raced down the track to alert on-coming trains. Moments later, out of the night, a whistle could be heard repeatedly. This sound was taken up and augmented by the sound of the other constable's whistle and, together, their combined cacophony succeeded in alerting the train driver. His train came flying towards us. It was quite frightening being so near such a large moving engine, to the extent that I could not think how the engineer could bring his huge, glistening and noisy steam locomotive to a halt. Miraculously, it seemed to me, the train stopped, shuddering, almost by where we were standing. The Inspector mounted the foot plate and in no uncertain terms told the train driver what he was to do regarding Holmes and myself:

"Get these men to Reading as soon as possible under the express orders of the Admiralty!"

We shook hands with the Inspector and climbed aboard into a First Class carriage and the train jolted off, aiding us in our mission.

"Needless to say Inspector, keep that surly Stephens under close lock and key," Holmes yelled down, from the open carriage window, "for he is not to be trusted!"

"You can be sure of that Mr Holmes. Stephens has got some heavy explaining to me that will take several days at least."

And with that parting remark Inspector Athelney Jones receded into the darkness and out of view as our train hurtled through the night.

After what seemed like an age, we eventually steamed into Reading, confident we were ahead of Moriarty's group by the action of stopping the train and arriving here in time to intercept one of the crack express trains bound for Paddington Station. We did not have long to wait and boarded a packed express train where we had to stand, crammed into a Second Class carriage of the Great Western Railway.

"Chasing after Moriarty, Holmes, is I think the least of our problems."

"Do not be ridiculous Watson. Have you lost your reason?"

"No, but I seem to recall that commandeering a train, at any rate in this country, is an offence leading to a trial at the Assizes court, is it not?"

I said this whilst keeping an eye out for the ticket inspector.

"To say nothing of the fact that we are on an non-stop express train to London without a valid ticket! And you know how parsimonious and vindictive the Great Western Railway can be, in avowing publicly their intention to '…make life extremely difficult and unpleasant for those persons caught riding our trains in the absence of a valid ticket for their journey…'

Notwithstanding that probability, the express thundered down the railway, pounding the steel tracks beneath us, tore through Maidenhead with its clock tower in a flash, then raced through Slough and onward as though unstoppable. This suited me very well, given the fact that a ticket inspector had now come into view and was conducting his business in a very officious manner and making his way up slowly from the far end of the packed carriage.

"Come on, come on," I mumbled to myself, and the train seemed to respond. I felt a jerk as the train took on more speed and we screamed through the Victorian-designed Acton Station and onward relentlessly to Paddington. By now the train was not only rocking and rolling from side to side but also making good progress. Alas so too was the ticket inspector and his gain made our situation perilous. However, we then passed Westbourne Park Metropolitan Railway Station adjacent to the permanent way of the Great Western Railway and steamed through Royal Oak Metropolitan Railway Station and I knew we were but minutes from our destination.

"What now to do about Moriarty?" I asked Holmes, promoting Moriarty back to the top of our priorities, now that the ticket inspector was occupied dealing officiously with a hapless, if ticket-less, individual.

"He will make for Victoria Station and avail himself of a Special Train."

"How can you be so sure?"

"Because I would do the same in his circumstances. Do you suppose that he is going to stand on a platform and wait for a train running to a timetable?"

At that moment our express passed Bishop's Road Metropolitan Station and entered Paddington Station and moments later ground to a halt. On our way out, passing the engineer on the locomotive, I felt compelled to thank him for his speedy efforts but desisted. Instead we bounded up the side ramp into Praed Street and climbed into a waiting Landau carriage with one explicit instruction.

"Victoria Station. A golden guinea if you get us there as soon as you are able!"

The carriage driver took us at our word and flicked his whip at his team immediately. Once again we were off, trotting briskly down Praed Street and into Spring Street. We continued into Sussex Gardens then around Lancaster Gate and into the Bayswater Road, turning right through the Victoria Gate into Hyde Park and down The Ring to the Serpentine Bridge. In the park the fog, as expected, was denser and more acrid, but nonetheless we made good progress and soon drove over the Serpentine Bridge. Within moments of doing so, we clattered at speed straight through the Alexandra Gate leading south out of Hyde Park, and over Kensington Gore.

Despite the dense fog, made more so by the proximity of Hyde Park, we raced down the Exhibition Road and then headed towards Knightsbridge by turning right into the Cromwell Road, dominated by the new Natural History Museum. Whilst looking at this huge Museum I remarked to Holmes.

"I remember reading an article in *The Times* recently, about why this Exhibition Road is called what it is, and the fate of a building that used to stand on that site," I said, pointing with my cane to the present Natural History Museum.

"Really?" drawled Holmes.

" 'The Great Exhibition of 1851', so the article informed me, 'introduced several building types, including that of its own famous 'Crystal Palace', constructed in its entirety of iron and glass. The Exhibition was indirectly responsible for the construction of the Exhibition Building of 1862, so named after the year in which it was constructed. The building was designed as an attempt to introduce the French style Neo-Classical based Beaux-Arts architecture into England. The attempt failed and its owners, in retaliation, pulled down their building which, shortly after completion, had been described as one of the ugliest public buildings that was ever raised in this country. It has now been replaced by the new Roman-esque-Gothic-style Natural History Museum.' "

Exhibition Building 1862

"Quite a short but dramatic life," responded Holmes.

"Indeed," I concurred.

Through a series of circuitous routes, which involved our driving down Beauchamp Place and beyond, past Hans Place, in which the home of Sir James is located and over Sloane Street, we eventually gained Chesham Place.

"Holmes, we are not far from Victoria for we have only Belgrave Place and Buckingham Palace Road to traverse before we are there. However, Holmes, I can also tell you that the last Continental Express departed twenty-three minutes ago."

A few minutes later we did enter the Victoria Railway Station, the West End terminus of the South-Eastern & Chatham Railway, from whence the Continental Expresses depart. Holmes immediately sought out the Station Manager

Exhibition Building 1862

and simply informed him that we wished to engage a Special Train, now, to take us to Folkestone.

"To Folkestone you say? Well, that is a co-incidence as I have just put a Special together for three gentlemen who also wished to get to Folkestone at their earliest. Pity you did not come earlier, otherwise you could have shared with them the carriage as well as the costs."

I looked, speechless, at Holmes.

"Are you able to have a Special Train made up now?" demanded Holmes in his most officious voice, which alerted me that he was at the end of his reserves of patience.

"Well, of course I can put a train together. We are, after all, a railway company running trains around the southern part of England. Of course I can make up a Special for you!"

"When?"

"Now. I will uncouple that wagon and locomotive. I am afraid we cannot give you a stabilising brake-van because it will take time in dislocating one from a train in the marshalling yards. The ride will be bumpy and your wagon will bounce around, but it will get you to Folkestone."

After some formalities had been gone through, as to who would be paying and what guarantees were being offered, we boarded our small non-stop express to Folkestone. For the first time, I actually felt we could capture Moriarty and was grateful I had brought my service revolver with me.

The journey was uneventful but extremely nauseating. The Station Manager was not exaggerating when he told us that, due to the absence of the stabilising brake-van, our ride would be turbulent and induce nausea.

"I hope that Sir James is a honourable man and prepared to meet our expenses, Watson. After all, engaging a Special Trains is no inexpensive matter."

"Do not fret, Holmes. Sir James is good for his word; he is after all a senior civil servant of the Crown."

"Yes," replied Holmes, "there is also that fact to be considered."

We arrived at Folkestone and, having asked various officials for directions to where the boats for the Continent depart made our way in great haste to those quays. We always knew in our hearts that the pursuit of this case was not going to be an easy one nor resolved within a short period of time. Indeed, it was more likely to be a long drawn-out affair with disappointment a real spectre and possibility at every turn, and with opportunities to bring matters to an early conclusion rarely, if ever, really present.

Such were the thoughts going through my mind as I watched the stern of a boat dip up and down on the tide as it sailed at full speed out of the Folkestone harbour. Upon its stern deck were three figures wearing top hats and capes flapping in the breeze.

* The Woman Without a Shadow

Chapter 7

The Vaulted Chamber

Our setback at Folkestone had affected Holmes, but not in the way one would have predicted. Instead it had the effect of galvanising his determination, as I realised the next day on entering our breakfast room back in 221b Baker Street, thoroughly exhausted from our efforts of the day before. Holmes, by contrast, appeared full of energy. He thrived in such circumstances.

"We must prepare for our journey to the New World, Watson, for it is there in the fair city of Chicago that we will seek and find our answers."

"Chicago? What the devil for?" I demanded, whilst pulling at the bell rope to summon breakfast.

"Why, to visit the *'City of Dreams'* of course."

"What, you mean the site of the World's Columbian Exposition?" I responded.

"And before you go on to extol the virtues, Watson, of that Exposition and its dazzling array of architecture, let me tell you it is not that which is of interest to me, but rather what was built there and *why*?"

Breakfast arrived and with a keen appetite I tucked eagerly into my Harrod's bacon and eggs.

"Despite your exertions of yesterday, do you feel equal to the task of continuing our quest abroad the Metropolis?"

"Rather!"

"The first thing is another visit to the offices of the infamous White Star Line in Pall Mall."

"What, to call upon that pompous Bruce Ismay again?"

"No, to purchase our tickets for a berth aboard the 'Olympic', which sails for New York the day after tomorrow."

Completing my breakfast with strong coffee and thoroughly replenishing my energy reserves with a grape or two, I rose from the table to inspect the weather conditions extant outside. The fog was still with us and looked more yellow than previously. The smoke causes this unappetising miasma from countless chimneys, which is not carried off by the wind, but mixes instead with the still and windless fog. This in turn becomes more dense and acrid. It is under such conditions that fog becomes injurious to health, and I was glad to be quitting the Metropolis for the cleaner and clearer air of the Atlantic Ocean – even at the risk of hitting something such as an iceberg and sinking. But first I had a task of my own to perform, and pulled twice at the bell rope to summon Billy our button pageboy.

"Ah Billy, please take this wire to the Sub-Telegraph Office at Wigmore Street and ask for the reply to be delivered by District Messenger as soon as it arrives."

Our pageboy both accepted my telegraph for dispatch and delivered one to Holmes, which he handed to him in his usual exaggerated and convoluted manner. Holmes tore open the envelope and looked surprised at what he read.

"Come, Watson, there is work to be done!"

Without ceremony we stepped out into Baker Street and headed north, crossing over Crawford Street en-route to York Place where we turned right into the Marylebone Road, heading east toward Harley Street.

"Are we going to that house in Harley Street?" I asked, somewhat perplexed.

"No," was Holmes' reply.

A few minutes later brought us to that very house in Harley Street. Through the fog I could just make out that distinctive protuberance that revealed the existence of the secret mezzanine floor that had contained the hidden art hoard. The plans of the art thief Lyon, I thought, were as daring as they were brilliant. Who would ever think of such a stratagem, especially when it came to defrauding the vindictive Moriarty, who ultimately revenged himself on Lyon with strychnine.

Continuing past the house, along the Marylebone Road, we paused at the junction of Park Crescent while a hearse and its Cortège of carriages went by in solemn procession. It was followed by a pantechnicon lumbering behind, bringing up the rear in a comparatively frivolous manner. As we crossed over Park Crescent, I became aware of the vague outline of a person, who was standing in the fog on the opposite corner. The fact of his not moving caused consternation in me to the extent that I touched Holmes' sleeve whilst pointing to the stationary apparition. Holmes too looked ahead with his face forward, peering into the fog. On reaching the figure I gripped my cane intending to bring down a blow on the person's head of such magnitude as to frustrate any intention of incommoding either Holmes or myself. To my surprise, Holmes started in first.

"Clay, John Clay?" inquired Holmes of the figure standing in the swirling fog.

"My dear Holmes, a pleasure to see you and is it the good Doctor Wilkins?"

I remembered this fellow as impertinent and unbearably confident. Only yesterday whilst in the Charing Cross Hotel, I had recalled his meeting with Holmes there a year ago and the fact that he caused me to spill my whisky, twice, onto my lap, and continually mispronounced my surname.

I assumed this meeting to be pre-arranged and not a

co-incidence. While waiting on Holmes who was deep in conversation with this fellow, I noticed that the junction of Park Crescent and the Marylebone Road was, in fact, the corner of a private garden. Dominating this corner was a small one-room stone pavilion, designed in the style of a classical temple such as one would see as a scenic focal point of beauty, especially on a country estate. It was about ten feet in height and each façade, about eight feet wide, had a recessed opening flanked by two columns with Doric capitals supporting a simple projecting pediment with a blank tympanum. The front façade had a door in its recess that led to the inside of the pavilion.

No sooner had I remarked on this to Holmes, than Clay, looking about in a furtive manner, moved quickly into this recess and, after a few moments, actually opened the door and ushered us into a small dank room. He then lead us out through another door into the garden which was swirling with fog that obscured the large overgrown laurel bushes that came into sight and as quickly receded from our vision. Following on behind, Holmes and I all of a sudden started to descend a flight of quite slippery steps and enter what looked like the entrance to a tunnel directly beneath the busy, traffic-laden Marylebone Road!

"Watch yourselves, gents, as the steps and ground are particularly slippery due to the fog," said Clay.

"Where does this tunnel lead?" I inquired of Clay.

"You will see, Doctor Watkins, you will see," he said, looking at Holmes even more furtively.

Abandoning caution to the Fates I followed behind. At length, we were about half way through the tunnel when I gradually became aware of the dull grey light emanating from its other entrance. It also came to my notice that somehow the traffic noise seemed powerless to invade this space. Time, so it seemed to me, appeared to stand still in the tunnel, the

Park Crescent Pavilion

walls of which were dripping with water, making for an unpleasant musty smell, the dankness of which was augmented by the fact that the fog pervading the subway hovered around us.

Clay stopped and looked both ways to either end of the tunnel, cocked his ears to listen out for any sound, and then pushed against the tunnel wall. Immediately, an opening appeared and a shaft of warm yellow light spilled out. Without further ado, Clay entered this doorway, pulling Holmes and myself after him, into what was an unbelievable sight!

This subterranean space was made up of a series of rusting cast iron walls supporting cast iron vaults, forming arches upon which the Marylebone Road above is constructed. Adorning the rusting cast-iron walls of the establishment, which gave off a reddish hue, were large pictures in gilt frames of ethereal and classical scenes reminiscent of Claude Lorrain. Other paintings, I recognised, were of known dignitaries and modern interpretations of concepts. Various polished brass objects were ranged around the large vaults, reflecting the light radiating from several chandeliers suspended from the curved cast-iron roofs. Upon the floor was laid a luxuriously thick red carpet punctuated with gold *fleurs de lys* in the pattern, which certainly added to the opulent ambience of the place.

The place was teeming with respectable professional gentlemen in frock-coats and top hats, some reading newspapers, others chatting amiably amongst themselves, and a few drinking at an extremely well appointed bar. The whole atmosphere was one that exuded understated gentility and good manners, in which the members of this unexpected assemblage were generally behaving as though they were in their own drawing rooms at home. They acted in a totally unabashed and relaxed manner, quite the epitome of a Gentleman's Club, albeit in an Iron Vault!

"When we last met a year ago in the Charing Cross Hotel you gave me information about Arthur Staunton that was useful but incomplete. I need to know more about the elusive Charles Peace."

"I believe, Holmes, you are engaged to continue to…" remarked Clay.

I heard no more since Clay's voice tapered off as they disappeared into the depths of a vault to gain privacy.

I approached the zinc-topped bar and sat on a stool whilst surveying the drinks on offer.

A bartender in a white jacket appeared in front of me and asked what I would have.

"Hmm," I said. "I see you have a bottle of that rare gold-leaf vodka; a glass of that liquor, neat, would be welcome, please."

And without any fuss or exhibitionism the bartender delivered a glass of pure nectar. Looking around the vaults I tried to assimilate in my mind the incongruous but real existence of this place, located below a major thoroughfare of the Metropolis that is the Marylebone Road. As I settled down to my drink I began to look more closely at the patrons using the place. One or two faces looked familiar, though from where I could not be certain. And then I saw it, a face about which I was most definitely sure!

It was that of the arrogant Sigmund Freud, the psychoanalyst and commentator on hysteria who had ignominiously thrown me out of his consulting rooms not these two days past. I felt sorely tempted to square up to Freud and have the goods on him but thought the better of it. After all, I reasoned, my presence here was that of a guest, aside from which I was anxious to join as a member.

Whilst I was ordering another drink, Holmes and Clay, having completed their deliberations, joined me just in time for me to include them in my order. Needless to say, the anecdotes and conviviality that accompany alcohol flowed in equal measure, and it was with reluctance that we bade our farewells and headed back out into the fog. Clay elected to stay on as he had other matters to attend to in this remarkable subterranean paradise. A kindly Bishop offered to take us out through the garden and pavilion back to the Marylebone Road, where Holmes immediately hailed a passing Hackney carriage.

"Oceanic House, Pall Mall, and step on it!"

"Oceanic what and where and do what?" replied the driver.

"Did you not hear me?" Holmes responded. "Oceanic House in Pall Mall!"

"And?" asked the driver, "Something about 'step on it'. Step on what exactly?"

Holmes stood there impassively and said, "Is there a problem with my simple instructions?"

The carriage driver looked at Holmes with a seasoned eye and replied, "Oceanic House, at least the one I know, is in Cockspur Street and not Pall Mall. And, as for step on it, I drive my carriage according to the Hackney Carriage Office

Regulations. Do you want me to take you to that address within the regulations or not?"

"Yes," I said, as both Holmes and I clambered into the carriage. Immediately, the carriage driver pulled his horse left round Park Crescent, skirting the garden we had just vacated, and turned into Portland Place. We appeared to be making good headway in the fog when suddenly the driver veered his carriage left into Cavendish Street.

"Was there something wrong with the *direct* route we were taking along the Portland Place?" asked Holmes through the open ceiling hatch in a manner pitched to irritate the driver.

"Yes. You do not know, but I do. A dray wagon has collided with a pantechnicon causing it to roll over onto its side that in turn has incommoded an omnibus, and now the carriageway into the Regent's Circus is blocked with wreckage, timber and warehouse goods."

"Cannot you pick your way around the wreckage?" inquired Holmes of the driver.

"You see that horse in front pulling this Hackney carriage? Well it is called a workhorse and it is used to pulling carriages such as this one, not vaulting over wreckage and obstacles. I have never entered this mare for the Grand National steeple-chase and I ain't never going to see it run at Aintree."

And with that Parthian shot, the Hackney carriage driver slammed shut the roof hatch preventing any further communication from taking place between him and either of us. We then turned sharply and with much jolting into the Portland Road, which eventually brought us to the Oxford Street, a street I detest and regretted having to use. I have mentioned before that the street's credibility deteriorates as one traverses east along it as we were now doing. The shops lining the front of the buildings appeared to be even more blatant about the low quality of goods and wares they were prepared to supply to an unsuspecting public. Needless to say, the traffic along this major thoroughfare running east-west was as heavy as it was slow, due to huge columns of omnibuses lumbering along with their human cargo. By now we had reached, albeit slowly, Dean Street, and into it our driver turned his carriage and clattered down toward Soho Square.

"This is the street," I recalled to Holmes, "where the infamous Colony Room Club is located. I wonder if it is still there, providing a refuge for those artists and tormented souls we had such pleasure in meeting and talking with?"

I was not to receive an answer. Instead Holmes directed a question not at me but rather at the driver.

"Driver, why have we driven into Soho Square, which is nowhere near the destination I gave you, and we are going east not south where Oceanic House is?"

"We are still west of Oceanic House and have not gone beyond it going east," replied the driver, marshalling as much contempt as possible for Holmes under the circumstances.

"Can you be sure, absolutely sure?" Asked Holmes.

"As sure as I am about what will happen to you come the Revolution," answered the carriage driver, with his voice laced with contempt.

"You could not organise a revolution on a merry-go-round!" I am certain Holmes replied.

The driver did not even bother to reply but, with a series of quick, desperate turns and reckless manoeuvres, took us dashing through alleyways and courtyards, finally bringing his carriage to an abrupt halt. He then said loudly in a Cockney accent, "I know my way around London, fog or no fog, and I do not take kindly to fares telling me how to do my job; so you can both get out of my cab right this moment."

I had known this would be the result of Holmes' encounter with that coachman, such was his character. One cannot win in these situations because carriage drivers invariably, have little else to do than to be Nihilist and cantankerous. Having been dismissed by him, we found ourselves in a street, or rather a cobbled stone yard, which was not immediately familiar, at least to me. The buildings, such as we could discern in the fog, were of a utility type, of very low quality and grimy, and seemed to rise through several floors up into the fog-laden sky.

By degrees we began to notice persons moving close by, some quickly, others with slower and measured steps as though stalking a prey. I continued to look up for a street nameplate but found none, and nor did I really expect to, for such places as this do not advertise their location. Then my mind flooded with memories of that peculiar incident of the dumb mute in the East End and the encounter we had with footpads. Was this going to be a repeat situation, I wondered?

"Well Holmes, what do you propose to do now, for I possess no clue as to where we are?"

"Have faith, Watson, and by deductive reasoning we shall navigate our way out of this labyrinth."

"By deductive what?" I asked with as much doubt in my voice as possible, as a way of indicating my despair.

"The carriage entered the yard from over there – or was it over there? Still, let us investigate this alleyway and see where it leads. Ah, nowhere. Right, let us try this one. After all, if all else fails, whatever remains must the solution."

It was not the solution and neither was the next one, and it became apparent to me that we were truly lost. I instinctively buttoned up my coat in order to create the vague dark outline of a bulky figure in the fog. I likewise removed my top hat to augment this anonymity in my attempt to blend in to our surroundings. The carriage driver, however, by his yelling at us, would have alerted anyone near-by as to our presence and, perforce, predicament. My suspicions proved to be correct, for within minutes of our arriving in the yard the place began to fill up with street-urchin types. Some merely looked at us, others were sizing us up. Above us people opened their windows and looked down on us.

There was a feeling of being in the wrong place at the wrong time. At that moment, however, Holmes pulled at my arm and led us through an archway that gave out onto a grubby side street comprised of dirty and bleak tenement buildings. We made our way along this street in the forlorn hope of finding salvation from our situation. Again Holmes' over confident treatment of the lower orders, in particular carriage drivers, has yet again resulted in our present dilemma which might conclude in our being inconvenienced at best or highly incommoded at worst.

My developing annoyance with Holmes at least took my mind off our predicament and instead compelled me to concentrate my mind on gaining a respectable and recognisable street from which we might continue our journey to Oceanic House. At length, we managed to extricate ourselves from this embroilment and eventually emerged in to the Charing Cross Road.

"I did not know such a place existed with minutes of the Charing Cross Road, Holmes."

How we got out remains a mystery to me, but I was grateful and vowed never to enter again such a place which, I now remembered from an article in the *Morning Chronicle*, was known as 'The Rookery'.* The name referred to a notorious slum between the Charing Cross Road and Seven Dials, in which were concentrated a general array of ambitious undesirables. These included thieves, footpads, dog stealers, prostitutes, pickpockets, and, more particularly, costermongers, speaking in their incomprehensible esoteric language designed to frustrate the uninitiated and keep their intentions secret.

"We are in Cambridge Circus, Watson. Let us see if we can find a carriage to take us to Oceanic House and…"

"No!" I interrupted Holmes. "Given our recent experience and your over-confident treatment of Hackney carriage drivers, I would prefer to walk, even in this fog, rather than risk another incident."

With that admonishing remark, I walked off uncertain of my decision into the all-embracing shrouds of fog, assuming Holmes would follow me. He did not.

Unperturbed, I turned into the Shaftesbury Avenue, past the Palace Theatre, known for its sumptuous bar decked out with its ubiquitous palm trees, and groped my way down this avenue towards Piccadilly Circus. My knowledge of the streets of the Metropolis is as good as any other, but in this blinding fog, confidence and the ability to recognise vague landmarks often desert me. I knew that, through keeping to the main thoroughfares and not resorting to unfamiliar back streets, I would arrive at my destination.

I therefore made my way down to the junction of Windmill Street where the London Pavilion is located opposite Monico's Restaurant, and a few moments later came to it. Looking up, I could just read the large sign poster that proclaimed 'London Pavilion – the House of Merriment – by the Brightest of Talent and the Best of Stars'. Given my recent experience in the 'Rookery', I could do with some outrageous humour, but resisted the urge to avail myself of a matinee ticket and continued instead down Windmill Street and over Coventry Street into the Haymarket, then down to Pall Mall. A rather circuitous route admittedly but one that was, with a betting certainty, bound to meet with success in getting me to Oceanic House. I wondered how Holmes was struggling, out of his depth, in the fog?

I eventually found Oceanic House and made my way into what was now the familiar territory of the main hall, and moved with confidence towards a commissionaire with the full expectation of having another misunderstanding as to my purpose here.

"I have come to make a reservation on the '*Olympic*' and am expecting a colleague to join me, though he may be some time," I said.

"Do you mean that gentleman over there who has been waiting some time for *his* colleague?" asked the commission-aire, pointing at Holmes who was sitting there with all the nonchalance of a Greek god, cigarette in one hand and a White Star Line brochure in the other.

"Good God Holmes, How did you get here before me?" I demanded to know.

"By a Carriage and Pair of course, however else?"

The commissionaire advised us that we should go up to the first floor in which the Commercial Department of the White Star Line is located. We did and upon entering the Shipping Office approached the counter. A clerk asked politely was he able to do anything for us?

"Yes," said Holmes. "We wish to book two berths on the '*Olympic*', sailing tomorrow evening from Liverpool for New York."

"What Class of berth did Sir have in mind?"

"Second Class for me and steerage for my valet here, Watson," said Holmes.

"Certainly Sir," said the clerk, whose look at me on hearing that facetious remark from Holmes showed clearly that he had relegated me downwards.

"Enough of this nonsense," I interjected, "I am a Doctor, Doctor John Watson, and this is my patient, Sherlock Holmes, and you might remember those two names when booking us both into Second Class berths my good man."

After much vacillation and form filling we eventually emerged back into Pall Mall with our Second Class tickets for travel on the infamous RMS '*Olympic*'. All of a sudden it dawned on me that we were off to the New World, to New

York *en-route* to Chicago! I am a seasoned traveller and have been to most of the provinces around our Empire whilst serving as an army doctor. Nonetheless, the prospect of visiting America filled me with fascination and I looked forward to it. Before we set off on that epic voyage, however, I had a small errand to run, and accordingly set off to Morel's Provisions Store, located at 210 Piccadilly.

We entered the high-class emporium of speciality foods and preserves, which included their infamous wooden boxes of *Glacé Fruits*, one of which I intended to purchase. In my endeavour to negotiate my way down the busy aisles to where the *Glacé Fruits* boxes were stacked in the shape of a pyramid, I inadvertently collided with a nanny and her charge, causing me to knock over a glass jar of boiled sweets.

"You will have to pay for that, Sir," came a lugubrious voice from the depths somewhere behind a highly polished mahogany counter dressed with a brass edge trim. "All breakages to be paid for by the customer," it continued.

"Oh very well then," I said handing a half-sovereign to a rather common and impudent shop assistant, clearly from the lower orders. I also noticed that the nanny's charge had no scruples about helping her little self to the boiled sweets now scattered on the floor.

"You are like a bull in a Chinese shop," remarked Holmes.

I chose on this occasion to ignore his sarcasm, which had rarely impressed me in the past, and decided to maintain a dignified silence. Having paid for my provisions, we made our way back into Piccadilly. Farther down the road, on the opposite side, our attention was arrested by the presence, just visible in the shrouds of fog, of the Egyptian Hall looking distinctly out of place and at odds in the vicinity of Piccadilly. It was built in the style of the ancient Egyptian cult Temple of Horus and typical of those found in the Valley of the Kings. It was constructed with walls into which the door and window reveals were set in slanting stone frames, wide at the base and narrowed toward the top, reflecting the overall trapezoid pyramid shape. The front entrance was located in between two broad columns which tapered upward to a capital in the style of the splayed leaves of a papyrus plant. The external walls and decoration of the structure supported a monstrously overhanging curved Egyptian architrave in the form of a hollow and roll that supported the stone slab roof.

The Egyptian Hall's design was in stark contrast to the elegant steel-framed Portland stone and Norwegian granite-clad building that was the Ritz Hotel, built opposite. Complete with its arcade fashioned on those of the Rue de Rivoli in Paris affording protection from the weather, it was built for the Blackpool Building & Vendor Company to be operated by Cesar Ritz.

We continued east down Piccadilly, eventually turning right into Air Street's short thoroughfare cut into a building, and paused to gather our wits before crossing the very busy Regent's Street. By dodging a series of military and commercial wagons and omnibuses, we achieved our goal and walked straight in through the front door of the Café Royal for luncheon.

Neither Holmes nor myself had any need to refer to the menu for we have dined there on innumerable occasions and for one good reason.

"Cholent and Latkes with Cumberland Sauce for both of us," instructed Holmes, "and your *specialité* of the Baked Ham *à la Café Royal* for the two of us, one with Tomato Sauce and the other with Mushroom Ketchup."

I followed him. "For dessert he will have the Warmed Eclairs and Madeira Sauce and I shall enjoy the Compote of Fruit, followed by, for both of us, *Café noir*, Brandy and the proprietor, Monsieur Nicolas Thévenon's choice of cigar."

"Now, what to drink? Always a difficult choice to make. Suppose we start off with chilled Chablis, then a Bordeaux, followed by Chianti?" Holmes suggested.

"Rather!" I concurred.

Whilst reflecting on the excellence of our meal over cigars and Brandy, Holmes suddenly said:

"We are making good progress in our quest in that John Clay has confirmed a couple of points, but there is, I believe, much more we need to learn and discover. All indications suggest that the situation is deeper than any of us thought, and has far implications reaching around the globe."

"Can you tell me anything at this stage, Holmes?" I begged.

"Well you know my methods, Watson. When all other facts have been eliminated, whatever remains must be the correct synthesis of the truth, however improbable," he said, more moved than I had ever seen him before.

And with that profound evasion of an answer to my question, he rose, leaving me to pay the bill for our luncheon!

* Now St. Giles' Circus.

Chapter 8

The Ghost of the Titanic

The next day, we were to begin our journey to the Herculaeneum Dock in Liverpool where the RMS '*Olympic*' was moored. I therefore spent the rest of the day relaxing with whisky and the *Daily Telegraph,* whilst Holmes busied himself referring to his notes and consigning bits of paper away for future use in what he refers to as a filing system, but to most people would seem a rubbish bin. Eventually, mentally exhausted, I retired to my room in readiness for the exertions that would inevitably be exacted upon my person on the morrow.

The next morning, refreshed, we breakfasted heartily on Harrod's bacon, eggs, and toasted bread with Marmalade, with strong Santiago coffee.

Apropos of nothing, I mentioned to Holmes, "I was thinking about our visit to the place beneath the Marylebone Road resembling a huge iron vault, as it were, and how utterly remarkable it is. I thought I dreamt it up but obviously I did not. How did it come into existence? What was the motivating force behind its creation, the creation of that iron vault, as I now term it, for that is what it is?"

"Quite simple. There are those who rebel at the very idea of being a member of a more formally established 'Gentleman's Club, the kind with which you are familiar and anxious to join. The members you observed in that establishment, remain a disparate lot and you will not find in their ranks a more diverse range of personality or character save perhaps in the Colony Room Club in the depths of Soho. In that respect one might find oneself talking with an artist, a Lord, a Barrister, a journalist, or indeed a criminal or musician!"

Holmes continued. "The style of the 'Iron Vault', as you call it, is conducive to reducing rigid social distinctions and allowing a certain cross-over of ideas and interests."

"Remarkable!" I applauded.

As Holmes walked off towards his room he casually said, "Moriarty is a member too."

I fell back into the chair from which I had just risen, my ranine eyes bulging with disbelief. A few moments later when Holmes reappeared I asked him how on earth could that be the case?

"Quite simply, said Holmes, "provided he does not break the golden rule of asking about or inquiring into any member's background or prospects, his membership is maintained as it is welcomed."

By now we had donned our coats and mufflers and I, clutching my portmanteau, and Holmes his Gladstone bag, ventured out into the fog. This time we walked to Baker Street Metropolitan Station to travel by the Underground Railway to the Gower Street Metropolitan Station.* After an uneventful ride, we walked through Thomas Hardwick's monumental Doric Arch and into the London & North Western Railway's Euston Square Railway Station. We entered the great terminus from High Seymour Street, located on the eastern side of the Station in order to gain the Liverpool-bound express train.

We arrived on time and at the right terminus, thanks to Bradshaw's indispensable Railway Guide. Excellent as the guide is though, it could not inform us from which platform the express train would depart. In order to ascertain this fact,

Doric Arch, Euston

we approached a railway servant upon the platform dressed in his uniform of black velveteen with red piping. He listened politely and attentively to our inquiry, then promptly informed us in an indifferent manner that it was from Platform 5 that the Liverpool Express left. He then turned on his heel and walked off smartly down the platform.

Our journey to Liverpool was without incident, as one comes to expect when travelling in a First Class carriage aboard an express train. Another redeeming factor was the fact that the London & North Western Railway uses the newly improved, patented, spring-loaded coupling gear. This ingenious gear assembly removes the dreaded jerks and knocks of carriages as they collide into each other every time the train starts or stops. These are familiar features that afflict carriages on other railways.

As we approached our destination, I pointed out to Holmes through the carriage window a partly constructed building as

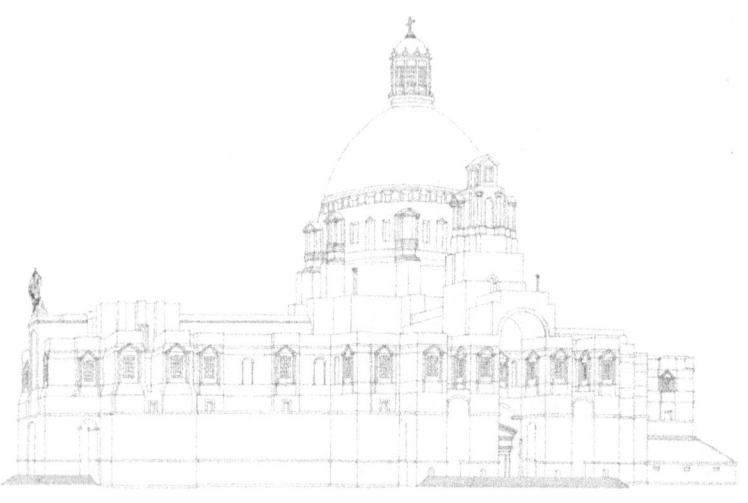

Ghost Cathedral, Liverpool

the site of a new Cathedral, hailed to be, when completed, the largest Cathedral in the world, ****** at least according to the *Daily Telegraph* or was it the *Morning Chronicle*? Though I seem to recall it has even at this early stage earned itself the sobriquet of Ghost Cathedral as a result of its incompleteness due to its vastness.

Our train eventually clanked into Liverpool's Lime Street Railway Station underneath a glazed screen, braced with iron tracery, which prevented inclement weather from entering the station. Alighting from the train carriage on to the platform we found ourselves beneath an extensive iron and glass canopy. From this station roof were suspended enormous town-gas globe lights. Though not of the chandelier type, they illuminated brightly a scene of chaos as various trade wagons, pantechnicon and delivery carts competed for precedence in the right of way for their horse-drawn vehicles amongst the piles of luggage and passengers.

I remembered Lime Street Railway Station. The last time

Holmes and I were here we witnessed an attempt to serve a writ on an individual, a pickpocket having a field day, being drenched with steam from an adjacent locomotive and enduring behaviour quite unacceptable and all before we had left the terminus! However, on our gaining the Lime Street Carriage stand, we climbed into a newly improved Clarence carriage, and instructed the coachman to take us to the Herculaeneum Dock and to the 'Olympic'.

It is hard to conceive of the scale or size of these White Star Line 'Wonder Ships' such as the 'Olympic', or as the ill-fated 'Titanic' was. However, whilst standing on the Hercu-laeneum Dock, to which the 'Olympic' boat was moored by adamantine chains, I tried to appreciate its immense size and sheer bulk. The vessel towered above me and its structure continued to my left and to my right blocking out everything else. It reminded me in a way of my first sight of Fonthill Abbey, when we stood outside waiting for a response to our summons at the front door. The building's huge scale had dominated and filled the immediate vicinity. As with the 'Olympic', both structures just seemed to continue to right and left in all their imposing, omni-presence. We ascended the gangplank, in itself capable if inducing vertigo, which led to a large door opening into the interior of the ship. We eventually made our way up to the upper section of this Royal Mail Steamer 'Olympic', the vessel that will take us to New York and to the New World aboard this 'Ship of Dreams'!

After what seemed like an inordinate length of time we found our berths. I assumed that by the time we had, the ship would be at least half way to the New World. It was therefore with disappointment that the seascape I expected to survey when coming onto deck comprised nothing more than the recently built largest ferro-concrete structure in the world, called the Liver Building, and other dockside edifices. However, a few minutes later after lots of shouting and general commotion on the dockside, the boat began imperceptibly to slip down the quayside and in doing so departed from the dock. Amongst a great deal of arm waving, verbal hopes and wishes, and insistences of *bon voyage*, mingled with the odd threat, the '*Olympic*' turned her stern to Liverpool and, facing the open sea, lurched forward on her voyage to the New World.

"Does one dress for dinner aboard these things?" I asked Holmes.

"Of course Watson. Civilisation does not cease on one's leaving Baker Street."

"That is not what you said when we were in Liverpool's Lime Street Railway Station!"

Accordingly, dressed in our jacket and tails we made our way through the iron chambers that constituted the boat and to the Grand Dining Room, whereupon we presented our berth tickets. A rather obsequious waiter offered to escort us to our table and led us into a dining room of such overwhelming sumptuousness and grandeur as to be oppressive, though impressive. The room was about two hundred feet long and as wide as the boat at seventy feet. Upon the floor was laid a red-and-gold patterned carpet and from it rose in three lines a series of square columns supporting an ornate stucco ceiling of filigree design that curved down to the columns' capitals, creating an impression of waves. We followed the waiter past large dining tables, which afforded spacious seating and elbowroom. Upon each table, covered in white linen cloth, were set glass vases bearing red roses, and sparkling carafes of water with matching silver accoutrements, all of which reflected the ornate glass light lanterns, set flat against the ceiling.

As we progressed though this luxurious Dining Room, I began to think we were being escorted quite to the end of the room, past several empty tables. Maybe this is where our berth number table is located, I thought. Suddenly, we came to a highly varnished, carved door and, upon reaching, it our waiter opened it and ushered us through, closing the door firmly behind us. We faced a sight to behold.

I have served in the British Army as surgeon and am used to bulk feeding in field tents made up as canteens, with all manner of standards being dispensed with, including persons smoking pipes whilst sitting next to a diner eating his food. In the room into which we had just been escorted, presumably, I thought, was our allocated dining table. People were walking about with plates of food in their hands searching for somewhere to sit. It was a scene of chaos and the noise was deafening. I also noticed that some diners were drinking warm beer straight out of the bottle in an abandoned manner. At length a portly servant came up to us and asked, in a demanding manner, to see our berth tickets.

I was not impressed with the way in which this flunky had addressed us and made my feelings known to him by deliberately taking time to reveal our tickets to him.

"I also notice you came into this room via that door," he said, whilst pointing to the door we had in fact entered through. "How did you manage that?"

"Quite simply, the servant escorting us pulled at the door handle and the door opened. How do you think we came through the door?" I informed this imbecile who by now was beginning to annoy even Holmes.

"No, no, no," he said. "This boat is compartmentalised. You should not have been able to gain access to the other side of that door! In fact, I remain surprised that you have been able to get by the elaborate segregation precautions that are in place on board the '*Olympic*'.

"What are you talking about? Kindly explain yourself, my good man."

"I am not your good man, Sir. And you will kindly restrict

yourself to addressing me as Steward since I am an *employé* of the White Star Line and you are both in the wrong area of the ship. Steerage passengers are located two decks below this deck."

"I beg your pardon, how?" I remonstrated.

"That is accepted. Now if you will follow me," interrupted the white linen-jacketed servant.

"Now listen here my good man. Listen! We are Second Class passengers and we were looking for our dining room table when our waiter delivered us here," I said, handing over Holmes' and my own ticket.

"Ah well yes, you see this is all wrong," he advised, whilst examining our documents, "you want the Second Class Dining Room!"

"Really?" said Holmes. "That is as profound a work of deductive reasoning as I have ever been privileged to experience at first hand. Perhaps you might just escort us through this boat to the appropriate place?"

"Follow me gentlemen, please."

"I did not realise a boat could have so many corridors, Holmes. Just think what it must have been like on board the ill-fated sister ship *'Titanic'* when it was in its death struggle and at a steep angle and sinking?"

"Well Watson, at least fifteen hundred souls could tell you what it was like before they all they went down with the ship."

At last we arrived at our dining room, less opulent than the Grand Dining Room from which we had been unceremoniously ejected, but infinitely better than the canteen we had just left.

"That canteen, Holmes, reminds me of all the trepidation, revulsion and systematic unpleasantness concentrated in an English parliamentary train in which we have had the misfortune to travel by."

Our waiter brought us the menu and wine list from which

we ordered immediately two bottles of Chardonnay.

I surveyed the menu headed 'Triple Screw Steamer *'Olympic'* Second Class Menu':

Luncheon

Hot Scotch Broth or Spaghetti au Gratin
Beef Steak & Kidney Pie or Roast Loin of Pork with Apple Sauce
Baked Jacket Potatoes
Cold York Ham or Roast Beef
Bologna Sausage or Brawn,
Pickles and Salad
Baked Apples or Blackberry Tart
Fresh Fruit
Cheese   Biscuits
Coffee

I was being to harbour concerns about the content of the menu, which seemed to me to be positively egalitarian. Had we paid for Second Class tickets to be offered this kind of food, I wondered.

"Waiter, do we have another menu from which we can select something edible? This menu looks as if it were designed for Third Class passengers or indeed those of steerage."

A somewhat perturbed waiter hurried off and shortly returned with two new menu cards:

Dinner

Consomme Tapioca
Baked Haddock Sharp Sauce
Curried Chicken & Rice
Spring Lamb Mint Sauce
Roast Turkey Cranberry Sauce
Green Peas Puree Turnips
Boiled Rice

Boiled & Roast Potatoes
Plum Puddings
Wine Jelly Coconut Sandwich
American Iced Cream
Nuts, assorted
Fresh Fruit
Cheese Biscuits
Coffee

"Good God Holmes, this may well be the '*Ship of Dreams*', but the items of food from this menu are rapidly turning it into a '*Ship of Nightmares*'," I said, repeating my observation to a passing waiter.

The servant stopped and suggested, "perhaps you might like to try the deluxe *à la Carte Restaurant* located aft on the Bridge Deck."

"How do we get there?" I asked.

"Forward Sir, please follow me."

We did so and Holmes, in appreciation of my initiative with the waiter, said approvingly, "Well done, Watson! Your belligerence has got us a decent menu from which we can select something edible."

"Rather!" I enthused.

Dinner
Sardines à l'imperiale
Consomme Petite Marmite
Saumon Naturale   Sauce Mousseline
Concombre
Chaudfroid de Volaille en Aspic
Filet de Mouton à la Sargent
Pommes Fridal Chouxfleur
Cailles au Canapes
Pomme Chateaux

Salade
Macedoine des Fruits en Gelée
Foie de Poulet et de Lard
Glace Pralinée
Dessert
Café

From this point onwards, life aboard the '*Olympic*' was one continuous round of fine dining, good drinks and witty conversation as we made our way around the Salon tables. Indeed, at one stage we were invited to join at his table, for dinner, the newly promoted Captain of the '*Olympic*', a pleasant fellow called Mr David Moody, who was one of the surviving officers from the ill-fated '*Titanic*'. All in all, the ship was, as the advertisements pronounced it to be '…a veritable floating palace, including her being the largest vessel in the world. It is not only in size, but also in the luxury of her appointments, that the '*Olympic*' takes first place among the big steamers of the world!' At least for us, but God help the Third Class passengers and those unfortunate souls travelling steerage in the bowels of the boat, who would only be released on sighting Ellis Island in New York bay.

* Now Euston Square Metropolitan Station.

** Metropolitan Cathedral of Christ the King – had it been built.

Chapter 9

The Largest Room on Earth

Whilst Holmes and I were promenading on deck and discussing our investigation, we became aware of a commotion at the front of the ship.

"Good God, Holmes, we have not hit an iceberg, I hope," I wondered fearfully, and began immediately to work out into which lifeboat I could scramble and how to operate the davits to lower it the down to the Ocean and effect my escape from the doomed boat.

"Do not panic Watson. It is only that a passenger has sighted the Statue of Liberty on the horizon. We both walked to the bow of the ship and, upon further observation, could indeed see Liberty on the horizon as if she were walking on the waters of the Atlantic! She stood there in splendid isolation, with no other structure or building to distract the observer from her stately poise and elegance, her eyes gazing out, looking east.

Of all the interpretations in stone or bronze of Greek goddesses, Liberty is by far the most dramatic and truly beautiful. She looks as if she has a determination in her facial features, as though pre-occupied with thought. In my travels around our Empire I have witnessed statues of mortals and immortals and most appear lifeless. Indeed, of course, they are, but I am reminded of the group of females, the Caryatids, carved as stone pillars on the Temple of Erechtheion* at the Acropolis in Athens. These women were reputedly turned into stone by the goddess Athena, who herself, as represented in stone and clad in an chryselephantine armour of gold and ivory, is ugly and devoid of the representation of life or movement. Liberty in comparison looks as if she can justify herself and her position by holding up high her flaming torch of liberty, whilst holding inviolate wisdom carved on the tablet she holds in her other arm, giving her meaning with benign purpose.

An age seemed to go by before we finally entered Lower New York Harbour, passing beneath the magnificence of the Statue of Liberty, then heading towards the newly constructed Brooklyn Bridge with its cobweb of steel cables glinting in the late Fall sunlight. In order to complete the docking, our boat began a series of sideways manoeuvres enabling the ship to line up its approach to the quay, on which it seemed hundreds of people were waiting to greet relatives from Europe. One immediately appreciated the colossal size and weight of the boat as it inched its way into the dock before being moored against the quayside.

We left the docks, heading straight into the hustle and bustle that the Lower East Side of New York is renowned for. After an inordinately long wait in the Customs Shed we were free to leave and, after some quite uncalled-for discourtesy, which seemed to be the normal behaviour hereabouts, availed ourselves of a carriage, the class of which I had no idea save that it only had two wheels. I knew with a betting certainty that it was not a buckboard or a Surrey. We clattered along a road, possibly South Street, adjacent to the East River. At length we drove under the Brooklyn Bridge and eventually emerged onto the infamous Bowery, then headed north over Delancey Street toward East Houston Street. Here our cab driver reined his horse left across Lafayette Street and then turned right into Broadway, where we continued at a brisk pace before turning right into West 4th Street and into Washington Square.

Whilst in the square we came to a halt, as a result of the vicissitudes of the traffic, and for a few minutes I was afforded the time to admire the Washington Square Arch, reminiscent of the Marble Arch in London. Eventually, leaving the north side of the square, we entered Fifth Avenue and proceeded in a stately fashion up to East 34th. Street. A few minutes later our driver deposited us at the Pennsylvania Railroad Station from where we would board our Empire State Express train to Chicago. Having paid our driver off with the usual attendant argument about cost and directness of route, we entered the 'Largest Room on Earth'. It is contained in the vast complex of buildings that is the Pennsylvania Rail Road Station located in between Seventh and Eighth Avenues on West 34th. Street. Whilst waiting in line for our tickets to Chicago, I consulted my Bäedeker's *Guide to the New World* about this famous Station. The article was quite illuminating, especially as we were actually standing in the building and could confirm visibly certain descriptive adjectives. The article read:

Pennsylvania Rail Road Station is deliberately designed in the impressive Beaux-Arts style. The building is constructed as a grand monumental entrance to the commercial Metropolis of the United States that at the same time conforms to the traditional aspects of a great Rail Road terminus. The Station remains to date the biggest building on earth, housing the 'largest and most monumental room in the world'; complete with sixty-foot-high Corinthian capped columns supporting a gigantic vaulted coffered ceiling. The Station's designs reflect those of the *Thermae* at Caracalla** in ancient Imperial Rome.

'The architect of the Pennsylvania Rail Road Station,

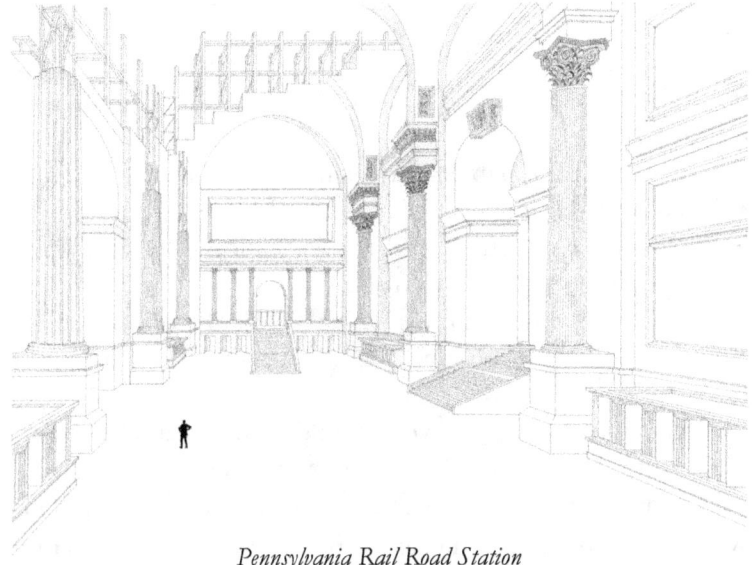

Pennsylvania Rail Road Station

Stanford 'Always Crazy' White, according to JP Morgan, owner of the ill-fated *'Titanic'*, did not witness the completion of his creation. He was alas, whilst dining in a restaurant in the Madison Square Tower that he also designed, shot dead by a jealous husband, a one Harry K Thaw – a major stockholder in the Pennsylvania Rail Road.

'A notable feature of the Pennsylvania Rail Road Station, located on the bustling Eighth Avenue, is the peculiar effect the Great Hall has on those who enter it, in making the visitor lower his voice and instilling a hushed reverence, as though entering a Cathedral.

'The facilities extant at Pennsylvania Railroad Station are remarkable. They include waiting parlors exclusively for women or for funeral parties in which mourners may wish to congregate prior to accompanying their coffins on eastbound electric trains to the Brooklyn Necropolis. In addition, there is a small infirmary for those in need of medical treatment.

Fresh-water drinking fountains supplied by the surprisingly clean tap water from New York's water mains are ranged throughout the Station's precincts.' So Bäedeker's guidebook informed us.

After an interminable wait queuing at the ticket office, a railroad servant informed us, with obvious delight in his manner, that we were at the wrong station and should get ourselves over to Grand Central.

"Do you not have here in New York the equivalent of Bradshaw's Railway Guide?" I asked loudly as I departed the from the ticket window.

"Yeah, we do, and *that* you should use it!" came the rapid staccato reply, to which I made no response.

We made our way out of the Station and started walking along 34th. Street, heading east to the corner of Fifth Avenue. Here is built the massive and imposing Waldorf Astoria Hotel, a favourite haunt of New York's high society.

"Watson, we have time to refresh ourselves with a drink, have we not?"

"I do not know but let us have one anyway!"

The Waldorf Astoria Hotel is built in the Victorian style of architecture that expresses opulence at every opportunity. Not one square inch of its surface had escaped the architects' designs for the interior finishes. Very beautiful, but it is as though the Baroque and Victorian styles have collided to create a grandiose though overpowering ambience within the spaces afforded by this huge Hotel, the largest in New York.

Various marble columns reaching up terminated in arches supporting ornate stucco ceilings with raised tracery designs. Some pilasters, flat columns, set flush against the walls, were performing the same role in creating a vaulted ceiling decorated with figurines and gold leaf. Statues looked down on us as we walked through the foyer on a deep-pile red carpet. Heavy, flocked silk wallpaper lined the walls, which intermittently gave way to highly polished mahogany doors set in wide door frames leading to other areas of the building with promises of even more splendour.

At last we threw open a massive double door clad in varnished walnut that gave us egress into a sumptuous bar covered with purple Fior Di Pesco Classico, the only marble to place one's drink on in style. Ranged upon the marble bar were huge gasogenes dispensing aërated water on an almost industrial scale! Competing for space on the bar were large bronze candelabra with candles giving out myriad points of light. The whole effect was of dazzling opulence. The room itself had not escaped the designer's attention. Suspended from the high, white, ornate stucco ceiling were acetylene-fuelled chandeliers radiating a powerfully brilliant light that illuminated the whole room. Laid out on the floor was a purple broadloom carpet with gold stars woven into its pattern, and upon it were large sofas covered in a deep red *moiré* silk. Next to each sofa were the ubiquitous palm trees very much in evidence. The whole place had an ambience of luxury where money was not a real option but imperial splendour was!

"What can I get you two gentlemen?" asked a friendly bartender.

These words heralded what I knew would be a very enjoyable time.

* Watson can only be referring to the replica of the Erechtheion at the side of St Pancras Church, Euston Road near the St Pancras Hotel.

** The vast Classical building housing heated bathing pools.

Chapter 10

The Hanker Fänners

Some time later we fell into Fifth Avenue and continued our by now much slower march north to the notoriously gaudy 42nd. Street, into which we turned left towards the Grand Central Terminal, home of the New York Central Rail Road and operator of the renowned Empire State Express. 42nd. Street turned out to be very similar to the Tottenham Court Road, in London, with reasonably large, glass-fronted shops selling clothing, books and furniture. The ground floors, I noticed, of the higher-class establishments had high ceilings, in fact quite obtrusively high ceilings. Other establishments were more suited to provisioning clients in search of Vaudeville, bordering as they did on the shallow and cheap. We made our way along its shabby elegance and finally came upon our destination.

As we approached the Terminal, the sheer size of yet another Beaux-Arts-designed Rail Road building was awe-inspiring. Even more impressive was the extravagant deco-ration of a carving of a monumental relief group dominated by the figure of Mercury, the Roman god of speed an, by implication, of Rail Roads. Here he is immortalised on the marble entablature displayed above the main portico adorning the buildings, whilst seemingly addressing 42nd. Street in all his god-like mute arrogance and impossible gesture. Suitably awe-struck we at length turned into its imposing portal and entered the Great Hall.

"First things first in getting our priorities right," I said responsibly to Holmes. "That bar upstairs looks suitable enough."

Holmes consented and we both eagerly ascended the polished limestone steps leading up to the bar. Having acquired our whiskies we surveyed the Grand Central Terminal's vast Great Hall. It is no co-incidence that it was designed by Whitney Warren, a cousin to William K Vanderbilt, owner of the New York Central Rail Road, so an adjacent commemorative plaque informed me.

The Terminal is designed in accordance with the impressive Beaux-Arts style. I believe the basic building method of Beaux-Arts construction is to affix imposing carved limestone masonry blocks to a building's metal frame – thus creating the impression of an edifice entirely built of stone. The resulting façade of this building displays ornate details, such as carvings, reliefs, statuary, crocketts, New York Central Rail Road corporation ciphers, bronze and nickel fixtures including window and door frames, ornamental lamps, emblems, signage and general ostentatious paraphernalia.

A huge four-faced bronze clock tower dominated the interior of the Great Hall. It was a feast for the eyes to see such beauty and strength combining to produce a truly monumental building. Sunlight streaming through the huge semicircular lunette window openings and reflecting off the Travertine stone floor dazzled the eyes. Even Holmes was impressed, as evinced by his roving eye. It was also evident to me that, in constructing this meretricious but impressive building, money was regarded as being no obstacle to design.

The Hall was dominated by a ceiling into which small electrically powered lights had been inserted to create the illusion of a celestial night sky with shining stars. The distinguishing feature of the interior of this Beaux-Arts building was the extravagant use of masonry blocks, I think of polished limestone or sandstone, to form internal walls, floors, arches and bridges, emphasising keystones, internal balconies, columns and stairs. The interior structure here incorporated wide low arches opening onto the different areas of the Terminal. The same technique, I noted, was deployed with stone balustrades on internal bridges linking one space with another. Broad staircases of polished limestone with intricate bronze railings ascended to the upper levels, including to the bar in which we were presently drinking.

Ornamental bronze and limestone statues on each of the landings supported globe lanterns that radiated electric light. Elaborate sections of cornice and architrave capped the stonework and walls, interrupted only by pilasters and piers supporting the decorative arches. The whole effect was one of a lavishly powerful interior of warm, pale yellow polished stone reflecting light from dazzling bronze light globes, reminiscent of the splendour of Imperial Rome that it emulates so successfully.

"I suppose we had better get our tickets and board the Express," I said with only the vaguest of intention, since I had neither the wish nor inclination to leave this fascinating location where I could watch the world go by. Looking at Holmes, I knew he felt the same. Nevertheless, we had descended the staircase from the bar down to the foyer level when suddenly a woman almost fell into me, causing me in turn to fall against a wall. It would have to have been with my right shoulder, and the knock immediately set off a deep pain that was the legacy of a wound received whilst serving during the Egyptian Emergency when attached to the Royal Berkshire Regiment.

"Oh pardon me sir," she said whilst gathering her wits, "I did not look where I was going, did I?"

"Oh think nothing of it Madam," I ventured, rubbing my shoulder.

"Oh you are so kind to me and I do declare you are a gentleman, Sir! There, I have caused you to soil your coat with soot from the wall," she said, brushing off with her hand the patches of soot from my coat.

"There you are, all nice and clean again, and even more handsome!"

I was flattered by this remark. She herself was quite a striking looking woman, not pretty but not unattractive either, with deep rouge-coloured lips. Her hair was dark and long, not styled, but worn rather loosely and tied with a purple velvet ribbon. Above this ensemble she wore a felt hat, almost it seemed as an afterthought, with a brown goose feather protruding from it. Her long dress of bright red was, I supposed, acceptable for the vicinity in which we found ourselves but it was difficult for me to ascertain the appropriateness. It is probable that such a dress would be out of place in the more fashionable parts of London. The blouse she wore was blue and she had covered it with a woollen shawl that appeared speckled with sequins. She then smiled at me, gave a shallow curtsey, and turned on her ankle, continuing her progress through Grand Central Terminal.

"We had better get our train tickets, Holmes," I said, reaching for my wallet.

"Hold on Holmes!" I said startled, whilst searching my person for the wallet.

"I cannot have left it in the bar at the Waldorf Astoria nor that bar we have just left. Oh no! That woman, that wretched woman has just picked my pocket and made off with my wallet."

Paying no heed to my weak thigh, another war wound sustained in creating our Empire, I immediately began to give chase and eventually succeeded in gaining upon the thief and confronted her outright.

"Young lady, you have just stolen a wallet from my pocket when you fell against me not these few minutes past."

"What, how dare you! Me steal your wallet? I am a fine, respectable lady, in fact a 'Southern Belle' just visiting New York," she protested.

I also noticed in the corner of my eye that another woman was coming to her aid, outraged at my very audible verbal accusation. Undeterred I repeated my allegation and approached the thief. What I failed to notice was that the other woman had by now moved to my right and, without any hesitation, landed an unerringly accurate punch on my face that left me smarting from the blow.

Both women were by now running away, with their voluminous dresses and petticoats flapping as they did so, but I was determined to retrieve my wallet. In giving chase, it occurred to me that the women were probably members of a notorious gang that Bäedeker's *Guide to the New World*, describes as being Hanker Fänners, who prey on strangers to New York and other large cities. They infest such places as Rail Road Stations, harbours and hotels, and have a reputation for violence and aggression of which they are proud. They often work their way along the New Jersey seaboard from Atlantic City to Jersey City, from whence most of them originate, and on into New York and other destinations. Their objective is the hapless male.

Undeterred by this unsettling thought, I kept the Hanker Fänners in sight and pursued them down a circular ramp into the depths of the Station, beneath the platforms. All was quiet as I surveyed this subterranean world of steel girders and forests of square iron lattice columns, unsure as to whether I was the pursuer or had become the pursued. Occasionally a train went rumbling by with it's driver looking at me askance, but apart from that all was quiet.

Then, out of nowhere, came a series of linked trolleys

trundling along a small conveyor track and piled high on them were valises, portmanteaus and trunks. The sight of this driver-less trolley train trundling along by itself momentarily unnerved me.

Suddenly the chase was on again as the two Hanker Fänners exposed their hidden position and made a break for it. By the time I had dodged in between the iron piers and reached their position they had disappeared again. Suddenly an iron bar went whizzing past my head. I instinctively ducked and dropped to the floor. Again the Hankers, who probably knew this subterranean realm quite well and used it as a resort to escape or avoid being apprehended, ran off. My comparative ignorance of my surroundings began to concern me. The chase was on again and the Hankers appeared to be making their way to what looked like a door giving access out of this subterranean world. I increased my speed in order to intercept them, for I was intent on retrieving my wallet at whatever cost. Whilst giving chase and gaining upon them both, however, one appeared to be slowing down, and then turned around to face me. It was the woman who had stolen my wallet.

"Hand over my wallet – now," I demanded

She smiled, reached down to the floor and picked up an iron wrench, which she then threw at me, missing my head by inches as it crashed into a nearby square iron latticed column. She continued her escape but I was having none of it and increased my pace, eventually catching up with her. Her accomplice re-appeared and an undignified struggle ensued as both Hanker Fänners fought with a viciousness I did not think possible from women. Needless to say my time as an army doctor had taught me a thing or two about close-quarter contact and I thus emerged victorious and with my wallet.

I rejoined Holmes, who appeared indifferent to my adventure and my close shave with a head injury or, possibly, death.

"I have remarked in the past, Watson, that you are too

trusting of women, especially those who flatter you. That woman was clearly a seasoned pickpocket and I am amazed you did not see that?"

"I am a doctor, Holmes, not a policeman and you might have said something or at least alerted me. And Holmes, notwithstanding that pickpocket who so nearly succeeded in dashing out my brains had that iron wrench made contact with my head, I, unlike you, do not have a warped view of the fair sex."

We purchased our Pullman tickets for the Express and made our way to the platform advised as being Platform No. 5.

Chapter 11

The Empire State Express

"Here we are Watson, it is from this platform that we board the Empire State Express for our trip to Chicago," said Holmes in a pensive manner.

Turning onto Platform No. 5 we walked past a huge thirty-seven-foot-long locomotive of the American Type 4-4-0 Class. Indeed, this locomotive engine was a sight to behold, with its tangle of highly polished brass and steel pipes, some of which were clamped to a gigantic boiler like protruding veins, and hissing steam fiercely. The cabin, with its tender, domes, smokestack, boiler, trim and light lantern in front, was painted in a black-satin finish, and constructed on eight steel wheels, four of which were over seven feet high. On the side of the black-painted tender in gold leaf lettering two-and-a-half feet high were the words, *'Empire State Express'*. The engine represented a terrific sight of colossal mechanical power concentrated and harnessed in order to haul this Express train of twelve carriages through the Allegheny Mountains. And, depending on the route, through the northern end of the beautiful Shenandoah Valley, at the tremendous speeds for which it is famously and justly renowned.

We presented our tickets to the conductor and he accordingly escorted us to our seats. On the way through the train carriages I picked up a small pamphlet that explained a few interesting facts about the Express.

The first of these stated that the 'Express is an all-Pullman train with no inexpensive coaches, comprising Dining, Parlor and Sleeping cars in addition to an Observation Carriage. In this carriage there is a Bar and a fully functioning, mechanically operated Aëolian Pianola for the enjoyment of those passengers holding First Class tickets'.

Whilst perusing other uplifting and informative facts, I became aware gradually of a commotion on the platform. It seemed to involve a group of rather angry-looking women, some of whom appeared to be trying to board the train.

The second fact informed me that the Express was named for the State of New York, the sobriquet of which is the 'Empire State'. Similarly, for example, the adjacent State of New Jersey is known affectionately as the 'Garden State', just as 'Key Stone State' is for the State of Pennsylvania.

At last the train began to glide imperceptibly along the platform and entered the tunnel through which the train would traverse up through Manhattan island, *en-route* to the Hell Gate Bridge, that spans the East River and over which the Express eventually progresses up into the 'Empire State'.

"I say, Holmes, this is the way to travel is it not? Mr George Mortimer Pullman certainly knows how to build luxury railroad carriages like this one in which we are now travelling. The attained levels of comfort in their appointments are as wonderful as they are resplendent!" I enthused definitively.

"I agree with the pamphlet you are quoting, Watson; compare the ignominious English parliamentary train or the Metropolitan Railway with the unbridled comfort of the upholstery in this carriage."

Presently a waiter in a white jacket appeared and asked if he could 'fix us a drink'?

"Rather," I enthused, "a large whisky – neat for me and a

large whisky with a dash of aërated water for my friend there"

"Would you like to try in your Scotch the new craze for the Coca-Cola?" asked the waiter.

"The new craze for what, the 'Coca-Cola'?"

"Yeah Sir, it is a dark, aërated beverage made with cocaine and sugar, and has more punch to it than aërated water."

That remark, I observed caught Holmes' attention.

"You think I would want to put a drink as that into my Scotch? Certainly not my good man!"

Our drinks, without the Coca-Cola, did arrive and, with our cigars, we enjoyed them in this unfamiliar world of opulence aboard the Empire State Express.

As the train made its way out of Manhattan, emerging at 97th Street, a huge parabolic railroad bridge came into sight. I knew it to be the Hell Gate Bridge that takes the train over the East River on the elevated railroad out to Long Island City located in eastern Metropolitan New York. It was certainly an impressive-looking bridge. I also noticed that, irrespective of the mighty engineering achievement of the parabolic steelwork which forms two huge arches, from which is suspended the bridge deck carrying the railroad, it is the massive abutments which, though playing no structural role, are impressive, representing a strong expression of Classicism.

The Classically ornate, granite-clad masonry abutment towers at either end of the bridge serve no real purpose other than creating the illusion that they are holding up the bridge by receiving the steel girder-work, although this is in fact anchored directly into the foundations of the abutments. The granite stone cladding is present merely to hide the collection of structural girders supporting the elevated section of the railroad. However, in typical Beaux-Arts style, the towers carry an array of design features, not least in the detailing of the almost cantilevered cornices to the upper sections of the towers. Both are completed with balustrades and arches,

Hell Gate Bridge

crowning deep vertical voids, some twenty feet wide, virtually forming two distinct piers to each of the masonry towers.

Before our train left Manhattan, I looked back in awe at the gigantic towers of the newly constructed Woolworth Building, affectionately known as the 'Cathedral to Commerce', which dominates lower Manhattan. The train carriages clattered and rumbled noisily over the bridge, whilst I watched through the steel lattice girders of the structure leading to the elevated railroad the fleeting vistas of Metropolitan New York, including its suburbs. As time went by, we glided through the State of New York, resplendent in the late Fall, with the blueness of the Allegheny Mountains in the deep background heralding our rapid approach to the State of Pennsylvania.

"Do you know Watson, that I am unable to eradicate from my mind the question of why Charles Peace was so eager for us to visit Lyon's house in Harley Street. Surely his death was a *fait accompli* and it was beyond our ability to do anything?"

"What can I say Holmes?"

I was somewhat perturbed by his line of inquiry, interfering as it did with my wish to experience the beauty of the rapidly passing countryside, and unwilling to consider the morbid facts surrounding the death months ago of a minor villain in the depths of a fog-bound London.

Holmes continued to mumble to himself in the absence of my invited response.

All of a sudden I became aware of a commotion coming from a couple of carriages away. I diverted my gaze down the carriage but could only hear loud voices. The noise seemed to have stopped and therefore I resume my gaze through the carriage window of the beautiful scenery rushing by resplendent in the late Fall. The blueness of the Allegheny Mountains seemed to have diminished almost imperceptibly as we raced toward them. Then it happened. The commotion all of a sudden erupted this time more vehemently and louder. At length, the reason for the noise that was becoming louder became all too apparent. It originated with a group of woman who, from their demeanour and attitude towards the other passengers, were looking for something or someone.

One of them, a rather vulpine-looking woman, approached and looked particularly hard at us. She then sat down next to Holmes, opposite me, and put her booted feet on the seat next to mine. In so doing she deliberately allowed her dress to creep back revealing to me her bare legs.

I repaired to my pamphlet about the Empire State Express, feigning absorption in its wealth of uplifting facts, especially the one informing me that each Pullman carriage weighs upwards of thirty-five tons. None-the-less, I still felt hotly embarrassed by the woman's blatant rudeness – and in public – on an Express of the New York Central Rail Road!

Then the inevitable happened and I could not quite bring myself to believe it. She deliberately let her foot drop sideways, bringing it into contact with my thigh, my injured thigh, a legacy of the Battle of Khandahar whilst serving in Afghanistan. No riveting or indispensable uplifting fact contained in my pamphlet about the Empire State Express could distract my mind from this outrageous behaviour – and on board a train!

I protested at this act of confidence, at which she appeared to feel no shame. I could hardly believe it was happening, even in America, and on a Chicago-bound train too.

"Please cease and desist from this over-confident behaviour in front of me, Madam." I said, with as much officiousness in my voice as I could muster.

"Over-confident what? What kinda spiel is that buster?"

Somewhat taken aback by her inelegant reply, I spluttered, "How dare you! How dare you speak to me like that and..."

"Yeah? Well how dare you rub your thigh against my aching foot which I just put there to rest on the bench you are sat on?" She interrupted.

Flabbergasted, I could barely contain my amazement at her behaviour, and even Holmes was compelled to intervene, but not in a way I anticipated. Rather, he was jerking his head in the direction behind me. I turned to see what had caught Holmes' attention. It was an ugly scene that manifested itself the form of a mob of rampaging Hanker Fänners, intent on trouble with anything or anyone and that, I immediately got the impression, included us. They had boarded the train intent on metering out violence to us and, in particular, to me as revenge for my encounter with their sister Hanker Fänners when retrieving my wallet from them in depths of Grand Central Terminal.

My heart began to pound against the wall of my chest.

"Come Watson, I think a strategic withdrawal is in order," commanded Holmes.

As I rose to comply with this welcome suggestion, the woman opposite me barred my exit from the seat with her partially bared legs. As I attempted to step over her she raised them accordingly and then grabbed me, yelling, "Here he is girls, I have got him!"

Never in my life, including during my service in the military, have I experienced a more instant dread as I did then, at the frightening sight of a mob of handbag-waving, hysterical women intent on my destruction, moving in towards me.

However, with the help of Holmes' hands around her throat, I managed to extricate myself from her lethal embrace.

As we passed down through the various carriages including the Dining Car, one of the pursuing Hankers picked up a long steak knife and threw it at Holmes. It pierced the back of his right arm but not, in my opinion, seriously. In retaliation, I picked up a large dinner plate with food on it, and without seeking permission from either the Rail Road company, the owners of the plate or the diner who was eating off it, tossed it, as one would throw a discus, back at the knife thrower. It made contact with her chin and she promptly collapsed to the Dining Car floor. By now other Hanker Fänners, incensed that yet another of their own had been downed, were clambering over her inert body in relentless pursuit of us. Another knife went whistling through the air, missing my head by inches. It pinned itself to the opulent mahogany and walnut-inlaid veneer wall cladding, on which was depicted a classical Greek scene of wood nymphs dancing gaily with trailing ribbons intertwined about their hands.

At length we reached the end of the third carriage, and here we turned to engage a few of the more intent Hankers on one of the exterior observation platforms that are located at the end of each carriage. A precarious place in which to make a stand, but necessary, as the pursuit was as relentless as it was threatening.

Then one of the more burly of the Hankers separated from

her comrades and launched her person at me with a foul curse, screaming that she intended to "throw you and your thin pal off this train – right now!"

The train was, I noted to my alarm, by now hurtling through the Pennsylvanian countryside approaching the Allegheny Mountains at a speed for which the Empire State Express is justly famous. That the Hanker intended to carry out her threat was never in doubt in my mind, because not only did she have the build, but also the vicious attitude to probably succeed in her intention. Moments later when she was attempting to carry out her threat I was able to dodge the repeated blows of her handbag to my person without recourse to undignified offensive re-action against her. Holmes had no such compunction, and unhesitatingly delivered an unerringly accurate Baritsu blow to the neck that incapacitated her, whereupon she promptly collapsed on to the observation platform.

Another Hanker, who had produced a not inconsiderably long knitting needle, started in to attack Holmes. She failed to notice my foot, however, and I was therefore able to trip her up on the deck and thus foil the violent attack upon Holmes. The presence of two inert bodies on the observation platform had the effect of slowing down the now incensed Hanker Fänners' progress in their vindictive pursuit of us.

We were accordingly able to escape into the next carriage, one that comprised Pullman sleeping berths. Here people were preparing to retire to bed and were dressed in white night gowns resembling so many shrouded ghosts. Their complacent lives were about to be interrupted horribly as Holmes and I went clattering through the carriage, chased by furious women screaming abuse and yelling oaths the likes of which I simply cannot bring to myself to chronicle. The Hankers were indiscriminately punching and lashing out with their weighted handbags at those passengers preparing to retire but unfortunate to enough to be in their way, most of who finished up not in their beds but on the floor bleeding.

We then entered or rather fell, into the ornately appointed Observation Carriage. There was little time available to take in the opulent interior of this carriage for obvious reasons. As the pamphlet promised, however, there was the fully functioning, mechanically operated Aëolian Pianola, now struggling with difficult arpeggios from some monumental piano transcription of the Prelude in C sharp minor by Rachmaninov.* I noted this whilst looking around for a suitable implement to use as a weapon. Not that this sublime and sensuous music, albeit mechanically contrived, made any impact on the Hankers who, immediately upon entering the carriage, made for this fully functioning, mechanically operated Aëolian Pianola, to strip it of any moving parts that could cause us injury. They found what they wanted and, within seconds, the rapturous ascent of arpeggios ceased abruptly, and an ornamental brass wind-up handle was briefly held high in the hand of one of the Hankers, and then thrown at us. Another managed to avail herself of a length of chord wire, from the Pianola, with which she made a noose and invited her sister Hankers to lynch us, "right here and now from the chandelier above!"

"This is rather reminiscent of the fracas we experienced at Moriarty's house in Well Road at Hampstead only a few months ago," remarked Holmes.

"Yes, but that was nowhere near as gratuitously violent as the one we are enduring at this very instant with these Hanker Fänners," I replied whilst dodging the brass sheet music rack ripped off the Pianola.

"Or as potentially murderous, even at Moriarty's instigation!" continued Holmes.

At that moment Holmes threw a bucket of ice at the women, who immediately retaliated by throwing any object that was not bolted down. At one stage, a few of the more masculine Hanker Fänners endeavoured to lift the now partially destroyed, non-functioning, mechanically inoperable Aëolian Pianola and propel it into Holmes. They would almost certainly have succeeded had they not been frustrated in their intent by one of the women falling in front of the advancing Pianola, causing the attack to fail.

By now the air was full of flying projectiles and Holmes pulled at my already aching left arm, from an injury received in the First Mesopotamian fiasco, and we managed to exit the Observation Car in the melée and shut the door behind us. In fact, we secured the door with a shutter bolt that could not be opened from inside the carriage. We both viewed our still-intent aggressors through the toughened glass window of the carriage door. I thought we were now secure, standing as we were on the comparative safety of the observation deck of our coupled carriage.

"Watson look!"

"Look at what?" I asked, knowing something to be wrong by the timbre of his voice.

My heart's action froze in my chest as the realisation of what I was seeing with my very eyes began to sink in, plunging me into abject fear. My attention was focused on the side window located at the very end of the carriage from which we had just escaped. We had bolted the carriage door from the outside preventing the Hankers from pursuing us, and had thought ourselves safe from further attack.

However, from that side window and hanging out of it was the bare leg of a woman wearing a laced up leather boot. Seconds later another leather-booted leg appeared, followed by a frilly petticoat blowing furiously in the wind as the train hurtled down the permanent way of the railroad. It was inevitable that, only moments later, a red velveteen waistcoat appeared, followed by a handbag and a head wearing a frilly blue bonnet, as a woman lowered herself down from the open window onto the running board alongside the carriage. She turned her face towards us and immediately the wind ripped the felt bonnet from her head, revealing a face of such repellent aspect and malevolence that, had my service revolver been with me, I would have shot her dead there and then.

I have heard learned people talk about the Valküre, the daughters of Wotan, who brave battlefields to retrieve the slain heroes and take them to Valhalla. This woman presented such a hideous spectre of both bravery and venality, that it would have disturbed Wotan himself and quite probably have precipitated *'Götterdämmerung'*. **

"Holmes, what are we to do? We can hardly incommode her lest she falls to her death, nor ignore her determined progress to that door, as she clearly intends to open it to allow her sisters to continue to hunt us down. They are clamouring for our blood. Holmes, what are we to do?"

"Watson, do you see that iron bar?"

"Holmes! You cannot be serious about my metering out injury to that woman?"

"No, but get it and follow me into the guard's brake-van, for it is in there that we shall have to defend ourselves and, if need be, incapacitate as many of these Hankers as possible before we succumb."

My reply reflected the audible trepidation in my voice.

"Holmes, I really do think our supreme moment has arrived and we shall be at the mercy of these Hanker Fänners. That worries me!"

"Watson, do what I propose now and, should it fail, the Hanker Fänners will be the least of our worries!"

And with that Parthian shot, he pulled me by my still-aching right shoulder down to the running board on the side of the brake-van. We began to make our way along this shelf located between the steel wheels and the carriage itself. We held on like grim death to any protuberance or fitting attached to the brake-van's timber sides that looked as if they could take our weight. A more frightening experience was hard to imagine, as the train rolled and rocked from side to side with the syncopated clanking of the steel wheels pounding the iron rails, racing round and round below us only inches from our precarious position.

At one stage, I seriously contemplated returning to the Hankers and engaging them in one final, if brutal, encounter, but there could be no winner, so I elected to continue to follow and support Holmes. Suddenly a telegraph pole placed adjacent to the track came racing towards us at tremendous speed. I flattened myself against the rough-hewn timber sides of the carriage and prayed as we rushed by it with only inches to spare. We continued to haul ourselves along the length of the brake-van's running board with my attention concentrated and looking ahead.

It was with blind panic, therefore, that I became aware that my ankle was caught by something. I turned my head to look behind me to see what the obstruction was. It was with abject horror I saw that a Hanker Fänner had also elected to risk death and to pursue us along this treacherous running board and had somehow grabbed my ankle. Indeed, she was leading two other Hankers, their dresses and bonnets flapping in the wind like the Furies riding a gale, creating a ghostly spectre of such enormity that it defied definition, except that this could only be the prelude to death. I looked into her Medusa-like face in a paroxysm of fear, frozen with indecision and expecting to turn into stone. Another Hanker supported her around the waist, aiding this vile woman's attempt to pull me off the running board and to my certain death.

"Kick her, Watson, kick her," came Holmes' words riding on the wind. "Kick her man, with all the vehement determination you can muster!"

I began to move my foot about, kicking at her grip as Holmes had suggested. After a few agonising moments of this action, a different expression overtook the features of my assailant's face. It showed me that it was she who was now in fear. I derived encouragement from this and began to kick all the more vigorously in the desperate hope of dislodging her grip. The more I kicked the more fearful she became. Then it happened. With a scream that surpassed that of the howling wind caused by the train's relentless speed, the Hanker let go her grip on my ankle and in so doing lost the hold she had on the running board.

The vision was terrible, as she appeared to float in the air and then a moment later she disappeared taking the other Hanker sister with her. Both flew into the gorse bushes alongside the permanent way, leaving a trail of torn dresses, scraps of velveteen and taffeta, felt bonnets and petticoats. At the same time, both Hankers' spacious handbags sprung open, disgorging their varied and surprising contents: an iron horseshoe, a small bottle of Bourbon, several sprigs of white heather and enough hardware to establish a thriving plumbing business, all now strewn along the railroad.

The remaining Hanker Fänner, utterly distressed at seeing her sister Hankers disappear into oblivion and certain death, looked at me with hatred in her smouldering eyes. This look made brace myself for what I thought was going to be the launch of a final and desperate suicidal attack upon my person.

She did not carry out her intention but instead thought the better of it and simply held her position on the running board with a grim determination. I continued to follow Holmes, looking back intermittently to assure myself that she was no longer hunting me. Eventually we reached the end of the brake-van carriage. God only knows how we achieved this death-defying feat but we did. With the help of Holmes, I clambered onto the rear observation platform deck at the end of the train. Never in my life have I felt relief as I did then. Our euphoria at surviving this ordeal was, however, to be short-lived, as we could hear distinctly that an attack on the front of the brake-van by the Hankers had begun.

We now entered the brake-van to defend ourselves to the death. We were in a slightly stronger position since we were in the brake-van behind the stout wooden door. This door was the only thing that separated us from the Hankers, who were now assembling, on the observation platform on the other side of the door. This fact became more audible by the second as we could hear the Hankers gathering in their preparation for their final assault on our persons. That attack would be almost certainly to the death, in revenge for the death of two of their sisters and injury to several others.

Though our predicament was unenviable, but real enough, I could scarcely believe the situation in which we found ourselves. Here we were, on an Express train of the New York Central Rail Road, one of Vanderbilt's finest, hurtling through Pennsylvania *en-route* to Chicago, being chased by a pack of rampaging Hanker Fänners intent on committing violent injury or probably death upon our persons.

It was not for the first time in my life I found myself experiencing pure fear. The last time was at the sight of the lined-up masses of the murderous Ghazis at the infamous battle of Maiwand, when I was with the Fifth Northumberland Fusiliers, where I received a shoulder wound as my reward for being there. But this was almost cast into the shade by the sight of these ladies chasing us mercilessly through the carriages of an Express train thundering through the night.

"Right Watson, time for action!"

"Time for what?" I wondered. "Have we not just fought a running battle through twelve railroad carriages, outnumbered at every stage? We now find ourselves holed up in the last wagon with no retreat or possibility of rescue from the murderous intentions of a bunch of extremely violent Hanker Fänners. The ancient Greeks, I think, had a term for such violent women; they called them Amazons. You say, 'time for action'; just what action did you have in mind, Holmes?"

"Watson do not panic! Treat these women as thugs and not as members of the fair sex as you always do, and, in showing no mercy, we shall prevail!"

"This is not the time to respond to such a remark, Holmes. However, it is my intention to prevail, if only to afford myself the opportunity to remonstrate with you at a later date," I said, barely hiding my disdain for Holmes' attitude, even in the face of this real and present danger.

At length, I heard the women's gathering crescendo of screams. I also witnessed the increasingly intense and very audible threats and oaths being freely bandied about amongst the Hanker Fänners, about precisely what they intended to do to our persons, bent as they were on total revenge. I now fully understood how General Custer must have felt during his supreme moment at his last stand.

The pounding commenced, as scores of female hands and handbags, horseshoes, knitting needles, steel-capped boots and hair combs began their relentless assault upon the timber door. Though the noise was tremendous, I did hear Holmes say distinctly:

"Do you realise a very singular fact, Watson? We have been here before, have we not?"

"Here before?"

"Yes, on that Necropolis Express railway train from London's Waterloo Station to the massive Brookwood Necropolis. Remember, we had broken our way into the brake-van full of corpse-filled coffins?"

"Well, if you are going to be facetious, Holmes, at a time as this, then the horror on that Necropolis Express, or indeed this Express train, pales into insignificance against some of our other experiences. Especially in comparison to that English parliamentary train attached to the Liverpool Express that we had to endure on our way back to London!"

We both laughed so heartily at our experiences of trains that, for a moment, the Hankers stopped their clamouring, perhaps confused by our humorous disrespect for their blood-curdling threats of death.

"It has started again, Watson. Do you hear the screaming, and the thudding against our locked door?"

"Yes, it sounds like the finalé to Act Two of Wagner's opera '*Götterdämmerung*', complete with all the attendant dread therein being released."

The attack continued in a determined fashion as several female, though not feminine, hands hacked away at the carriage door. At one stage, an axe was deployed in their attempts to get at us. A hole appeared about three feet above the deck of the brake-van. Immediately, Holmes rammed the iron bar into it with the intention of disrupting those attempting to force their way in. The language and cursing in response to this act was such that I felt weak at the knees and did my best to consign the memory of it to oblivion. Holmes' action had, however, not deterred the women and soon a knitting needle was brought into play, in order to create another opening.

"This is serious Watson"

"I know!

"No, I mean have you noticed anything?"

"No, only that we are but minutes away from being brutally murdered."

"The train is slowing down."

"Good God Holmes, do not tell me those Hanker Fänners have got to the engine at the other end and are stopping the train?"

Holmes looked concerned in a way that I had not seen

before. At that instant a bell was heard, the kind of bell that heralds a train's approach to a station or depot.

"We are entering a station," I proposed, "but listen, the hammering has ceased!"

"Possibly, but we are not opening that brake-van door until I hear a male voice on the other side of it."

We did not have long to wait. The voices of three police officers could be heard on the observation deck and so we opened the door. We were then escorted through the train. The amount of wreckage was colossal and we had, in comparison, escaped with little injury where others did not fare so well. Several passengers were nursing bruises, wounds or cuts. Others were surveying the damage to their possessions and clothing. We walked through the Observation Car where the Aëolian Pianola had been smashed to pieces. Even its internal wires had been removed, for what purpose I dread to think.

The whole train had been so systematically vandalised that the New York Central Rail Road had decided to terminate it there at Pittsburgh. We also learned that the train had only barely steamed to into the Pittsburgh Station, because three of the Hankers had actually managed to gain the coal tender located immediately behind the American Type 4-4-0 locomotive. Imagine if they had clambered onto the engine foot plate, I thought, and interfered with the train driver or incommoded his engineer?

"Mr Holmes, Mr Sherlock Holmes?"

We both turned around to face our inquisitor who wore a fine coat with an Astrakhan collar and a shiny silk top hat.

"Mr Holmes my name is Carnegie, Andrew Carnegie. You may not have heard of me, but I am a businessman and live here in Pittsburgh. You are welcome to stay as my guest this evening."

The police had diverted the Express to Pittsburgh, where

we now were, because of a telegraphed message from the New York Police Department, the officers of which had watched an inordinate number of Hankers board the train at Grand Central Terminal, and knowing that this could only mean trouble. The Hanker Fänners, including the few who had attempted to escape arrest by running away down the railroad track, were now being rounded up by Pittsburgh police officers.

It was patently obvious to me that the Pittsburgh police had some expertise in riot control, for they had penned in most of the Hankers using their Billy clubs and Nightsticks. Some of the Hankers were looking at me with smouldering eyes set deep in their powdered faces beneath their frilly bonnets. One even made a final break for it in her forlorn attempt to land at least one blow to my person.

Looking towards Andrew Carnegie, I said eagerly to Holmes, "I think we had better accept this gentleman's kind invitation and quit this place before our luck changes."

* That Prelude in C# minor had not been composed – it was a paraphrase for Pianola of Chopin's Etude No.12 in C minor Op.10

** Twilight of the Gods

Chapter 12

The Titan of Iron

The name of this fellow meant nothing to me nor, I suspect, to Holmes, but at any rate he had offered to remove us from the vicinity of the Hanker Fänners, who still posed a threat in my opinion, and that was good enough for me. And, in a flawless application of deductive reasoning, I noted that, in addition to the fine clothes he wore, he had invited us to be his guests in a strange city and owned an expensive American Town Carriage. The liveried coachman and four horses were standing at the ready by this very opulent and grandiose glass-panelled carriage, into which I climbed eagerly, followed by Holmes and Carnegie, and we pulled smartly away from the Hanker Fänners.

"Your reputations proceed you," said Carnegie in an ingratiating manner to Holmes, "but the New York police could hardly fail to notice a huge contingent of what we call in America, 'Hanker Fänners', boarding that Express out of Grand Central Terminal we knew there could only be trouble. The train would have been, as a matter of course, diverted to Pittsburgh and inspected. It was purely fortuitous that a detective on duty at Grand Central recognised you, Mr Holmes. Immediately, that information was wired through to us here. Together with other reports of incidents taking place on the Express, including sightings of women hanging off the side of the train, we had ample reason to divert it. I was advised by Pittsburgh's Chief of Police, as a matter of routine, of your presence on the train and now, here we are."

"Mr Andrew Carnegie, the 'Iron Titan'?" inquired Holmes.

"Well, some call me 'King of the Vulcans', but I'd prefer it if you were to call me Andrew."

It was obvious to me that 'Andrew' clearly enjoyed his sobriquet 'King of the Vulcans' as the foremost Ironmaster of Pennsylvania.

We rattled through the streets of the city with its steel mills, furnaces and forges billowing out smoke. The occasional glimpse of an erupting furnace afforded through the windows of the carriage made the scene look more like Dante's 'Inferno' or the domain of Pluto, wherein Vulcan might well have wrought his metallic objects for the gods, than a Pennsylvanian town.

"Were you able to take dinner on the train?" asked Carnegie.

"Not exactly," I fielded, "though we did most certainly enter the Dining Car, not for the purpose of dining, however, but rather for the preservation of life, whilst battling with the Hanker Fänners."

Carnegie looked at me as if to question just whom, in fact, he had invited into his expensive carriage, then smiled and reached for a flexible tube which communicated with the driver and into which he gave an instruction. Almost immediately, the driver wheeled his four-in-hand carriage in a different direction and, within minutes, we pulled up outside an impressive stone-built edifice with the name 'Duquesne Club' emblazoned above the main entrance.

"Welcome to the Duquesne Club, gentlemen. I think you will find it comfortable and we can dine here," said Carnegie.

Indeed, the club was well appointed and comfortable. The interior was designed in an overtly masculine manner. No lady would feel comfortable in this establishment, I thought. Still, it was in keeping with what I was beginning to understand to be the Pittsburgh style: tough, decisive and determined. Carnegie re-joined us and led us into an impressively decorated Dining Room.

"Let me be frank with you, Mr Holmes. It is indeed fortuitous you being here in connection with Moriarty and other matters. I do not have just a passing interest in him, but rather a deep concern, since I believe he has perpetrated fraud upon me, in addition to trying to wreck my business. I made my money," Carnegie continued, "by founding the Union Iron Mills, later Carnegie Steel, which, at the time, were able to roll out the huge steel girders needed to bridge the mighty western rivers of America over which the Union Pacific Rail Road needed to lay its track.

"Henry Clay Frick, who, in conjunction with investment from the wealthy Thaw family was able to start his coke-supply business, including supplying me amongst other companies, eventually came to work at the Carnegie Steel Company. Frick, as manager, instigated wage cuts at the Carnegie Homestead Steel Works for economic reasons. A strike resulted and, to impose order, Frick called in three hundred guards from the Pinkerton National Detective Agency, which resulted in an escalation of violence and fourteen deaths. In a way, I feel kind of responsible as President, even though I was away at the time of the incident. Later, Frick himself was shot twice and stabbed by a deranged anarchist in the pay of Moriarty, so the Pinkerton Agency suspect."

Carnegie stopped talking as a waiter appeared at our table with a trolley. We did not so much order our food as accept what we were given. This consisted of a thick, rare sirloin steak, a large glass of iced water, a bowl of freshly grated horseradish and an empty glass that could be filled readily from a large bottle of whisky placed strategically in the middle of the table. Very civilised, I thought.

"It is because of those incidents," he continued, "that I started the Carnegie Trust, in an attempt to make reparation to the city of Pittsburgh. This inevitably means the acquisition and display of art for the benefit of all, hence my interest in the World's Columbian Exposition, where I wished to inspect a vast display of paintings and sculpture. I still want the works of art that I have paid Moriarty for, and to get him for probably shooting my business partner Frick. Clearly, Moriarty has been acting on several levels against various industrial Titans by causing strikes and unrest, together with bankrupting companies.

"In my own case, JP Morgan, the banker who will act for anyone, certainly acted against me in trying to acquire my steel works, having failed to take over a little outfit called Standard Oil or something, owned by a John Davison Rockefeller, or some such name. Morgan's motive was 'to organise steel production into a competition-free trust combine'. What Morgan is referring to by 'competition-free trust combine' is a self-regulating pricing monopoly. To achieve this 'eminent and laudable state of affairs', Morgan set up a rival company called Federal Steel, headed by a judge, Elbert Gary.

Not long afterwards, my customers began going elsewhere. He also caused a rift between Frick, my partner of many years, and myself. Inevitably, the inevitable did happen and I was forced to sell my holdings for only one-and-a-half billion dollars to Morgan – or to whomever he was acting for, no doubt some *eminence grise*. On the first of April, 1901, the US Steel Corporation came into existence, the creation of a combine of all steel manufacturing companies, including mine, headed by Elbert Gary.

"You see, gentlemen, we Robber Barons and Industrial Titans exist in a rarefied world, which is incomprehensible to the ordinary person, where literally might is the law, irrespective of its being right or wrong. We are not accountable to anyone except our Profit & Loss Account, and remain above public opinion and the law, as witness the brutal suppression of strikes. With this arrogance, do you honestly think that sinking a boat in the middle of the Atlantic Ocean, to answer your question Mr Holmes, fifteen hundred miles away from these United States, is going to in any way cause anxiety? Furthermore, I understand that Morgan was in England at the time, and was booked on the maiden voyage of that '*Titanic*' since he owned the ship, but cancelled at the last minute."

To my request to a passing waiter for coffee, he replied, without stopping, that 'coffee is something you drink in the morning' and continued on by.

"Gentlemen, the reason I am saying all this is because quite simply I recognise an opportunity in you. Take some facts about Pittsburgh, for example, and you may perceive what we are about.

"Pittsburgh is the fifth-largest city in America, and Millionaire's Row is located in a district called East End. In that district are concentrated more millionaire industrial magnates than *anywhere* else on earth. Pittsburgh is not just a steel town but the centre of *industrial capitalism,* making profit by controlling 60 per cent of American assets. Unlike the speculators in New York who make money from stock transactions, a fraction here and a fraction there, here in Pittsburgh we made America what it is today.

"Numerous great industrial magnates and investment Bankers like Andrew Mellon live in East End. Some are Presidents of major corporations in America, including James McCrae, President of the Pennsylvania Rail Road, and Robert Pitcairne, Vice-President of the same. The industrialist George Westinghouse has his own railroad station and track to his house. In fact, all the magnates have their own private railroad carriages, often Pullmans, waiting in stations for their exclusive use.

"Pittsburgh is the focal point for industrial power, finance, capitalism and politics, representing a lethal mixture of envy, wealth and ambition. Countless Republican Presidents have visited and stayed in private houses here on several occasions. We can make or break Presidents, indeed, the real decisions are made here in the mansions on Highland Avenue and Fifth Avenue here in Pittsburgh or during poker games to which only important Titans of industry are invited. The 'Titanic' was, as it were, a pawn in a poker game.

"There is one and only one drawback to living in Pittsburgh: the sulphur in the smoky air causes the silverware to tarnish quickly, and that is a real tragedy!"

I looked at Carnegie after this insensitive comment and showed my feelings by sucking in my breath, in so doing raising my chest, and rubbing my palms on my knees. 'Silverware to tarnish quickly', I thought, how inane! Not in the least put out, Carnegie continued with his, admittedly, interesting, narrative.

"Allow me to demonstrate an example of our arrogance," said Carnegie.

"In 1870, the residents of Liberty, Forbes, Highland and Fifth Avenues, in the millionaires' area of Pittsburgh called the East End, in order to improve their district property values, submitted to the City Council the Penn Avenue Improvement Bill 1879. It was duly passed and improvement works totalling $5 million were carried out. When City Hall attempted to increase their city taxes accordingly, the residents took the City to the Supreme Court, claiming that the Improvement Act 1879 was unconstitutional and not valid, and won, meaning they paid no taxes for the improvements!

"Mr Holmes, Doctor Watson, this shows a contempt and disdain for any form of government at any level. It is not just the 'Titanic', but much more besides. The 'Titanic' was a mere symptom. We have other industries looking for markets for their wares. In particular, we have an armaments industry looking for outlets for its guns and ammunition. The two major companies involved in armaments are based right here in Pittsburgh. If you think the sinking of the *'Titanic'* was a major disaster then be prepared for a far worse one in the next two years, 1914 at the latest." Thus spoke Andrew Carnegie.

After dinner we assembled in a large comfortable drawing room to enjoy our brandy and cigars. Our host introduced us to a number of gentlemen standing around a large marble fireplace.

"Gentlemen, this is Mr Sherlock Holmes and his colleague Doctor John Watson. They are both from London, England," said Carnegie, pointing to us.

"My name is Mellon, Andrew Mellon*. Is your friend such a valetudinarian that he requires a doctor with him at all times?" he asked, with such a profound look of concern on his face that I was lost for words and froze speechless on the spot. When I did regain my composure I noticed that Mellon was not only quite thin but looked as if he were in the latter stages of inanition. Indeed I would venture to suggest that there was more meat on an Oxo cube than on this fellow.

"Doctor Watson, do come and meet Henry Clay Frick, my old partner, and Phillip Armour from the Armour Canning Corporation," urged Carnegie.

Later, I was introduced to a George Westinghouse, who chatted about his innovative railroad carriage braking system and how many lives, to say nothing of railroad stock, had been saved as a result of its application.

"Of course you know Mr HJ Heinz, the food manufacturer?" asked our host.

After introductions were exchanged and glasses refilled, I found myself talking with a very loquacious fellow by the name of Alex Peacock. He used to work as a manager for Carnegie, but went on to describe in fascinating detail his project to construct a huge mansion called *Rowanlea* here in Pittsburgh.

"I intend," he explained, "to construct a gigantic mansion

house for no other reason than to enjoy building it, and no amount of funding will be denied in its ostentatious creation!"

I confess to becoming rather envious of this fellow and his unashamedly ambitious plans to construct his equivalent of Fonthill Abbey in England. America seemed a place where megalomania and wealth could combine easily to create such fantastic structures as this fellow was envisaging and one could well imagine.

Eventually, however, Carnegie came over to us and said that we ought to be going. I wished my friend good luck with his great plans for *Rowanlea* and he responded by inviting me to stay in the house when built. I might just take him up on that offer!

It was with great reluctance that I left the 'Duquesne Club' and its august list of members. It was a place I could easily have become accustomed to but alas, leave we had to. Thirty or so minutes later, we entered the East End District and gradually our carriage began the ascent up a roadway called Highland Avenue. I now knew that along this avenue, lived most of the wealthy industrial and banking magnates, in houses built to the size of palaces, including the one we drew up to, belonging to our host. We entered a large hallway, clad totally in polished wood. Wooden floorboards, wooden wall panels and a light-coloured timber ceiling. The whole effect was surprisingly warm and mellow, especially as a strong smell of beeswax pervaded the air. Continuing down the hallway, we turned into a sumptuously decorated drawing room, and it was here that Carnegie showed us some of his prize collection of paintings, which could rival any city's art gallery.

Somewhat exhausted, we sat down on buttoned Chesterfield sofas and drank whisky whilst smoking our cigars.

"I have arranged a First Class berth for you on the *Iron City Express,* leaving tomorrow, which will get you into Chicago by early evening."

"We are appreciative of your time, hospitality and the concerns you have shared with us this evening regarding events surrounding the *Titanic'* and other matters. Allow me be equally frank with you. I am engaged to look into a certain matter for a certain reason for a certain person. I am not constrained in my investigation, nor prohibited from advising persons of my choice regarding information gleaned as a result of those inquiries. In the meantime, it will be useful to me if you would jot down on that piece of paper the names of the paintings expected to be delivered to you, which had been reserved and paid for," replied Holmes at some length.

We talked further into the night about *objets d'art* and other acquired cultural status symbols, in particular Carnegie's unique plan to build a series of libraries – 'for the Benefit of Mankind' - not just here in the United States, but in England too. Or rather, as he said wisely, he would construct the actual impressive buildings and it would be up to the city fathers to stock them with books, thus forcing them to carry out their civic duty in educating their citizens. With this insight, I could see how the man had become the 'Iron Titan'.

The next morning we breakfasted and bade farewell to Carnegie, who would not be joining us on the trip to Pittsburgh Station, but hoped to meet up with us again, perhaps in England, then closed the door of our Roofseat Break carriage. We clattered down the drive into Highland Avenue, resplendent in the subdued sunlight of late autumn beneath a powder-blue sky. We progressed in style along this very elegant Avenue, gazing on either side at the mansions of differing design and size.

The huge Gothic houses were built to a formula, complete with elegant round towers capped with battlements and arched openings in the limestone-block façades for door or window reveals. Various steeply pitched blue slate roofs were adorned with ornate crenellated gable ends adjacent to castellated turrets with wide verandas linking bay windows.

Set among the Gothic residences were houses that were designed in the French Second Empire style, with their mansard roofs surrounded by intricate and ornate metal fencing. Some of the larger mansions reflected a Neo-Classic or even Greek influence in their architecture when being built. Most of the buildings were of limestone, easily quarried in Indiana, and consequently conveyed an image of profound wealth that is the salient hallmark of this Avenue.

One peculiar architectural observation I made was of the Victorian neo-Gothic Revival mansions as interpreted through the Queen Anne style. Nothing epitomises the Victorian style better than a Queen Anne house. Complete with dormer and bay windows, towers or turrets, cross gables and fish-scale tiles adorning steeply pitched roofs, crowned with metal fencing. They were in the majority by far and the preferred choice of residents along this thoroughfare of the wealthy.

All the mansions were impressive, and their being set back in their own extensive gardens, imparted a image of importance. Despite the various European styles in their design, all clearly sought to outshine each other, as though in an architectural competition. Most of the houses featured an elaborate carriage vestibule irrespective of the architectural style, either simply attached to the front entrance or at the base of a substantial tower. It was a betting certainty that each residence would have the latest in mechanical innovation such as butane gas lighting, indoor plumbing, central heat and electricity, all to promote a comfortable style of living. This approach to living invariably includes the ability to pay for that kind of existence and the access to necessities.

* Banker and Secretary of the US Treasury

Chapter 13

The City of Dreams

We at last arrived at the LaSalle Railroad Station in Chicago and, upon doing so, were immediately surrounded by yet another powerful Beaux-Arts building. This is the architecture of the New World and I could only imagine what wonders would be conjured up to create the '*City of Dreams*' at the World's Columbian Exposition here.

"First things first, Holmes, where is the bar, the 'Central Bar'?" I said, looking around this cavernous space enclosed by delightful architectural styles based on those designs of ancient Imperial Rome. Holmes led the way through the terminal to a limestone-built bar of grand proportions.

"This will do," said Holmes, dumping our luggage in the corner, whist I caught the bartender's attention.

Two... ah no... one large vodka with aërated water on the rocks and a dash of crushed lime, and for me, a large whisky on the rocks with half the 'Coca-Cola'."

"'The Coca-' what?" asked the bartender.

"Yes, my good man. It is a dark aërated beverage made with cocaine and sugar, and has more punch to it than aërated water."

"Never heard of it, but do you want that I should put sugar in your whisky?" came the bartender's reply, and I pretended to be more interested in the Station's well-appointed architectural features than in formulating a response to his facetiousness.

I checked my gold Hunter to ascertain the correct time and re-joined Holmes. We chatted about the train journey from Pittsburgh to Chicago, how it was, in comparison, rather boring and uneventful. We even regretted not having may be just a couple of Hanker Fänners on board just to create some anxious moments and excitement – or even here, to give us a run for our money, I thought, looking around the Station. Then it happened; I could not believe my eyes.

She came gliding across the smooth limestone-covered floor of the foyer like a goddess riding the zephyrs, with a determined look of pleasure upon her face below an Alice band that held back her long dark hair. She now looked hard in our direction to make sure that it was really I. My heart felt as if it had stopped momentarily as she approached me, then it started to race wildly, pounding against my chest. I froze and words failed to leave my mouth, while I attempted to gain Holmes' attention.

"John, John Watson!" she cried, whilst completing her advance towards me. Holmes, totally unaware of this assignation, turned, then dropped onto the polished limestone floor, his by now half-depleted glass of vodka and whatever, lime or something, he had in it, looking as if he were about to endure an apoplexy.

"Katherine!" I replied, rushing to greet her. "You look radiant, still with that smile of yours. Absolutely a joy to see you again after nearly a year!"

"John, your features look much nicer when not surrounded by that clammy fog you have in London. I did not get to see a single view of a London street, due to the fog, when I was there last year."

"Katherine, you remember Sherlock, whom you engaged last year?"

"Yes I do," she said coolly. "I do indeed."

Holmes, presumably having recovered from his apoplectic fit, could barely conceal his surprise, concern or disgust at the unexpected arrival of *that* woman from Eureka Springs, and here in Chicago of all places.

"I got your wire, John, and have booked you into the same hotel I am staying in, the Auditorium Building on Michigan and Wabash, and, you will be pleased to know, it is Chicago's largest building since the fire of 1871."

"Watson you said you had organised our hotel arrangements?" said a bewildered Holmes.

"I did, through Katherine."

"I have a Rockaway carriage outside to take us to the hotel."

We chatted and made our way through LaSalle Station concourse and out into LaSalle Street through its massive arched portal entrance.

"What have you been doing with yourself, Katherine, since last we met?" I asked.

"Well, I did go to Europe and to Vienna, where I fell in love with the place. I then travelled to Berlin and stayed there for some considerable time, attending regular Philharmonic Concerts at the *Schauspielhaus*, for I am, as you know John, passionate about music, especially music from the late nineteenth century."

"In that case I shall book tickets here and see what the Chicago Symphony Orchestra can offer us."

"I look forward to the concert."

Holmes followed behind, struggling with our luggage.

I did not quite realise what or how big a Rockaway carriage can be but, suffice to say, it easily contained our luggage and the three of us. My first impression of Chicago was that of a pleasant and civilised city with pride emanating from everywhere; cleanliness, order and courtesy were the norm. It was a pleasure cantering down LaSalle Street from the Station into

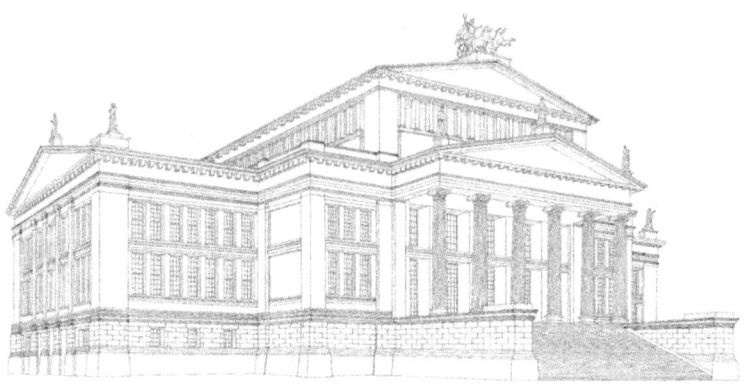

Schauspielhaus, Berlin

Van Buren and past The Rookery Building on South LaSalle Street. I had heard that term before but where?

We passed the Pullman Building on Michigan Avenue and later a rather ornate and unusual large Gothic tower on North Michigan Avenue.

Katherine pointed out the Chicago Opera House to me, adding that it was to be pulled down.

"Why?" I inquired.

"I do not know. Progress, I guess, but it sure is scheduled for demolition."

We arrived at our hotel on Wabash, whereupon Holmes confirmed our reservation by checking us in. After which he turned to me and said, "Right! Back to reality and the game is afoot, eh Watson?"

I was not quite certain what to make of this outburst by Holmes but went to my room with mixed thoughts and a promise to meet at the bar before dinner.

I was in the mood for pre-dinner drinks and so came down early but, on my way to the bar, bought a copy of both *The Times* of London and the *Chicago Tribune*. In the *Tribune*, I scanned the columns for Philharmonic concerts in Chicago.

I found one, an interesting-looking one, one that Katherine would like, I postulated. All of a sudden, Katherine appeared, looking even more radiant in an electric-blue satin dress, complemented by a deep red silk moiré sash. She wore black velvet gloves, which reached to her elbows, matching her black velvet Alice band, which she wore in place of the usual silver tiara to hold back her dark black hair. Around her throat was a golden chain bearing a dazzling blue stone of Lapis Lazuli that set her whole ensemble off to such magnificence.

She climbed onto a stool next to the bar and ordered drinks for us.

"What can I get you John?"

"That is very kind of you, Katherine. I will try a small spritzer made with a dash of that new crazy drink, the Coca-Cola, on the rocks!"

"The Coca- what, in your spritzer?" Katherine asked, expecting an answer, as did the bartender.

"It is a new-fangled drink and all the rage back East in New York."

"What is this, the 'Coca-Cola'?" inquired the bartender.

"Well, it is a dark aërated beverage made with cocaine and sugar, and has more punch to it than aërated water.

"What is it, an English beer? I have never heard of it," offered the bartender.

"I agree," said Katherine. "I too have never heard of nor seen it, and I have been in England!"

"Let me replenish your drink, Katherine, and, bartender, I will just have a spritzer with aërated water."

"With aërated... what?"

At that moment, Holmes came in and seated himself to my left, not realising Katherine was sitting to my right. Holmes started in about "...the objectivity of analysis; when all else is eradicated whatever remains must..."

"Good evening Holmes! I thought there for a moment you

were trying to avoid telling me how charming I look this evening."

As Holmes opened his mouth to reply, Katherine turned to me and said.

"Do tell me John, what musical concert have you chosen for us to witness together this evening?"

"The *Chicago Tribune* carries a schedule showing that the Chicago Symphony Society Orchestra will this evening be playing, in their newly built Orchestral Hall, the largest auditorium in the world, on Michigan Avenue, the *'Planets Suite'* Op 32 by Gustav Holst. Holmes and I heard it in London a few days ago and it really is a fascinating work, especially his interpretation of the planet Uranus."

Uranus? I pondered for a moment, then turned and said to Holmes.

"Do you remember the Principal in that laudanum den in the East End of London, the Diogenes Club or whatever, talking about the World's Columbian Exposition and, in particular, a symphony composed by Dvorak, his Ninth in E minor, called *'From the New World'*, written especially to commemorate this Exposition? Well, it too is going to be performed this evening at the same concert."

"I cannot wait to hear the Symphony," said Katherine.

At which response, Holmes looked away.

"In that case, we should all avail ourselves of this musical interpretation of the World's Columbian Exposition and of the Planets in the Orchestral Hall this evening," I announced, as we all in turn repaired to our rooms. Whilst changing into evening dress, I could not help but think of our taking that express back to New York. For some reason, the thought of it filled me with a nameless dread and foreboding.

Whilst waiting in the foyer, Holmes was first to join me, followed by Katherine looking, again, resplendent in that electric-blue satin dress, now complemented by a white fur stole accompanied by the faint aroma of Attar of Roses, Wagner's favourite scent. Holmes and I escorted Katherine from the hotel to our waiting Brett carriage for the short drive to the entrance to the auditorium and moments afterwards, we took our seats in the Dress Circle.

As my eyes took in the ornate interior of the auditorium, I reminded myself that tonight was indeed our first and last in Chicago, and possibly in this place, for tomorrow we would take the evening train back to New York.

The concert opened with a work by Dvorak, which was not in the schedule. It was his *Opus 98*, the Suite in A major, '*The American*', which concluded to thunderous applause from a delighted, if unsuspecting, audience for this musical treat. The Holst work was less impressive on this occasion and, in any case, it would have been over-shadowed by the Ninth Symphony.

Dvorak's Ninth Symphony in E-minor called '*From the New World*' opened with a slow but rising crescendo, inviting the listener on a journey through various musical landscapes. The power of the music portrayed in the minor idiom is immediately obvious to any trained musical ear. It promises to be the precursor of a monumental harmonic journey of discovery. As it played on, the ideas encapsulated within the symphony, I felt, expressed very succinctly the hopes, aspirations, dreams and optimism that we too were to experience the next day at the World's Columbian Exposition. Among the musical abilities radiating from Dvorak is a characteristic, yet unexpected, harmonic development, together with the fresh and vital application of orchestral forces in expressing a coherent melodic progression which, in so doing, achieves a rich intensity of feeling.

The concert was a resounding success and the symphony played to great applause. I was especially pleased to witness the Dvorak with Katherine at my side. What Holmes thought of it, being as he was seated on Katherine's other side, I cannot venture to say, save that he looked thoroughly bored, and possibly slept throughout at least part of it. I, for one, will always associate this Symphony with our experiences in Chicago.

Afterwards we climbed into a Stanhope Phäeton and repaired to the hotel for drinks and dinner. It is to be remembered that, the following day, we were to visit the Exposition and then leave for New York in the evening.

Whilst Holmes was momentarily absent, Katherine confided to me and said, "I am very happy to be here in Chicago with you, and that we will experience the *'City of Dreams'* together."

I noticed that Katherine then blushed; it could have been her innate gauche shyness or it may have been the whisky she had consumed.

After two or so more drinks we decided to go into dinner. Apparently, in this hotel things are quite relaxed in that one does not wait to be shown to a table by a waiter. Rather, one just looks around for a free table and effectively claims it by sitting down at it. There were of course waiters taking orders from the tables and waiting on people. Some diners, however, because of the vogue or impatience, were actually helping themselves to all types of cooked food from a long, linen-covered mess table. The same principle of helping oneself, it seemed, was applied to dining, where the whole ethos appeared to be one of organised self-improvisation in satisfy-ing one's order.

"I cannot for the life of me imagine serving myself at that mess table," I remarked to Katherine. "For one thing it defeats the object of trying to confuse the waiter when giving our orders from the menu."

Alas, we did have a waiter serve us a splendid dinner, which we all completed with cigars and brandy. At the end of a pleasant evening, we rose to retire to our respective rooms.

"Well good night, Miss Katherine, so nice..." faltered Holmes.

"Do you not mean, '*au revoir*', Holmes? After all, I shall be joining you both at breakfast at eight o'clock sharp, for we have work to do and no time for revelry!"

And with that Parthian shot, she turned on her ankle and marched off smartly down the red-carpeted corridor.

The next morning, having breakfasted, we made our way to the front of the hotel in search of a carriage to take us to the World's Columbia Exposition located near Jackson Park, in between North Central Chicago and Lake Michigan to the east. The doorman advised us that the crowds going to the Exposition were such that we would be better off riding Mr Charles Yerkes' 'Union Loop' Elevated Rail Road to get there, rather than get embroiled in the heavy road traffic. He then whistled over a Brett carriage and told the driver to take us to the nearest elevated station on van Buren, where we could take the Intramural Elevated Rail Road to Southern Colonnade Station at the Exposition.

The doorman did not over-estimate the traffic; it was appalling. It took us five-and-forty minutes to cover a distance of no more than one mile, but at length we gained the Van Buren Elevated Rail Road Station. Travelling north from Central Chicago, we looked down from our high position in the train on a variety of buildings of diverse styles, showing that the city was indeed going through rapid expansion with a terrific rate of progress since the devastating conflagration of 1871. We proceeded along the railroad track above the seething traffic and took in the vistas afforded through our carriage windows. Then we saw them. Rising above the haze coming off Lake Michigan to our right, the gleaming splendour of a series of white stucco-clad buildings, one by one, came into focus. As we approached, the buildings

World's Columbian Exposition ticket

took on a monumental appearance due to their size and grandeur. This indeed was the '*City of Dreams*'!

"Would you look at that! What a magnificent site!" said Katherine.

I could only sit there in awe at what was unfolding before our very eyes, made all the more spectacular by the views from our carriage high up on the Intramural Elevated Rail Road, so much more impressive than if we had come in at ground level in a carriage. Our train began slowing down and eventually ground to a screeching stop as we had arrived at the Southern Colonnade Intramural Elevated Railroad Station. Alas, we had to come down to earth and so descended the steps in order to do so, and were immediately absorbed into a dense crowd, the surge from which propelled us past various buildings.

"Looking through the official guide to the Exposition," said Holmes, leaning against a stucco-clad, fluted column, "it would appear that there are several buildings dedicated to a single function or exhibit. We need to inspect them if we are to discover the clue to our investigation which, I believe, lies within these exhibition buildings."

Holmes went on to read from the official handbook and explain the relevance of the World's Columbian Exposition and the opportunities it afforded.

He read allowed to Katherine and me.

"'The World's Columbian Exposition at the Chicago Fair has been organised to nominally celebrate Columbus' discovery, four hundred years ago, of the New World of America, and particularly to give recognition to the achievements of the American people. This Exposition will accelerate the growth of civilization in these United States. The promoters of the World's Columbian Exposition in Chicago are especially eager to establish the fact that there are numerous wealthy Americans who consider themselves a significant force in the art world and are willing to purchase art work, especially from England or Europe.

"'There will be ten thousand items of art on display from the eighteenth and nineteenth centuries, from private and public collections around the world, making it the largest exhibition of art ever held in the United States. The exhibition is expected to attract upwards of twenty-seven millions of visitors, one half the total population of the United States. Even the composer Antonin Dvorak, to celebrate and mark the occasion of the Chicago World's Columbian Exposition, has written a symphony, his ninth in E-Minor, and he calls it *'From the New World'*.

"'It is a testament to its importance that the World's Columbian Exposition in Chicago is generating massive interest, not only in terms of art, but also other disciplines such as engineering, architecture and manufacturing. Indeed, the whole site, comprising over six hundred acres, is a fantastic collection of Beaux-Arts inspired buildings, based on designs emanating from Neo-Classical designs. The eminent American architect, D H Burnham, a great exponent of the Beaux-Arts style, is leading the architectural designs, including reproductions of huge buildings based on European palaces.

"'One of the entrances into the area in which the World's Columbian Exposition buildings are located is dominated by

Gothic Water Tower

the hundred-and-fifty-foot-high Gothic Water Tower. The
Tower was designed as a practical solution to the problem of
equalising the piped water pressure in central Chicago. Despite
its highly Romantic design, built of Illinois limestone blocks,
complete with turrets, pinnacles and crenellations, the Tower
survived the Great Fire that engulfed and destroyed the city
of Chicago in 1871. As a result of that calamity, all new
buildings in Metropolitan Chicago have now to be constructed
using fire-resistant materials, including stone or iron, in order
to prevent a repeat of that disaster. The construction of the
Tower using iron and stone is in a class of structures, which

includes the St Pancras Hotel in London, that are pioneering the way for the evolution of iron-framed, fire-proof buildings for the safety of all.

"'Located around a vast lake are structures with names such as the Palace of Fine Arts and the Federal Government Building. Other buildings are dedicated to Transportation, Manufacturing and Liberal Arts, Agriculture and Horticulture, these last three of which are modelled on the *Petit Palais* in Paris. Added to this collection is a huge structure they call the Court of Honor. As part of this Court exists the huge, magnificent and impressive Administration Building which, with its enormous grand dome, dominates the structure, and is illuminated at night by electricity-powered Edison illuminating light bulbs.

"'This vast collection of over two hundred classically styled buildings, clad in white-painted stucco or staff, has earned itself the sobriquet of *'City of Dreams'*, and is reminiscent of the Forum in the ancient city of Imperial Rome. The buildings are, of course, much larger and are erected clearly as symbols of America's intellectual succession to European Classical architecture. In this respect, it is an auxiliary requirement that the World's Columbian Exposition will effectively civilize the world and complete the work started elsewhere. This goal will be achieved by combining art, especially paintings, with the untold wealth in America, which is available to commission new works of art and to purchase old and modern paintings.'"

Holmes completed his lengthy reading.

We wandered past the Court of Honor, the centrepiece of which was the Grand Basin, a large man-made lake containing an immense gilded statue of the Republic. It is framed to the east by an impressive, colonnaded Peristyle structure, from behind which, the Columbian Orchestra and Chorus was playing music that could be heard emanating from an auditorium beside the lake. It then struck me that the music being played, albeit not very well, was Holst's *'Planets Suite'*! Nothing unusual in that, I thought, it has after all become a popular work for orchestra. Again though, it was Uranus from the *'Planets Suite'* they were playing and Uranus still haunts me for some reason.

We entered several buildings, including the ornate Hall of Machines, designed in the classical style with the uniform white stucco façades common to all the main buildings. Inside, it was anything but classical but resembled a very modern iron-framed structure, creating an impressive open space without the interruption of columns. Likewise, the imposing Agricultural Building, designed by McKim, Mead & White, the same architects who had designed the Pennsylvania Rail Road Station, was the epitome of the excess displayed in the exhibition buildings. The Electricity Building, complete with several square-towered belfries, resembled more a Baroque-style palace than an exhibition hall and matched the three-domed Baroque Horticultural Building.

When eventually we did emerged from the Electricity Building a sign outside proclaimed the following fact:

'A telephone will be deployed within the confines of an orchestra playing in New York. The sound of that music being played will be conducted along wires all the way to this Electricity Building, in which a great horn will throw out the melody for the benefit of all who care to hear this marvel!'

Most of the edifices conformed to a uniform cornice height, geometrically logical, and were covered in the same white staff finish, creating a similarity of style within this magnificent collection of buildings.

The whole site had a magical feel to it, created by its huge buildings with columns and colonnades, plazas, protruding cornices and pediments. Most of the buildings were of the Neo-Classical style or their architectural successor, reflected in Beaux-Arts design. Both styles of structure complemented each other by composing, in their entirety, an ethereal *'City of Dreams'* the memory of which would last a lifetime.

We headed north passing the extensive stone-colonnaded Peristyle, embellished with statues, but punctuated at the centre with a huge dominating Arch, four times the size of the one at Marble Arch in London, supporting an equestrian sculptural group. We progressed along and in so doing was confronted by the enormous expanse of the Manufactures and Liberal Arts Building. This remarkable structure, covering over eleven acres, exhibited objects ranging from the University of Chicago's Charles Yerkes' telescope, all seventy tons of it, to one of Johann Sebastian Bach's fully-functioning clavichords.

However, it was the one-hundred-and-forty-room structure of the beautiful Palace of Fine Arts that arrested Holmes's attention. By now, I too was beginning to understand Holmes' line of inquiry.

"There is more to these buildings than just exhibiting," I began to think.

The Beaux-Arts-designed Palace of Fine Arts, with its white columns and large dome, contained an array of well known artistic masterpieces from around the world, covering the disciplines of painting, decorative arts, sculpture, and drawing and etching. The paintings included those by John Singer Sergeant, Winslow Homer and Thomas Eakins together with paintings from private collection of art by Pisarro, Renoir and Cassatt.

Holmes led us to the Intake Desk and asked the commissionaire on duty for the Curator. After a few minutes he appeared and, having been shown our group, walked up to us asking for a Mr Sherlock Holmes.

"Ah, Mr Holmes, my name is Peerelle, Stephen Peerelle, and I am the curator of the Palace of Fine Arts. I got your cable, though I remain uncertain as to what assistance I can lend you."

"Thank you for receiving me and my colleague Doctor Watson."

Holmes did not introduce Katherine despite the fact that Peerelle was leaning forward, evidently anxious to make her acquaintance.

"What does come as a surprise to me," continued Holmes, "is the fact that the Exposition is still running. Was it not supposed to have been concluded some time ago?"

"Yes, you are correct, but such is the popularity of the event that its extension has been demanded by a very enthusiastic and supportive public, who are attending the event in their thousands, making our Exposition a resounding success in establishing two distinct statements. American international business superiority asserted as indicated by the exhibits of the Manufactures' Building and cultural parity with Europe.

"I understand each pavilion or exhibition hall was sponsored by an organisation or individual benefactor," said Holmes to Peerelle.

"That is true, Mr Holmes, and we were extremely fortunate to have a wealthy banker sponsoring us, and indeed, what is now the Transportation Building."

"You say *now* the Transportation Building; what was its designated use before it became that?" asked Holmes.

"Well, it was designed as a place to display Old Masters and new works of art, especially from England, including an extensive collection from the Pre-Raphaelites, Whistler and Millais, and some European artists, such as Böcklin and Lorrain."

"So why was the art work not displayed in the designated hall?"

"Because of that dread-filled calamity that was the ill-fated '*Titanic*' when it sank! In so doing, it took with it to the depths of the Atlantic a prize collection of works of art and, even more regrettably, a number of promising artists too. Who knows what art we could have experienced had those artists been spared? That is why the hall was given over to another use." So said Peerelle, who appeared still moved by the tragedy of the *'Titanic'* and its impact on the exhibition of art work of which he is Curator. He walked up to a nearby bench and sat down with his elbows resting on his knees and holding his head in his hands. Katherine immediately recognised the sense loss and feelings of desolation still fuelling his deep sadness. She approached him and rested her hand upon his shoulder. A few moments later, he came to.

"Oh please forgive me," said Peerelle, "I still cannot think of those souls who perished with such hopes and dreams in their hearts without a profound sadness attending me."

"One final question, Curator, are you able to divulge the name of the wealthy banker who sponsored this Palace of Fine Arts *and* the Transportation Building?"

"Why yes, of course, and with pride and delight. A local resident who has amassed a fortune in New York, a financier by the name of Adam Worth."

Holmes stood there, transfixed by a huge painting of an ethereal classical scene that was directly in his sight.

"Oh, I see you like the *Architect's Dream* by Thomas Cole," suggested Peerelle.

"I was just thinking. Could I ask you to escort us over to the Transportation Building to enable us to look over that structure and, in particular, its interior appointments?"

"I think that is possible, if you will but give me a few minutes to collect my hat and stick," replied Peerelle, disappearing into the depths of his Palace.

"Well Watson, do you see any significance in the statement Peerelle has imparted to us?"

"I confess, Holmes, that nothing Peerelle has said makes me any the wiser, other than that the Transportation Building was used for anther purpose because of the sinking of the

'*Titanic*'. Where does that leave us in our quest?" I asked, looking at Holmes and then Katherine in turn.

"It was a long-standing plan," said Katherine incisively, whilst turning her head and attention to concentrate on a large painting of a serene classical landscape by Claude Lorrain.

Despite the pervasive presence of the crowd, the walk from the Palace of Fine Arts to the Transportation Building was not a long one. Our route took us past the American Cereal Company's small but exquisitely charming Pavilion, built of decorated timber and glass, looking somewhat out of place amongst the white-stuccoed giant structures which surrounded it. On two occasions I had to resort to referring to the *Chicago Tribune's* New Improved Miniature Guide Map and Index Diagram of the vast expanse of the Exposition, without which we would surely have become lost. Peerelle, I think, had a vague idea where we were headed, but on those two occasions, I pointed to my Map to advise him and thus correct our progress. Most of the buildings, with their wide colonnades, offered welcome shade from the effects of the blistering sunlight reflecting off the stucco-clad, white-painted buildings.

On entering the Transportation Building through its impressive great portal, comprising a series of recessed arches framing the famous Golden Door to the pavilion, we were introduced to its Curator. I noticed Katherine looking earnestly at the metal girders rising from the walls supporting the not insubstantial, intricate trelliswork and transoms of the ferro-vitreous vaulting system that comprised the glazed roof structure.

"What is it, Katherine?" I asked, noting the puzzled expression upon her normally intelligent and radiant face.

"You remember, John, when we first met in the fog-bound Baker Street, I explained to you my thoughts about that White Star Liner the '*Olympic*', or whatever it was called, and my being from an oil-bearing part of the Oklahoma Territory? Well, we did not become wealthy by being ignorant. No Sir, we learned about the source of our fortune, including a basic understanding of the engineering of our oilrigs and derricks. I am no engineer, but I have been around scores of art galleries and I learn quickly. I can tell you John; this hall was not designed to show off paintings or sculpture. What I would like to know is the answer to one simple question."

And with that remark, Katherine marched up to the Curator, who was deep in conversation with Holmes and, without introducing herself, butted into their discourse and asked simply, "Who was the architect of this beautiful and practical building?"

The Curator was stunned momentarily by her adroitness and confidence, rather than by the question she had asked. Holmes gave her a piercing, if questioning, look.

"As it happens," said the Curator, recovering his composure, "the architects of this fine building are the firm of Adler & Sullivan out of Chicago, the same architects who designed the famous Wainwright Building – the first true skyscraper - in St Louis, Missouri."

"Good, then let us visit these architects and congratulate them on the excellence of their design of this temple to Transportation, complete with its Golden Doors." said Katherine, triumphantly.

I could detect in Katherine's manner that she had figured out a singular fact from her observation of the structure, and had understood the significance and the wider implications of that revelation before Holmes!

Looking around this building, it became evident, even to my untrained eye, that this building was not really designed to receive works of art, but rather built to the commission of a financier called Adam Worth to receive agricultural machinery or something similar.

Clearly, our investigations were proceeding successfully, if

I could but see it. Katherine had observed something, and before Holmes! With that degree of satisfaction, we elected to spend a while longer looking at the stupendous buildings and exhibits that truly make this a place a *'City of Dreams'*. I was pleased and grateful to be able to experience the once-in-a-lifetime opportunity that it afforded.

Later we decided to take the steam packet boat over Lake Michigan back to Central Chicago, believing it would be an enjoyable experience. We had made some progress today, according to Holmes, who appeared more confident about reaching a solution. However, it was Katherine's thoughts and appreciation of the situation that I felt were more relevant to the matter in hand. Accordingly, we all jumped on board the moving sidewalk on the pier jutting out into Lake Michigan. After a short wait, we boarded the packet steamer and headed into its ornately appointed bar for refreshments.

Our journey south across Lake Michigan could not be said to be in any way as exciting as the *'Olympic'* crossing of the Atlantic, but the bar functioned extremely efficiently, with little or no waiting for service. Needless to say, having disembarked on to the quayside, we had to hail a passing Barouche carriage. Having climbed in we gave instructions to the coachman to take us to the architectural firm of Adler & Sullivan at the Steinway Hall Building at 17 Van Buren Street, to keep the appointment Katherine had arranged by cable previously.

Louis Sullivan turned out to be a rather genial character, and motioned us to make ourselves comfortable on chairs ranged around his office. Ironically, the Victorian interior of his office resembled that of a prosperous banker's, rather than an architect's.

"Yes," said Sullivan, answering Katherine's inquiry, "a rich financier, Mr Adam Worth, did come to see Adler & Sullivan some time ago and commissioned us to design what is now called the Transportation Building. I, as a senior partner, attended the first meeting that was concerned with general ideas, budgets and concepts. At the time our practice was very busy with several commissions, so I assigned one of our talented young architects, a Frank Lloyd Wright, to carry out the brief. In all honesty I paid little attention to the ideas expressed by Worth, but was aware of the fact that he did not really want a gallery for the exhibition of paintings. His wishes seemed to reflect an ulterior design not in keeping with the traditional design for picture galleries, at least, as I perceive them."

"Would you agree the glazed fenestration is too much, in that the large window areas would reflect daylight onto the glass-fronted paintings?" continued Katherine.

"Quite!" responded Sullivan, clearly impressed with Katherine's intelligent observation.

"Also, when we ascended the steps leading into the Main Hall of the pavilion, it was evident to me that the floor slab was at least eleven inches thick. Is this not a somewhat over-use of concrete for what is essentially a floor designed for people to walk upon?"

"Again Ma'am, you have a very keen eye in observing that particular detail. However, clients often have fads or foibles of their own and, if those are what they want incorporated into the design, then so be it. We can advise but not instruct," answered Sullivan.

"Is such a variation on the eventual use of a building normal?" Katherine asked Sullivan.

"It is possible that the client may have wished the building to be designed in a certain way so as to enable it to be used for another purpose after the Exposition. I assume this is what Adam Worth had in mind for the eventual use of his Transportation Building," informed Sullivan.

"Finally, Mr Sullivan, what do you make of the wide

double-leaf doors connecting the various galleries, not to mention your famous Golden Door entrance into the pavilion?" inquired Katherine.

"Good point," replied Sullivan, "though it is not uncommon to have large doors in galleries, after all some paintings can be quite sizeable."

"Yes, but paintings are carried sideways not front facing. That Transportation Building has all the hallmarks of being designed deliberately as a hall to exhibit large items of heavy transport machinery, which is precisely what is on exhibition currently. I do not think Worth had any intention of displaying art in that building!"

"I agree with you. I noticed this intention when I went with Lloyd Wright to the site to see how the structure was progressing. When I ask Lloyd Wright about this, he replied that the client, Adam Worth, had told him that there might be a more economically lucrative use for the structure, and that the designs should be flexible and capable of being amended accordingly. In carrying out the client's wish, the designs were, of course, perforce amended."

"When did this change of brief take place?" asked Katherine, leaning forward from her chair.

"Let me see now, about a year ago," said Sullivan. "I remember the change because not long afterwards, ten days or so, we all learned of the dreadful sinking of the ill-fated '*Titanic*.'"

"*Res ipsa loquitur*,"* said Katherine, looking at me.

After much hand shaking and offers to look over the architects' office and at the other exciting projects they were engaged upon, we found our selves back outside the Steinway Hall Building in Van Buren. We looked around for a carriage to take us back to the Auditorium Hotel to change and pack, ready to intercept our express train back to New York this evening. Katherine spotted one and, with a piercing whistle,

summoned a Rockaway four-wheeler over in our direction.
"Auditorium please," came the injunction.

* The thing speaks for itself.

Chapter 14

The Curious Tale of William Vanderbilt

Our journey on the express train back to New York, despite my misgivings, was as uneventful as one ought to expect. I still have difficulty believing our experiences with those Hanker Fänners and their murderous intentions towards Holmes and myself. Nor did it escape me that we were now thundering down the permanent way headed for New York – home of that violent gang of women. Would they, I wondered, be sauntering around looking for further opportunities to pickpocket and offer gratuitous violence to all and sundry? Probably, but more importantly, would they be looking for us and would they recognise both Holmes and me? I dreaded to think what the implications would afford us now that we had Katherine to look after. Somehow, ironically, I felt safer for her being with us!

At length, we started to race through Metropolitan New York and, in the distance, we could make out the Woolworth Building towering above the New York skyline, adjacent to the distinctive stepped pyramid-shaped top of the Banker's Trust Building in downtown Manhattan. Surveying the middle distance around East 23rd. Street I recognised, referring to my indispensable Bäedeker's *Guide to the New World*, 'The Three Graces' in the ornate tower of Madison Square Garden, the beautiful Metropolitan Life Assurance Building, clearly modelled on the Campanile of St Mark's Cathedral in Venice, Italy. And, finally, the ornate Fuller Building on Broadway, the twenty-one-storey skyscraper that is affectionately known as the Flatiron, due to its triangular shape.

From the windows of our express, hurtling down along the East River, I caught glimpses of the huge Byzantine-Romanesque Cathedral to St John the Divine, which was in the process of being created to the glory of God.

A few minutes later, the speed of the train began to ease back as we rumbled over the Hell Gate Bridge and started to enter a series of tunnels on our descent into Grand Central Terminal, and the territory of Hanker Fänners. A bell could be heard in the tunnel, heralding our approach to the platforms. Without much palaver or ceremony, we walked briskly out of the Terminal into 42nd. Street and immediately stopped a Bronson wagon by walking in front of it.

"This carriage, or whatever it is, will do," I said to Katherine, throwing my portmanteau and her valise into the back, then, with Holmes Gladstone bag, we clattered off in the direction of the Plaza Hotel on Fifth Avenue and Central Park South. On our journey we went by the Dakota Building, looking forlorn as if holding a terrible secret within its precinct.

Arriving at the Plaza Hotel was quite a shock. The building looked more like a stretched-up French Chateau, as if the building owners had decided to add a further ten floors to an existing well-balanced and designed edifice. Still, we checked in and freshened up, for we now had a meeting with another Titan, the Rail Road tycoon William Vanderbilt.

Presently, we assembled in the foyer and, whilst I was speaking with Katherine, Holmes arrived so we made our way out into Fifth Avenue, whereupon a Barouche, or Caleche carriage as they are known here, took us up. On our way south I noticed something.

"Look Holmes, the Carnegie Hall," I cried, as we pulled

into West 57th. Street on Seventh Avenue. "We should avail ourselves of a concert and see Andrew Carnegie's much-vaunted generosity in action!"

"You would like the interior of the auditorium, John," Katherine said, "very Victorian, with red plush everywhere. Do we have time to attend a concert before we sail back to England?"

"Hopefully."

We pulled up at the not insubstantial and imposing Vanderbilt mansion at No. 10 Washington Place, home of William Vanderbilt, President of the New York Central Rail Road.

After introductions had been made, Vanderbilt launched directly into what was on his mind.

"I do not approve of private detectives, Mr Holmes, however I am prepared to tolerate you for I invested in that art work and prepaid for it. The insurance cover is not what I want as my wife wants the art she decided upon. Ergo, I am prepared to listen to what you have to say."

Eventually Holmes replied to this unexpected outburst from our host.

"I am not retained to search out the missing works of art, but rather to determine other matters relating to the apparent sinking of the 'Titanic'. If you coöperate with me, then I may be able to assist you in your quest."

Clearly Vanderbilt was not used to receiving such direct suggestion from anyone, let alone a comparative stranger, but there was such self-assurance and authority in Holmes' voice that he compelled attention and compliance.

"Well yes, Holmes. Pleasing my wife's insatiable appetite for art is the more important right now. May I offer you people a drink. Wine for you perhaps, madam?"

"No. Neat whisky, large, and thank you," answered Katherine.

"Whisky, neat for me too, please," Holmes countered.

"Doctor Watson?"

"Whisky and a dash of the 'Coca-Cola'" I replied with ease and confidence.

The order was taken and our drinks arrived on a silver tray, together with cigars that we all enjoyed from our comfortable buttoned down leather armchairs. I noticed, however, that my whisky was not complemented with the Coca-Cola, as requested, but merely made up with cubes of ice, enough, I thought, to sink another '*Titanic*'.

"Tell me about Gould," asked Holmes, unexpectedly.

"Jay Gould died some years ago and, when he did, a loud cheer erupted, the likes of which we shall never hear again in our lifetimes. Gould was a predator on anyone and anything. However clever and resourceful he could be, however, I was always conscious of a hidden hand, a force, and an *eminence grise* as it were, behind him, controlling events and secreted in the background. I now know that this *eminence grise* was bankrolling Gould in his bid to bankrupt my New York Central Rail Road, aided and abetted by JP Morgan, that other shadowy figure in the background. These two financiers destroy Rail Roads!

" I understand that you have recently been in Chicago. Well you would have certainly seen, if not actually ridden, the Union Loop Elevated Rail Road operating in central Chicago. Charles Yerkes, a Chicago industrialist, built that urban railroad and, in so doing, attracted the attention of JP Morgan. Yerkes not only managed to protect his railroad, he also did something else that would have affected you as residents of London, England.

"Some years ago, Yerkes decided to become involved in the extension and development of the London Underground Railway. He established the Underground Electric Railways Company of London to manage the Metropolitan District Railway, the Baker Street & Waterloo Railway, currently under construction, and the proposed Great Northern, Piccadilly and Brompton Railway. Yerkes used labyrinthine financial arrangements to fund the construction of the new lines and to electrify the District Railway. In so doing, he frustrated an attempt by JP Morgan to become involved with the London Underground, and for that you should be grateful to Yerkes, otherwise you would have no viable underground railroad operating in London.

"Whilst none of us Robber Barons and Industrial Titans are angels, Mr Holmes, Gould was most certainly not. In part, he was responsible for the stock and gold market crash known as Black Friday, out of which he made a fortune by manipulating stock prices, again with information supplied by this *eminence grise*. He was also responsible, by his manipulation of the stock values, for the crash in the value of the New York & Erie Rail Road, thus initiating the 'Erie War', for which he was never forgiven. A hated man, he was often attacked in the streets of New York, especially outside his famed sumptuous mansion on 47th. Street and Fifth Avenue.

"Let me tell you of an incident and you will judge for yourself what kind of vituperative an individual he is. I shall make no comment to influence you, other than to point out that what I say is true. A few years ago, Gould decided to gain control of a new form of transport in New York City called the Manhattan Elevated Rail Road, which was as the name suggests, raised above the city's streets. Gould started his campaign to discredit this profitable company, through a newspaper he owned, by accusing it of insolvency, corruption and being generally inefficient and not worthy of the franchise it held to operate the Elevated Rail Road. Soon after, the value of its stock began to fall and Gould bought the deflated stock well below par through an intermediary. Eventually his stock accumulation enabled him to take control and he installed a compliant Cyrus Field, respected in Wall Street, as the new

President to lend verisimilitude, as it were, to the venture.

"The Elevated Rail Road issued more stock under the new regime and the value was manipulated upwards, whilst the fares were doubled! However, Field, because of his civic conscience and connections, would not sanction this and cancelled the increase in fares. It is to be remembered that Gould made his fortune by stock mismanagement of companies he was involved with. Accordingly, he decided to remove Field, in a very dramatic way, even by his standards. He first of all persuaded him to buy more 'lucrative' stock, which he did and, in so doing, became over- extended in the event of default. Gould and his cohorts then raided the stock market by dumping their shares and causing the price to collapse, leaving Field ruined and destitute. That is how he acted. When he died some years' ago his funeral was attended by no other than JP Morgan to whom he was very close."

"Are you suggesting this *eminence grise* is JP Morgan?" asked Holmes.

"Oh no," said Vanderbilt, "it is a fellow called Moriarty, a Professor James Moriarty."

"Why would Moriarty need Gould? As a very able lieutenant, to lend verisimilitude, as it were?" I asked.

"He did not, it was Gould who needed Moriarty," replied Vanderbilt.

Vanderbilt became increasingly emollient as our conversation progressed and, typical of Titans, could be bearable when he chose to be.

After a few more details were exchanged and another drink organised, without any warning Vanderbilt invited us to join him on his yacht and go to his Rhode Island residence, 'The Breakers', for the night. Holmes wavered in uncertainty, but I accepted immediately as a once-in-a-lifetime opportunity to experience something more exciting than a fog-bound Baker Street, to which, as far as I was concerned, I was in no desperate hurry to return. Katherine concurred with me in this decision.

Vanderbilt left the huge drawing room to make arrangements.

"Watson," said Holmes, "you know, I am uncertain as to who is my arch nemesis, Morgan or Moriarty. Moriarty clearly now has access to Gould's wealth and is using it in various schemes. Let us consider the situation. Moriarty, Morgan and the late Gould are linked with each other for the purpose of ruthless deception leading to colossal financial gain, with no fear of anyone or anything. After Gould's death, Moriarty now remains unchallenged, certainly not by Morgan, and is financed by Gould's wealth, which he administrates as the successor to Gould's business. Vanderbilt and Carnegie want revenge on Moriarty and Morgan.

"Interesting. One can now actually feel the kind of power emanating out of these dealings, where sinking a capital ship of the line such as the *'Titanic'* would present not the slightest qualm, as these people are answerable to no one!" I said.

"We have got to work out who is doing what to whom, when, where and why, Watson."

"I agree, and perhaps our visit to JP Morgan might well provide some answers, though for the life of me, I cannot imagine why he has granted us an audience."

"I can," replied Holmes. "Morgan is scared and I do not suspect it to be of Moriarty!"

"The *eminence grise* again? Good God, Holmes! It is as though a hidden power, this *eminence grise*, has opened a Vault of Madness on to an unsuspecting world. When will this insanity end and upon whom does one wage war?" I asked of Holmes.

Presently Vanderbilt joined us in the Main Hall of his rambling Washington Place mansion, ushered us through the main doors, held open for us by two liveried servants, and down to the street, into a waiting, highly polished Barouche with two more liveried coachmen sitting high on the front bench. We clattered out of Washington Place and, with a few turns, found ourselves in Fifth Avenue being pulled by four magnificent horses all the way to East 96th. Street, where we turned toward the East River to board Vanderbilt's yacht.

Once inside his luxurious boat, we weighed anchor and cruised at quite a rate of knots up the East River.

"It should not take us long to get to my cosy little den, as I call 'The Breakers', near Newport, Rhode Island," said Vanderbilt as we progressed into Long Island Sound and headed eastwards. As we did so, Vanderbilt pointed with his cigar to a large residence facing out over the Sound.

"That over there is Glen Cove, that ostentatious house you can see is the residence of JP Morgan." After some considerable time, and drink, we arrived at Newport and clambered into an elegant Long Island Carriage, pulled by four horses and driven by liveried coachmen.

The cosy little den called 'The Breakers' that Vanderbilt referred to, after we had eventually progressed up the majestic sweep of the front drive, turned out, upon arriving, to be a huge mansion house built in the styles of Italianate and Renaissance. It looked quite impressive, with numerous arches punctuated with recessed roundels, balconies and terraces, and large circular rooms with colonnades supporting verandas.

The main entrance to the building was within a portico, comprising four fluted columns rising to at least thirty feet and capped with Corinthian capitals, which supported an ornate flat-topped pediment with a low crowning balustrade above a deep architrave. Surrounding the house were large sculpted bronze lantern stands, on the top of which rested clusters of glass globes issuing forth a gentle, soft light. The house was covered in white stucco with stone corner dressings that contrasted with the shallow incline of the red terracotta roof tiles. This arrangement augmented the concept of a villa - as a place of relaxation and escape from the cares of business.

Our stay was to be overnight only, so Vanderbilt was unable to show us over the house to the extent I think he would have liked to. Still, he turned out to be an amiable host, very considerate in attending to our every whim and fad. Dinner was a sumptuous occasion served with wines I did not know existed. After dinner, Vanderbilt showed us his various collections of art and manuscripts, and then trailed off with Holmes to talk further about this Moriarty affair.

This left Katherine and I to wander around the house and, in the end, we went for a walk along the various terraces surrounding the house. Walking down one particular one, we came across the large curved wall of the house and, as we passed, we gazed through the window, only to see Holmes deep in conversation with Vanderbilt. Both seemed agitated and their furrowed brows, evident from where we were standing, expressed concern. We continued to promenade down the terraces illuminated by acetylene-fuelled ornate glass lanterns, leaving Holmes and Vanderbilt in conference.

When we did meet up eventually in the main Drawing Room, Holmes repeated to Vanderbilt the offer he had made to Carnegie, in that of his being engaged to look into certain affairs for reasons which concern a certain person.

"It remains at my discretion to whom I may advise and impart information obtained as a result of those inquiries. As I asked of Carnegie, it would be useful to me if you would provide me with a list of the paintings you were expecting to be delivered to you, that you reserved and paid for," advised Holmes.

We all retired to our appointed staterooms since we had had a busy day and, on the morrow, our journey would take us back to New York.

At breakfast we discussed other subjects and topics of

mutual interest. Vanderbilt was clearly a very cultured individual, but also a very sharp and clever operator. It was easy to see how he had built up his powerful New York Central Rail Road and to understand his avowed intent to defend it from predators such as Morgan or Jay Gould.

It was a fine experience being in Vanderbilt's yacht heading back to New York, and I think Holmes was glad that we had effectively forced him to go to 'The Breakers'.

Chapter 15

The Marble Library

Arriving at JP Morgan's residence at 219 Madison Avenue and 35th. Street, two imponderables presented themselves to my mind. Firstly, why should a very wealthy banker choose to live in a brownstone house in a neighbourhood like Madison Avenue, especially that particular stretch of the Avenue and, secondly, grant us an audience; was he not, after all, our quarry?

Holmes pulled at the bell wire and, after some considerable time, a deliberate amount of time in my opinion, a servant of the house opened the door.

"May I be of assistance?" Came a lugubrious voice that sounded as though it emanated from the tomb.

"We have an appointment with your master – Morgan," said Holmes.

"If you mean Mr Jean Pierpont Morgan, Junior, he is hardly my *master*, for I am an *employé* in his service."

"Well, perhaps, but we have come to talk with him not you."

"Possibly, but I understood that a private detecting person had an appointment with Mr Jean Pierpont Morgan, Junior. He is not expecting this group of persons, whom I am reluctant to allow admittance into this house. For Mr Jean Pierpont Morgan, Junior, follows an inflexible routine, allowing no uninvited persons to disturb him."

"I beg your pardon!" I exploded, enraged by this servant's

confident attitude in front of us. "Does the name Sherlock Holmes mean nothing to you?"

"I cannot say it does, but then I do not read cheap, sensational literature, the kind of which your friend is likely to appear in."

I could not believe the encounter we were enduring with this, this truculent flunkey behaving in such a confident manner in front of us all – and with no shame.

"Do you propose to leave this young lady in the doorway? Have you no courtesy, no manners?" I asked.

"I will confer with Mr Jean Pierpont Morgan, Junior," he said, stifling our protest at the ill-treatment meted out to us, and promptly slammed the front door in our faces.

A full twenty minutes elapsed before we heard a shuffling noise from behind us. It was the servant and he took his time in reaching us.

"I have conferred with Mr Jean Pierpont Morgan, Junior, and he will see you, not in his house but in his Library, which is located next door, and there he is prepared to tolerate members of the public such as yourselves."

We followed this individual through a garden area and eventually through a stone doorway into another set of grounds, in which the Library building was situated. The building of the Library looked more like a fortress, built to keep people out, and had a low architrave running around its cornice giving a sinister, almost minatory, aspect to its appearance.

At length, we entered a portal dominated by two gigantic bronze doors of monumental proportions, which led us through into the main hall, built in the style of a Rotunda, the floor of which was made up of marble slabs set in an intricate pattern. The walls of the Rotunda were lined with Repen Classico marble, punctuated with flat column pilasters capped with ornate Corinthian capitals. These were augmented by fully rounded columns of Verde Vecchia Chiesa marble, supporting a white stucco architrave, that gave way to a quatro-vaulted ceiling, resplendent with murals depicting mythological scenes and in which obtrusive power was paramount.

Morgan had not so much constructed a library, but rather a Mausoleum. In it, pride of place would be given to his sarcophagus resting in the middle of the Rotunda, surrounded by his symbolic and allegorical paraphernalia. With this and in the hope that his condemned soul might find salvation and rise up through the central oculus window opening set in the ceiling immediately above. The presence of four exquisite, bowled lantern stands made of Travertino Rosso Persiano marble, acting almost as a guard in waiting for the inevitable arrival of the sarcophagus, augmented the feeling of a Mausoleum.

"Clearly a man with imperial ambitions," said Katherine, as we entered the East Room, formerly the Treasury, which housed quite a considerable collection of books.

This library was constructed of walnut shelving ranged over three storeys, upon which were placed books of the kind one buys by the yard, rather than considered purchase or family inheritance. The inlaid walnut shelving was more a triumph of structural engineering than elevated balconies of learning. Each book, I noticed, was in pristine condition and some, in fact, had not even had their pages cut open!

Above the fireplace hung a tapestry, of dubious origin, that depicted one of the deadly sins, that of Avarice as personified by Midas, the mythological king of greed, upon whose touch objects would turn into gold. This included food, which then of course he could not eat, and so precipitated his collapse.

The upper section of the walls of the room depicted scenes of historical characters engaged in the serious business of making money. Crowning the wall of the room was an architrave that resembled an Egyptian hollow-and-roll curve, progressing to the ceiling, which was decorated with the twelve zodiacal signs, reflecting Morgan's obsession with the figure twelve, rather like Holmes' fear of the figure five.*

The place was full of allegorical meaning, which was reënforced in the art displayed on the walls, to the point of defeating, obviously, the original concept. Ranged around the place were paintings of dubious origin, merit and acquisition, including Jean Baptiste Greuze's '*La fille a l'Agneau*' and Gainsborough's 'Duchess of Devonshire', the originals of which, I knew, with a betting certainty, existed in Staunton's establishment in the Tottenham Court Road in London. Morgan's building exuded a feeling, not of learning, but of mass acquisition for the sake of undiscerning hoarding, displayed throughout rooms, which were fit more for the execution of Masonic Temple rites, than they were for a domestic library or art gallery.

"Look, John, an original Gutenberg Bible from the fifteenth century! Does it not seem at variance with the establishment we are in, with its ornate ceiling depicting the zodiac rising above all and indeed looking down on us?" said Katherine, in hushed tones.

Despite the Beaux-Arts exterior of the place, designed by McKim, the creator of the Pennsylvania Rail Road Station located but a few blocks away from here, the interior of the place was very much different. It conformed to an overbearing neo-Mediaeval opulence so often displayed by many successful Victorian Titans. In evidence were mural and *trompe-l'oeil* paintings depicting scenes straight out of Wagnerian opera. Scenes from '*Tristan und Isolde*', perhaps, '*Tännhauser*' probably, or the Sacred Music Dramas as '*Parsifal*' or '*Lohengrin*'- certainly. Not one square inch had escaped the interior decorator's attention, in that every surface was overlaid with sumptuous decoration as if to extract every ounce of value from their investment. We had observed this trait of megalomania when at the residence of Carnegie and, more so, when staying with Vanderbilt.

Passing through the elm-panelled North Room, containing even more books ranged on double-tiered, bookshelf balconies, we were ushered into the lush Drawing Room. This room was lined with red velvet, flock-patterned, silk wallpaper with a matching full-size broadloom scarlet silk carpet. Against the walls were fitted dado-high, glass-fronted bookcases, upon which were placed Carrara marble figurines from classical antiquity

Positioned in the middle of one wall was a fireplace surrounded by the biggest stone-carved chimney-piece I ever wish to see, standing at least seven feet high. Perched on top at each end were figures of winged angels kneeling down and supporting two-foot-high candlesticks. Despite these heavenly reminders, the chimney-piece was not something one would leave one's tobacco pouch on, I thought.

In the middle of the room was a large, deep red, velvet-covered sofa with two matching armchairs, lending a sense of comfortable, if condescending, opulence to the richly appointed room. The armchairs were ranged in such a position facing the sofa as to appear almost inquisitorial, as if to intimidate the sitter. Not deterred by this arrangement, Katherine and I sat on the sofa, and Holmes positioned himself in one of the armchairs. We had not long to wait before we heard the sound of a door being opened. We all looked to the left of the fireplace towards the corner of the room from whence the noise originated.

Then, to my utter astonishment, part of the wall moved out, creating an opening in it and revealing a hidden room. The red velvet, flocked silk wallpaper, together with the low glass- fronted book cabinets had camouflaged the door very effectively. Then, though this secret aperture, stepped

Morgan and, with his shoulder, started to close the door, but not before I had noticed quite clearly that the walls of that secret vault were lined with steel!

Holmes and I rose from our seats. Katherine did not, but remained seated, looking at Morgan as hunter views his quarry.

"I see you are recovered from the assassination attempt on your life at your country retreat in Glen Cove, Nassau County, Long Island. Shot twice, I believe, by the deranged Erich Meunter, a German national and doctor of *mathematics*," said Holmes stressing the word 'mathematics'.

"This Britisher Holmes might want to pussyfoot around with you, Morgan. I do not wish to, but what I do want to know is why you had my fiancé done away with," interjected Katherine.

"An unfortunate occurrence," replied Morgan, still startled by this outburst from a woman he had never met before nor been formally introduced to.

"An unfortunate what? Asked Katherine, rising from the sofa. "That so-called occurrence involved the deliberate murder of the man I was to marry!"

"I am a banker and not used to being addressed in quite this manner by a woman I do not even know," responded Morgan.

"The lady is quite correct," I said, coming to Katherine's aid. "You may be a banker but you are, Sir, implicated in the callous death in Eureka Springs of an *employé* of yours. After all, did he not work for you?"

Katherine had not quite finished.

"You have an awful lot to answer for, Morgan, and these two gentlemen are going to expose you for what you are and, not only that, but the bloodhounds of the press are loosed upon you. What did the *New York Times* print? 'Thoughtless disregard for life we can with equanimity accept, but the reckless disregard for capitalism we certainly cannot.'"

That last remark visibly disturbed Morgan. '...reckless disregard for capitalism...' the credo by which he lived cast into doubt.

"Your involvement with Moriarty, was it on a professional or social basis?" asked Holmes.

"Neither," came Morgan's reply, "I was never introduced to the man."

"What about Adam Worth, the *eminence grise*, the prime mover, the power in the background, as I understand it?" I asked.

"The *eminence grise*, as you call him, Doctor Watkins, is a rather fanciful term for a man of unimpeachable character and a fellow financier by the name of Adam Worth. I have had dealings with him, but only in business terms. You probably do not know, but he had to earn his fortune!"

I interjected, "Morgan you too were cheated by Moriarty, and you know your Nemesis ** is upon you!"

At that juncture, a knock on the door was heard and the truculent servant of our previous encounter came in to the room. He shuffled up to Morgan and whispered something in his ear, whereupon Morgan dismissed him with a wave of his arm.

"I will have to terminate this conversation as I have more urgent matters to attend to in receiving a deputation from my board of directors."

I certainly realised, as did Holmes, that there had been some double-dealing against Morgan, who must also be irritated with Worth, as well as in danger of being done away with by him. It was obvious that Worth was on a mission to eradicate all threats against him, and determined that no evidence or witnesses were extant to potentially testify against him.

"Worth has Gould's fortune to propel him on his quest to achieve his aims," said Holmes. "He has taken on Carnegie and Vanderbilt and has subdued the Professor Moriarty. Good day, Mr Morgan."

And with that Parthian shot, which surprised not only Katherine and Morgan but myself too, Holmes then gathered up his hat and cane and made towards the Drawing Room door.

I looked at Morgan and detected in his countenance a very visibly concerned person, who was experiencing difficulty discerning the facts in a series of events affecting him. What was evident to me was that Holmes' final remark to Morgan had delighted Katherine, who clearly revelled in the fact that Morgan was now made to feel uncomfortable.

As we left Morgan's temple to his vanity, I said to Katherine, "I note that there is a performance of Gustav Mahler's '*Auferstehungs-Symphonie*'*** being performed at the Carnegie Hall this evening."

"In that case we should all avail ourselves of this musical interpretation of Mahler's Second Symphony at the Carnegie Hall of Charitable Bequest, and see for ourselves the measure of this legacy and the extent of the generosity of Mr Carnegie!" she replied.

"We will, I feel confident, appreciate this Symphony, and perhaps take dinner afterwards at PJ Carney's on 57th. Street opposite the Carnegie Hall," I continued.

Upon arriving at the chateau-styled Plaza Hotel, we all three of us repaired to our rooms and agreed to meet in the foyer later, ready for our departure for the Carnegie Hall. Within the space of one hour we found ourselves seated in Carnegie's bequest to the American people.

The conductor, a diminutive fellow walked on to the platform and ascended the podium, from which he directed the orchestra with a wave of his baton, to commence playing the opening movement of Mahler's Symphony No. 2 in C minor.

The concert was disappointing, to say the least. One ex-

Gustav Mahler

pects the Metropolitan orchestra of any nation to be up to a certain standard. The conductor spent more time jumping around the podium than he did conducting. Had he spent a fraction of his undoubted and very obvious gymnastic ability and energy in organising and marshalling the inherent force of any Mahler symphony, then he might have succeeded in interpreting this complex C minor work in an innovative and uplifting manner.

After some slight, undignified pushing, we managed to quit the Hall, and headed across 57th. Street into PJ Carney's renowned bar-restaurant, I believe the term is. In this type of establishment there is very little ceremony and one merely sits in a row, usually at the bar, with waitresses moving up and down taking orders from customers as and when they require beverages or food.

"I must say, this bar-restaurant, as they call it, is an apt term for what is, on the face of it, quite a civilised way to prepare and serve food and drink, with none of the fancy ritual normally associated with eating food in order to live," announced Holmes

"How is that, Holmes?"

I could detect that Holmes was still rendered uncomfortable by the fact that Katherine referred to him by his surname, as indeed do I.

"Because people make too much of what is, after all, a necessary bodily requirement in order to acquire the energy to live," said Holmes, deliberately looking at me.

"But Holmes," I said, "the idea of eating food is to enjoy the flavours and tastes. Surely this desire cannot affect your clinical approach to food?"

"What do you not like eating, Holmes?" asked Katherine.

"Offal and, in particular, liver."

"No doubt you will eat an alternative to offal, in which case John is right. One is guided by taste and preference in *order* to enjoy the food for the purpose of eating to exist…" delivered Katherine.

This dialogue may well have gone on. However, at that particular moment a waitress appeared, looking as though she was ready, not so much to take our order, but rather to serve up an argument.

"What can I get you to drink and eat?" was the opening salvo from the waitress.

I cannot bring myself to chronicle the performance that erupted at this juncture between Holmes and the waitress, save to God that I wished Katherine and I had not been compelled to experience it.

The next morning we all breakfasted heartily in preparation for our journey, later that evening, back to England. I felt saddened by the idea of leaving New York, but happy that Katherine had consented to accompany us in order to be in on the conclusion to our investigation. It is, of course, to be remembered that Katherine's fiancé, who worked for JP Morgan at the time, had been done in, at the behest of Moriarty, whilst they were taking the waters at Eureka Springs in the Oklahoma Territory some fifteen months ago.

Again, and for the last time, we climbed into a Rockaway carriage and proceeded down Broadway towards our destination at the dockside and our rendezvous with the pride of the White Star Line, the Royal Mail Steamer '*Olympic*'. *En-route* I noticed an article in the *New York Times* and remarked to both Katherine and Holmes, "Morgan has got his just rewards." I pointed with my index finger to an article headed:

'Morgan Removed by Board'. It continued, 'JP Morgan has been relieved of his position as Chairman of the International Mercantile & Marine combine, owners of the '*Titanic*', by a unanimous decision of the board. An officer of the company informed the *New York Times* that this unprecedented action was in response to information received that the calamitous sinking of the ship '*Titanic*' some months previously may not have been the result of an accident, as originally supposed. There is information that the sinking may have been planned.'

"That is the best bit of news I have heard in ages!" announced Katherine.

"Interesting," remarked Holmes, "you can be certain who supplied that information to the board, our old friend Worth, who clearly now has Morgan in his sights for removal."

"One cannot condone Worth's action, but ought not we to warn Morgan, even anonymously?" I ventured.

"I imagine Morgan will be the first to realise his predicament, and will need no urging from us, even if we were predisposed to advise him," replied Holmes.

"Nevertheless though, Holmes, ought not we, at least, to set a guard upon him if only for the preservation of life?"

"I think a guard has already been set upon Morgan in the form of that supercilious servant we met at the front door to

Morgan's mansion in Madison Avenue. Indeed I venture to say that it is a brave assassin who would have a verbal encounter with him."

Our conversation died down as our Rockaway carriage made its way down to the Lower East Side for embarkation. I was sorry to be leaving New York, not least because, bathed, as it is by the Atlantic breeze, it very rarely becomes fog-bound, unlike London, to where we were headed.

Arriving at the Customs Shed, we made our way through the chaos it contained to the pier where the huge '*Olympic*' was moored. Despite its history, the boat appeared to me, at least viewed from the dock looking up, to be unsinkable.

"How could something as big as a ship like the '*Titanic*' sink?" I mused to Katherine as we ascended the gangplank and entered the ship through a large door in the side. "It just seems to me to be too improbable, and yet the '*Titanic*' went down."

Katherine did not reply, but continued to read the *New York Times* she was holding.

It was at that moment, I realised, that Katherine looked ashen and was staring intensely at another banner headline in the *New York Times,* in addition to the one regarding JP Morgan's removal from the Board.

"Katherine, are you alright?" I asked.

"John, see what has become of our '*City of Dreams*'! It is ruined!" she exclaimed, handing the paper to me.

My heart sank as I read the news that indeed the Exposition site was a sea of flames, with whole swathes of the area and the buildings therein destroyed. Those buildings, echoing the glory of ancient Roman imperial architecture, now alas, were in ruin and ashes.

"Do you remember when we were walking arm-in-arm down the colonnade of the Peristyle building, with its views of Lake Michigan between the sets of columns? How we felt it was so magical to be in a classical building looking out onto the blue waters of the lake? How the colonnade we were in, seemingly endless, disappeared into the haze, as if into eternity?"

"We are destined to destroy the things we love," I replied, knowing it to be a feeble response, given the enormity and magnitude of the calamity that had befallen the World's Columbian Exposition at Chicago. I also realised it was a weak re-action to Katherine's feelings, so clearly reflected in her moist eyes. I knew the Exposition meant something to her in terms of a celebration of achievement, an awakening, an appreciation, a consolidation, a desire to aspire, to improve, to give hope and deliver happiness!

Katherine looked at me and I returned her gaze. We both knew that something we held dear in our hearts had been destroyed and reduced to smoke and ashes.

I searched the front page for more details. The fact that the '*City of Dreams*' was now a massive conflagration was the last in a series of disasters befalling the city, starting with civil disorder leading to riots, culminating in the assassination of the mayor of Chicago, and an outbreak of smallpox.

"We have gained something from that experience, Katherine, and it will remain the '*City of our Dreams*', and so dwell in our memories to cherish for the rest of our lives!"

"True, John. We are now on board another dream. This boat, this '*Ship of Dreams*," said Katherine.

A few minutes later we stepped onto the upper deck of the RMS '*Olympic*'. We stood on the deck talking about New York and the New World. It was there that our wishes were made, in that '*City of Dreams*' in far-away Chicago, still brilliant and magical in our minds. We looked at each other, knowing something between us to be indestructible. We both looked ahead as the boat slipped its moorings and, eventually gliding past Liberty holding her illuminated Torch of Freedom,

headed out into the cold dark waters of the Atlantic on that
November evening.

* The case of the Five Orange Pips resulted in the death of a client.

** The avenging Greek goddess of truth and reckoning.

*** The Resurrection Symphony in C minor.

Chapter 16

The Flight to London

Our journey back across the Atlantic Ocean was less adventurous than our outward-bound trip. Possibly the thought of being back in fog-bound London filled me with a nameless foreboding. Even Holmes spent an inordinate amount of time in his cabin sending and receiving cables via the Marconi apparatus located in the Wireless Room.

On the one occasion I did find Holmes taking the air on the forward deck, he was standing on the very front apex of the ship, peering over the prow into the distance as if expecting to see England come looming up from the horizon. He noticed me and raised his outstretched arms.

"I wish to God, Watson, we could get to England earlier, for I can think of no better reason now than that of ours at this time to break all speed records and risk an iceberg collision in pushing this ship across the Atlantic!"

"We can do nothing whilst we are at sea, Holmes, so you may as well relax and gather your reserves of strength, for I suspect recourse to such will be necessary, once we are back in London."

I left Holmes brooding and searching the blood-red horizon.

Katherine and I, in contrast, waltzed our way across the Ocean to the music being played in the Grand Salon. The band played a selection of music from the *'Planets Suite'* including the haunting 'Uranus' and *'Music of the Spheres'.* Waltzes were played frequently, including *'Roses from the South',* a personal favourite of Katherine's. We danced until we were too exhausted to stand up, let alone propel our persons across the Ballroom floor in syncopation to the harmonic rhythm.

"Is this not the way to live, Katherine?"

"Rather, I could do this forever! I now understand why people elect to spend their lives floating around the Seven Seas."

"I agree, Katherine, this is too good to last, but we shall enjoy it whilst we may."

We did, at least for a while longer, as we experienced the splendid isolation the Ocean can induce in one. There is, of course, no reference to anything, just the heaving waters upon which one momentarily exists. Consequently, this situation can augment inner feelings and compress into a clearer perception the concept of one's own existence, and the indescribable feeling of being able to enjoy it with someone.

Our sentiment that this was too good to last, was alas, rather too abruptly implemented. Within no time, all three of us found ourselves in the Liverpool Customs Shed explaining various facts, including why a lady from the Oklahoma Territory wished to enter England. I lent support to Katherine's replies. Holmes, I noted, did not. Eventually, having secured Katherine's permission to proceed, we found ourselves on the railway platform at Liverpool's Lime Street Railway Station, waiting to board an express train bound for London. We boarded the express and had an indifferent journey back to London. At length, we arrived back in the Metropolis, which was still shrouded in fog, much to Katherine's and my dismay. However, I managed to engage a Hansom carriage to take Katherine and I from Euston Station to the St Pancras Hotel, and check her in.

"Watson, where are you going?" asked Holmes.

"Since you ask, Holmes, where would you think I am going? Your deductive reasoning appears to have abandoned you on this occasion. I am going to escort and check Katherine into the St Pancras Hotel. After that, we are to attend the Queen's Hall, for Katherine has expressed an interest in witnessing a performance of the mighty Eighth Symphony by Anton Bruckner. You know the one, the C minor Symphony, in which the structure of the music is said to resemble the architectural proportions of a Cathedral."

As we set off, I noticed Holmes hail a Phäeton carriage to take him and my luggage back to Baker Street. A few minutes later Katherine and I pulled into the sweeping driveway of the Hotel, punctuated with gas lamps pouring out their weak blue light. In front of us was the phäntasmagoric and cliff-like façade that is the imposing magnificence of the London Midland Railway's St Pancras Hotel looming up out of the fog that seemed powerless to shroud it. The sight of that splendid romantic Gothic structure dominating the fog brought a smile to her face and I knew she was glad to be back at this Hotel, of which we both have fond memories.

I waited down in the Main Reception, remembering the time I was last here, on my first visit to Katherine, who was staying at the time, and how impressed I was with the Hotel's appointments. Indeed, I remain so. I then suddenly caught sight of the supercilious concierge who was still dressed in his red tail-coat and black top hat, and who treated me in a less than courteous manner when I presented my credentials to him.

"Hello John, are we ready to leave?" asked Katherine, who had returned looking very elegant.

"Yes let us engage a carriage to take us to the Queen's Hall. I think you will like it there. It is one of London's favourite concert halls, with its sumptuous red-plush interior and gold detailing set in a Victorian-Baroque style of architecture."

St Pancras Hotel

"Carriage!" cried Katherine, and climbed into the vacant Brougham that drew up immediately. "Queen's Hall, Portland Place."

"Where did you get your fondness for music, especially the later Romantics and, indeed, contemporary composers as Mahler or Schönberg, whose epic work *'Gurrelieder'* you have referred to on numerous occasions? One day I should like to hear that monumental work," I said.

"I have always been fond of music and it is the one art form I can relate to, enjoy and appreciate. It has become such an integral part of my life that I would be lost without recourse to it."

Our Brougham carriage had by now traversed the Euston Road and was progressing down the Tottenham Court Road, still lively and bustling with life and activity. Street urchins, including cotton-dressed and booted girls and Cockney boys of precocious disposition, were everywhere to be seen. Some were clearly engaged in street business. Others, one instinctively knew, were keeping a look out for the law or, better still, richer opportunities.

It was along this thoroughfare, at the junction with Goodge Street, I informed Katherine, that Holmes and I had investigated the curious circumstances of a bowler hat, a goose and a precious stone. Which, in turn, led to the singular case of the jilted fiancée, a broken shop window hereabouts, and the disappearance of a bridegroom as he stepped out of his Hackney carriage into oblivion, when arriving at the St Pancras Hotel to attend his own wedding breakfast!

"What! The same hotel I am staying in? Asked Katherine.

"Yes," I replied. "And, here at No. 35 is Arthur Staunton's so-called Picture Gallery. I desisted, however, from chronicling the details of Staunton's nefarious activities and occupation to Katherine.

Eventually we turned into Tottenham Street, made our way via a circuitous route to Riding House Street, and headed westward. The street is quite narrow and twists and turns and, as we clattered down its cobblestones, we witnessed a series of ghostly lights emanating from the gas lamps that swirled by us as we passed. After a few minutes of this surreal experience, we arrived at the Queen's Hall to witness a performance of the mighty Eighth Symphony in C minor by Anton Bruckner, complete with sonorous scales and harmony, indeed resembling in its construction the architectural proportions of a Cathedral!"

After the concert, we decided to dine at the Vienna Café Restaurant at 24 Oxford Street. For some reason we elected to walk there in the fog, arm-in-arm for mutual support.

"I do so much adore Bruckner and his control when marshalling huge orchestral forces in order to develop such sublime and sonorous music," said Katherine.

"I agree. It is the nearest to combining two art forms successfully, those of music and architecture."

Having groped our way through the fog, we managed to find the Vienna Café Restaurant in the bustling Oxford Street.

"That music and our short walk have given me quite an appetite," remarked Katherine, as I held the door open for her.

"Right, what have we got here?" said Katherine, having secured our seats. "Waiter, I think the Mixed Grill with Devilled Butter looks good, with an inch-thick chop of centre-loin lamb, calves liver, lamb's kidneys, and rashers of bacon with grilled mushrooms. For dessert I will elect to go for the Lord Mayor's Trifle. And wine, let me see, yes, I will try the Burgundy, Volnay Beaune."

I followed in by ordering, "Lamb Chops in Tomato Sauce, together with Roast Pork with raisins and apples to complement. For dessert I shall have the Wine Jelly with Brandied Peaches and, to drink, a bottle of Chablis."

We enjoyed our dinner as we had the concert, and chatted amiably *en-route* back to Katherine's hotel, where we agreed to meet the following day to see how the case was progressing.

Back in Baker Street I entered our drawing room, only to be informed by Holmes, "The game is afoot, Watson! Whilst you were gallivanting around the Metropolis, with, with that, that woman, this wire from the Admiralty was delivered by Government Dispatch Messenger not one hour ago. Holmes handed the slip of paper to me. It read:

'...BELIEVE MORIARTY AT REICHENBACH.
PINKERTON THERE... .....SO ARE JESUITS...
HOPKINS EN-ROUTE...WILL YOU GO? END.'

"Watson, there is work to be done and not much time to do it. We start for Reichenbach first thing in the morning," he said, disappearing into his room.

Not much time, I thought, pulling the bell-rope to summon our pageboy, who appeared a few moments later.

"Billy, take this telegram to the Crown Post Office around the corner as quickly as you can," I said handing him a half-sovereign. I then retired to my own room to pack, picking up the bottle of whisky *en-route*. The night dragged on as I slept only intermittently because my thoughts were concentrated on Moriarty and, especially, the fact that Meiringen was in Europe and therefore somewhat beyond English justice. Were we to intercept him, what precisely would be our options when confronting him, I pondered repeatedly.

Breakfast the next morning was a rushed affair since we had to catch the Dover boat train of the South Eastern Railway operating out of Charing Cross Station. Eventually we managed to secure a returning Landau carriage and with the usual injunction of, 'a guinea if you take us to Charing Cross as quickly as possible', climbed into it and made ourselves comfortable on its buttoned-down leather seats. It was early in the morning and the usual vicissitudes of traffic had not quite started, so the drive to our destination was without incident and unimpeded as our horses glided through the fog-bound streets of London.

We arrived just in time and, as we made our way down the platform, I looked about me. Holmes called me and said he had found an empty First Class compartment. I found what I was searching for too.

"Katherine! Over here, Katherine!"

"I got your telegram last night about the trip to Meiringen and meeting you here. And yes, I have made the hotel arrangements there as you asked."

"Good," I said helping her onto the train.

"Good morning, Mr Holmes, how are we today?" asked Katherine.

Holmes looked up and, with a visibly pained expression on his face and ignoring her polite inquiry, restricted himself to diverting his gaze by staring out of the window.

The train began to move jerkily down the platform, and soon we were rumbling across the Hungerford Railway Bridge over the Thames in the direction of Waterloo.

"This is where the Admiralty clerk, Cadogan West, met his supreme moment, on these very railway tracks below us, and in so doing triggered off this investigation in which we all find ourselves involved," I said to Katherine.

Chapter 17

The Reichenbach Incident

Eventually we arrived at Meiringen, in the middle of a major tempest with the wind blowing furiously and rain lashing down. We were not the only visitors to step down onto the wet station platform, I noticed. The storm, which showed no signs of abating, had accompanied us through the Hasle Valley alongside the swollen waters of the Aar River. There was some confusion with the ticket collector over our tickets, the resolution of which I gladly left to Holmes' deductive reasoning, especially his ability to express it to the now irate railway servant.

I stepped out, not really prepared for this weather, to hail a carriage of sorts to take us to the Englischer Hof, with the vague hope that they had received and acted upon our reservation. At length, an empty carriage came into view through the rain and I flagged it down. On turning around to reënter the Station to alert the others, I noticed to my dismay that the carriage, rather than stopping as hailed, just went cantering on by!

I retraced my footsteps back to the station's *Porte Cochere* to seek shelter from the rain under its canopy.

"It kind of rains a lot in this part of Europe," said Katherine, smiling at my sodden attire whilst walking to join me.

Suddenly, she darted out from beneath the *Porte Cochere* and whistled loudly at a passing carriage, nearly deafening me in the process, such was the piercing shrill of her whistle. Whatever effect it had on my ears must have also affected the carriage driver, because he immediately reined in his horses and headed towards us. The horses' hooves echoed as they clattered on the flagstones under the *Porte Cochere*. Having loaded our luggage onto the open-top carriage without the assistance of the coachman, who just sat there looking on impassively as we did his work, prompted me to remember 'an extra tip for you, my good man, upon arrival'.

Having dismissed our carriage driver, *sans* tip, and thanked him heartily, we eventually gained the foyer of the hotel, all rather dishevelled. Katherine took care of the registration and checked us in.

"*Guten abend,*" she started in with the concierge.

"Ah good evening, Madam," came the reply. "You are the *Amerikanische* dame we have been expecting?"

"Yes, you are correct, and this is Herr Doktor Watson and that is Holmes. You have rooms for us I believe."

"Yes, your room is on the *piano nobile* as is Herr Doktor Watson's and his patient, a Herr Holmes, as you specified in your cable, is not bothered where his room will be. We therefore have put Herr Holmes at the back of the hotel on the fourth floor, and Hans will now escort Herr Doctor's patient there. Madam and Herr Doktor please to follow me to your rooms," said the concierge, leading us to a broad red-carpeted staircase to the upper floors.

On ascending the staircase, I was aware that a commotion had broken out in the foyer and, thinking it might involve Holmes dissatisfied with his room, looked back to see what could be the cause of it. From my vantage point on the stairs it appeared that two gentlemen with pronounced American accents, which Katherine turning her head noted too, were arguing with two priests, as to who had the prior rightful claim to a double-booked room. The priests, in a dazzling display of intellectual prowess, were laying claim on the *à priori* basis of simply their being there first.

On entering my hotel room, I went straight to the window to ascertain what view I could expect to see of the locality. None, as my window opened onto the side tower of an adjacent church. The building being almost Lutheran did not display any interesting architectural detail, just a blank wall. The teeming rain coming in from the open window prevented any further visual exploration.

I did not feel like taking dinner tonight as hunger did not affect me at the moment, and the journey across Europe had the effect of making me feel weary, though not tired. Perhaps a small drink to be sociable and keep Katherine company, lest she find herself deadlocked with Holmes.

Katherine was already in the Salon at the bar, considering the wine list.

"What do you think, given what small choice there is? The Montrachet, the most expensive white Burgundy wine there is here, or shall we explore the Claret, the non-Burgundy red wines of France?"

"Rather," I tried to enthuse.

Holmes deigned to join us some time later and, upon looking at the empty bottles in front of us on the bar, remarked:

"We have been busy."

"Yes," said Katherine, "waiting on you for your decisive and intuitive analysis on the challenges we face, for we are convinced, are we not John, that you and only you can determine the correct solution."

"I am honoured," said Holmes, with a searching sideways glance in our direction, "but we have to tread carefully in order to arrive at the right solution."

"You are absolutely correct about treading carefully!" said Katherine, to my surprise.

"It is a question of logical deduction," said Holmes.

"Do you not mean 'reduction'?" asked Katherine.

Holmes, somewhat put out by this interjection, restricted himself to giving her a withering look which made no impact upon Katherine.

Holmes continued, "…logical deduction…"

"What can you be talking about?" she interrupted. "The reason John and I ask," she said, incorporating me into her attack upon Holmes, "is because we were discussing the challenges afforded to wine makers when trampling down the grape and how they might affect the taste. You said just now, 'but we have to tread carefully in order to arrive at the right solution'. In that remark about treading carefully on the grapes, I can agree. All this talk about 'logical deduction, conclusion and synthesis', the right whatever, it is pure conjecture, as my High School Ma'am could have told you!"

"Well Holmes, what do you think about the bouquet of this Montrachet?" I said, pushing a filled glass along the bar to Holmes in a doomed attempt to change the subject and engage his interest.

"I am afraid my considered opinion will be of little help to you as I have no experience and therefore knowledge of the inferior wines that you two clearly enjoy," he answered, ordering a chilled bottle of Veuve Clicquot champagne.

Looking around the Salon in order to break off the encounter, I noticed that the two priests had taken up position in a small alcove with a good strategic view of the Salon. A few moments later, the American fellows strutted in, looked around, and sat down at a table positioned between the priests and us. Both parties expected waiters to attend upon them but none came. For some unfathomable reason, all of a sudden the atmosphere in the hotel Salon became such as to induce a sensation of anxiety, a tension as it were, producing a feeling of expectation as if this were the overture of a grand opera, about to unfold.

Katherine, who by now had turned away from Holmes, was looking at me. Our eyes met and we both knew we were experiencing the instant change in the atmosphere of the Salon.

It was for good reason the atmosphere in the Salon had changed, for at that instant in stepped James Moriarty, Professor of Mathematics, flanked on either side by two gentlemen, and all three were wearing top hats and black capes!

From that moment, the consumption of alcohol increased immeasurably, as people reverted to talking quietly amongst themselves as heads came together in an overtly conspiratorial manner.

It was after some considerable time that I regained my room and, thankfully, collapsed onto the bed, thoroughly exhausted, probably due to the tiring journey we had made that day across Europe.

The next morning I drew back the curtains concealing the window, expecting to find an overcast sky and dull rainy day. It was and so I closed the curtain and instead lit a gas mantle on the wall for illumination, whilst I consulted my diary. Eventually, I went down to breakfast.

"Good morning, Katherine. Did you sleep well?" I inquired.

"Yeah, like a groundhog in winter! I did ask, because I know you like it, whether or not they have any smoked bacon here. The waiter seemed a bit confused."

"I will ask him when he re-appears, whenever that will be."

"Waiter," said Katherine, "more hot coffee, and this gentleman wants to order from you, *verstehen?*"

I started in with what I considered to be a recognisable English breakfast, including lamb chops and smoked bacon.

The waiter listened attentively and politely to my order, writing down carefully everything that I had asked for.

"Will that be all and some sauce, yes?" he said, and disappeared in the general direction of the kitchen.

In the meantime, the Pinkerton agents came into the breakfast room looking a bit piqued, followed by the Jesuits, who nodded to us as they made their way to a vacant table.

"Whatever could those devout Fathers be doing here?" asked Katherine.

"They have an interest in Moriarty because he has caused them financial injury in the recent past by substituting their collection of original paintings, including some famous Old Masters, with counterfeit copies. Their collection, which was used as collateral for loans for their College when required, is now worthless and could bankrupt them."

"Moriarty is braver than I thought," said Katherine. "It must take nerves of steel to be at variance with the Jesuit Order."

"I do not for a moment think the Jesuits intend to extend so much Apostolic Benediction to Moriarty, as Compelled Redemption and *res communis* to the Jesuit Order!"

"Good morning. May I join you, or is this a private rendezvous?"

"Oh, have you got our breakfast order?" asked Katherine, without looking up. "Oh it is you, Holmes. I thought you sounded like the waiter. Of course you may join us. Please do sit down."

Presently the waiter re-appeared with Katherine's order and mine, at least so I thought, but I could not be bothered to argue. Holmes placed his order of Emmental cheese and grapes with Parma ham.

Moriarty entered the breakfast room and suddenly the clatter of cutlery in contact with china plates stoped, as did conversation. Such, however, was my annoyance with what the waiter had brought me under the guise of breakfast, that the advent of Moriarty was of supreme indifference to me at that precise moment.

"Look at this," I said, to either Katherine or Holmes, without diverting my gaze from the plate. "See what the waiter has delivered. Eggs, not grilled, smoked bacon, but cold ham of sorts, tomato, kidney, and what is this, fried potato? * And what has he done to my lamb chops; what is this sauce ** he has drenched my breakfast in?" I asked, knowing no answer could come forward from either Katherine or Holmes.

Later on in the morning, when the rain had eased off somewhat allowing the sun to make an anaemic appearance, I climbed the steps to the top of the tower of the hotel in order, out of interest, to survey the surrounding countryside. Despite inclement weather, this was a popular area for hiking and persons could often be seen tramping around the hills, seemingly walking without direction.

This was the case when I looked out from the tower. Upon focusing in on them, I realised that two of the figures were the Jesuit priests, with their black cassocks flapping around in the wind and very distinctive against the green grass. In a different direction, the Pinkerton agents in their white ankle-length coats, looking out of place, were combing the hills as if looking for someone. Just then, out of the corner of my eye, I saw a figure darting across an open stretch of grass. It was Holmes! I then descended the steps to meet Katherine and, eventually, Holmes for luncheon at noon. Since breakfast had not been successful, I hoped this meal would be, for I now had quite a keen appetite.

Luncheon was a fiasco to the extent that I cannot bring myself to chronicle the experience, save to say that I am starving and uncertain as to what precisely we are doing in this hotel, and for how long is it our intention to stay? The parties booked into Meiringen were not here 'to take the waters', that much was certain to me. They all appeared to be manoeuvring around waiting for their avowed wish, the opportunity to 'incommode' Moriarty. It was more reminiscent of musical chairs, but with a touch of the farce, especially given the setting of the Swiss town of Meiringen.

Whilst we were all walking, in between showers of rain, Holmes, for no apparent reason, asked, "When do you expect to go back to your United States?"

"Why, that is so very charming of you to ask, Sherlock," replied Katherine. "I may call you Sherlock, mayn't I? I will go back to America when I choose to do so, is that not the case, John?"

"Such a facile question from Holmes is not worthy of your consideration," I assured her.

We walked for some miles, then turned and headed home as the sky was beginning to darken, heralding yet more rain. We just made it to a large chalet not far from the hotel and decided to take afternoon tea there. So had the Jesuits and the Pinkerton agents, in addition to Moriarty and his group. We found a table and I immediately searched the menu for something edible. The best I could find was pickled walnuts, sauerkraut and black rye bread. The drinks tariff was even worse. I looked around to see what others were drinking for inspiration and got none. I noticed the Jesuits took sweet sherry, whilst Katherine, Holmes and myself had to make do with neat Vodka without so much as aërated water. The Pinkerton agents were struggling with some indifferent, warm lager-beer. I could not quite hear what Moriarty and his henchmen had ordered, but it sounded like tea with a diffusion of milk.

After some considerable time, Moriarty got up to leave and, in so doing prompted everybody else to do the same, causing an undignified struggle at the doorway leading out of the chalet. We left some time later and retired to our hotel rooms.

I decided to forego dinner as a predictable waste of time, and instead went for an evening walk with Katherine now that the skies were slightly clearer if doom-laden, with streaks of speckled red. We talked of Chicago and of the Hanker Fänners' avowed intention to batter Holmes and myself to death on board that Empire State Express. Katherine described Eureka Springs in the Ozark Mountains near the Oklahoma Territory, and how much she loved the people there and the town itself.

"You should go out there and see for yourself, John."

"I shall go there!" I replied, earnestly.

"You know, John, according to this handbill I picked up from the hotel foyer, there is a small concert being got up this evening in the Pump Room, whatever that is. The music features Haydn's String Quartet in G major, Op. 77 No. 1, and Mozart's String Quartet in B flat Major."

Having alerted Holmes to this programme and changed into evening dress, we all three took our seats in the Pump Room, a modestly designed concert hall with classical pretensions. The music was performed to a decent level but not to the standard one expects at the Wigmore Hall in London. It was not the music that occupied our attention, however, but rather certain members of the audience.

The Jesuits were in attendance and appeared enthralled by the serenity and ethereal sonority of the music, almost as though in a trance. Whereas the Pinkerton agents, in their ill-fitting dinner suits, kept looking at their steel pocket watches, uncertain how long this recital would last, or indeed if they could cope with it. Moriarty also looked as if in deep communication with the music. His being a Professor of Mathematics could, I reasoned, afford him such ability.

The interval came and people made for the crush bar, where the language was surprisingly genteel: "Oh please do let me help you," I overheard one of the Pinkerton agents say, and the other went out of his way with, "Please do have my seat, no, no, I insist." Even Moriarty was heard saying, "Please, after you Sir."

The second half of the concert was a qualified success, after which we repaired to the hotel Salon and to the bar. The usual regulars were in attendance having a late evening drink.

The next morning I rose early and went for a stroll around Meiringen. I did have an ulterior motive of looking for a telegraph office from which I could send a cable telegram regarding a race I was interested in backing. I did find such an office and scribbled out a note for the clerk to transcribe.

...MRS HUDSON - STOP - ...EIGHT SHILLINGS EACH WAY ON RASPER - EPSOM AT FOUR - WATSON ....STOP.

On my way back to the hotel, the skies looked ominous and red, almost menacing, but still the rain did not come. Once inside, I made for the breakfast room and joined Katherine. Holmes eventually deigned to join us too. We chatted about the race to be run at Epsom that day and my stake in it, and what appalling weather we were enduring. After breakfast we made ourselves comfortable in the hotel reading room, catching up on the news and generally relaxing.

I suggested a walk whilst the rain held off, and perhaps tea in the Pump Room. We all agreed and so we walked for some considerable distance before we decided to turn around and take tea. On entering the Pump Room, we saw Moriarty who, to my surprise, came up to Holmes, though without his henchmen. I immediately grabbed my cane and motioned Katherine behind me, expecting as I did something untoward about to erupt.

Instead Moriarty merely looked at Holmes and then said something to him. I could not hear what was said, but Holmes replied. A few moments later both turned and departed. It was Katherine who broke the silence when we received our refreshing tea and biscuits.

"Well, Holmes, do have some tea; and how do you take

your milk, a concoction or a diffusion, and what did that Moriarty want?"

"I merely advised Moriarty that his life was in danger, certainly here at the Reichenbach Falls, but in fact anywhere. He agreed, and thanked me for my observation. In addition, I mentioned that he had caused to have opened the 'Vault of Madness', for which the consequences will be for him to deal with. He also acknowledged that. We then, as you saw, departed each other's company, I walking away from Moriarty."

After tea, we decided to continue our walks again while the rain held off. Katherine elected not to come with us, but instead to make her way back to the hotel on the pretence of a headache. Holmes and I set off into the dull, overcast day and headed instinctively toward the crevasse in the mountainside that is home to the Reichenbach Falls, which comprise three distinct waterfalls. The first, Lower Fall, is but ten minutes up the chasm and the second, the Central or Kessel Fall is fifteen minutes into the gorge. The Upper Fall is still higher and takes about thirty minutes to reach.

Whilst we were making our way along the narrow pathway at the side of which was a steep drop into the swirling waters beneath, I was aware of other figures slipping in and out of view between crags and scrub bushes. We eventually reached the highest of the falls, the Upper Fall. Undoubtedly the view and experience were impressive, though it was without doubt an extremely dangerous place to be. The water, having travelled at speed down the mountain, hits a jagged shelf that shoots it into a cascade away from the mountainside and into the air, from whence it then drops, pounding onto the rocks below.

The power of the water hitting those black rocks below causes a spray to come rising up like smoke from an eternal abyss. Indeed to fall into that chasm would ensure a certain, if terrifying, death. The place was steeped in danger, not only from the chasm, but also from rocks intermittently rolling down the hill and bouncing off the pathway and into the abyss and oblivion. Not for the first time did a boulder come bounding down from the hillside above us missing Holmes and myself by only a few feet. And, though I knew such occurrences were usual, it did little to decrease my sense of insecurity.

We decided to retrace our footsteps along the narrow path from whence we had come and back through the Kessel Fall. Our attention was focused on the pathway in front of the adjacent chasm, whilst also keeping a careful vigil on the hillside for falling rocks. While we walked, I noticed the two Jesuit priests with their cassocks flapping in the wind. Not only they, but the Pinkerton agents too, had decided on an outing to the falls. It came as no surprise, however, to see Inspector Hopkins farther down the chasm, obviously in search of Holmes and myself, as his frantic arm waving at us so indicated.

Also of no surprise to me was the sight of Moriarty taking his afternoon constitution, flanked by his henchmen in top hats and capes, progressing towards us along the same path. A slight anxiety griped my heart at the prospect of being within inches of that loathsome creature, and the consequent opportunity to push him over the edge and thereby do society a favour and risk the verdict of the jury at a subsequent trial for his murder. We continued to where the Kessel Fall is at it's most awesome and terrifying, mingling the constant spray of water with the thunderous sound of the water pounding mercilessly against the rocks in the abyss below.

Then it happened! In full view of Holmes, the Jesuits, Hopkins, the Pinkerton agents and myself, a sizeable boulder came rumbling down the hillside, out of sight from Moriarty, but in full view of the others in the locality. The boulder continued hurtling down, then crashed noisily onto a rock sticking out from the hill and bounced out just above a now-alerted Moriarty, who turned to face the boulder falling towards him. Everything stopped and then, as if in slow motion, I saw with my bulging eyes the rock strike Moriarty. He appeared to grab the boulder in a death struggle, which was yet a desperate attempt to hang on to the rock for life. With a sickening grimace upon his face, Moriarty, whilst still holding the boulder, disappeared over the edge into the abyss that is the Kessel Fall, from which there can be no escape from certain death! We all stood there stunned, looking into space in utter disbelief.

Then, gradually galvanised into action, some of us went to where Moriarty had stood; others, including myself, bounded up the hill to the position from whence the boulder had come. The place was deserted, so we commenced our journey down to where Hopkins was peering into the abyss into which Moriarty had fallen. Suddenly, my eye caught something the colour of which was at variance with the surrounding green grass and moss. It was an object I recognised! I knelt down to feign re-tying my bootlace and surreptitiously picked it up and secreted it about my person. I joined the others at the edge of the abyss, where the Jesuits were on their knees offering prayers for the soul of the recently departed. The gentlemen in capes and top hats were nowhere to be seen, their services perforce no longer required.

I went up to Hopkins and said, "Good God Hopkins! Did you witness that?"

"Yes, Doctor, I did," he replied, visibly stunned by what he had seen. Indeed we were all in a state of anxiety over what we had witnessed.

"You are representing the government, I suppose."

"No Doctor, representing Scotland Yard."

I accompanied Hopkins back to the hotel as Holmes returned with the Jesuits.

It was a pensive crowd that returned to the *Englishcher Hof* late that afternoon and, whether it was the unsettling experience or just a thirst developed from the walk, I could not say, but we all instinctively repaired to the Salon and to the bar. A few minutes later Katherine joined us, looking particularly fresh, as if she had been just recently walking. I then remembered that, of course, her being from Eureka Springs meant that she has always had a healthy complexion. It must be, I concluded, all that walking and country air that they are used to.

* Rösti

** Sauce Bernaise

Chapter 18

The Reckoning of Eternity

It was to a clammy and fog-bound Victoria Station that we arrived from our sojourn in Switzerland. I would always prefer our Empire and London, even in fog, to European countries, which hold very little appeal for me. We made our way outside into Terminus Place and managed to secure a vacant Brougham carriage.

"221b Baker Street," instructed Holmes.

Having arrived at Baker Street exhausted, we entered our drawing room and collapsed into chairs. Presently, Mrs Hudson came in and inquired of us did we like refreshment, "a pot of tea and bloater *paté* sandwiches?"

Katherine and Mrs Hudson appeared to have become soul mates, brought together no doubt through their mutual animosity towards Holmes.

"No, Mrs Hudson, we are fine," said Holmes, closing the door firmly on her whilst I opened a bottle of whisky and started to fill the expectant glasses I had handed out to the assembled group.

"I suppose you will probably want the 'Coca-Cola' in your whisky, Watson," said Holmes.

"Do not be facetious, Holmes, it neither becomes you, nor is it relevant. As you know the Coca-Cola is an American drink; I could not possibly have it in my whisky here in

London. What would Mrs Hudson think?" I interjected.

What was of more immediate concern was, I noted, that Mrs Hudson's 'Bloater Delight', as she termed it, had miraculously now transmuted into a fish based '*paté*', and by what manner of progression of metamorphosis I had neither desire to explore nor experience.

Presently, a knock was heard at our door and in walked Sir James Walter of the British Admiralty, followed by Stanley Hopkins from Scotland Yard, who closed our drawing room door and pulled back the *portière* door curtain in his attempt to keep our conversation confidential.

We all of us seated ourselves on chairs ranged around the drawing room.

"Well Holmes, what have you discovered? The Inspector here has advised me of the good news regarding Moriarty. Please tell me now that this saga is at an end, and that there will be no further outrages."

"Gentlemen," said Holmes, "there is in existence a new 'Napoleon of Crime', whose actions in the annals of criminality surpass even those of Moriarty's!"

"Good God Holmes – who?" demanded Sir James, visibly disturbed by such a revelation.

"His name is Adam Worth and he has quite a chequered history, but remains a more daunting an adversary than Moriarty ever was, and has very little regard for life. Allow me to inform you of a few illuminating, if disturbing, facts about this individual.

"Worth organised a robbery in the vault of a bank in Boston, Massachusetts, some years ago by tunnelling in from a neighbouring shop. The bank, on being robbed, alerted the Pinkerton Detective Agency, which tracked Worth and the shipment of trunks in which the stolen gold bullion was kept, to New York. Worth then left New York aboard the '*Olympic*' arriving at Liverpool, where he assumed the alias of a financier called Henry Judson Raymond.

"Worth then moved to London, where he took rooms in Mayfair and, with associates from New York, formed his own criminal gang. At this stage he probably had an encounter with Moriarty and a power struggle ensued, with Worth coming out the victor. He then employed Moriarty, as a 'tool of convenience' to administer their combined criminal empire. Accordingly, Worth, through Moriarty, organised major robberies and burglaries using a series of subordinates, none of whom ever knew Worth personally, or indeed even his name. His skill here was to detach himself from any potentially incriminating evidence, accept in one singular case.

"We know that Worth was personally responsible for the theft of the painting of the Duchess of Devonshire by Gainsborough in a daring raid on the London gallery of Agnew & Sons in Bond Street. His confederates in the crime later grew impatient with Worth's reluctance to fence the painting for money, from which they expected their share. In retaliation, Worth fired one and sent the other back to the United States where, on trying to rob the Union Trust Company Bank, he was arrested. The criminal later confessed to his and Worth's role in the theft of the painting to the Pinkerton Detective Agency, which in turn alerted Scotland Yard, but they in turn were still unable to prove anything against Worth.

"Worth was very much attached to the painting, keeping it with him, at risk, on his various travels whilst organising new schemes and robberies, one of which was perpetrated in South Africa. There, he stole a valuable quantity of uncut diamonds that he proceeded to sell through a firm he founded in London called Wynert & Co. The company sold the diamonds cheaper than its competitors could ever do, since Worth had paid nothing for them! As to the painting of the Duchess, it is believed that he eventually sent it to Chicago, where after some time the owner of the White Star Line, JP Morgan, purchased it. It is certainly a fake though, as the original never left these shores and is in London," said Holmes.

"The audacity of this scoundrel is contemptible, though one must credit his nerve," remarked Sir James.

"Worth, having established himself in London," continued Holmes, "as a respectable financier using his London alias of Henry Judson Raymond, returned to America, leaving Moriarty as his lieutenant in charge.

"Whilst in America, Worth meets up with the banker, Jay Gould and together they manipulate Rail Road stock and attempt hostile bids in order to gain control of profitable companies. Companies owned by such Titans as Vanderbilt, Rockefeller and Carnegie. So here we see a criminal in the making, aiming high, with no lack of confidence and with fear of no one.

"The catalyst came when Worth met JP Morgan. Whatever they got up to, one thing is for certain, they would have discussed Morgan's continuing concern about the effect the White Star Line and its '*Olympic*' ship was having on his International Mercantile & Marine combine. The plot to remove this cumbersome piece of redundant capital equipment called the '*Olympic*', by whatever means necessary, would not have presented a problem for Worth, according to Carnegie. What did he say when we were in the Duquesne Club at dinner? Something along the lines of:

"'…we can make or break Presidents, indeed, the real decisions are made here in the mansions on Highland Avenue and Fifth Avenue here in Pittsburgh or during poker games to which only important Titans of industry are invited. The '*Titanic*' was, as it were, a pawn in a poker game.'

"That plot began to take shape in conjunction with another development to make money, that of the World's Columbian Exposition in Chicago. Worth conceived a plan of startling proportions. The first part of the plan was based on the Titans' desire to acquire art. As we have seen most Titans salve their conscience by buying art as a reflection of their perceived established status.

"Morgan's Library is a classic example of this psychotic trait, as is Carnegie and his Libraries, even more so. Can you really imagine Morgan sitting down in his Library one evening and reading the first edition, he possesses, of Charles Dickens' 'Little Dorrit'? The more art they possess, and they adore possessions as a reflection of their success, the better they feel as reaction to their dubious origins in their remorseless conquest of wealth. In this respect the acquisition of art lends, as it were, verisimilitude to their existence. This desire for recognition and acceptance as *connoisseur* is alas their weakness, their Achilles' heal and Worth capitalised precisely on that one fact.

"To execute his plan Worth prevailed upon Moriarty to use his contacts in the art world to organise an exhibition of English and some European paintings – new and old, modern and classical. All to be exhibited in the Transportation Building that Worth commissioned to be built with funds from Gould's company," said Holmes.

"Ah," said Katherine, "when we spoke with the architect Sullivan about the design and *use* of the Transportation Building, both John and I noticed that the hall was not designed to receive paintings. The layout and reflected daylight would have precluded such a function. The hall was very definitely designed with an ulterior purpose in mind."

"That much is true," remarked Holmes, in his first admission that Katherine might be correct in her observations.

"Our discussions with Vanderbilt, Morgan and Carnegie," continued Holmes, "indicated to me that a new *eminence grise* was in the background, instilling fear into all that came before him, including Moriarty and Morgan, both of whom had grown to fear him.

"Moriarty was in fear of his life, as I discussed briefly with him at Reichenbach, and he thanked me for my advice, despite knowing it to be too late. Moriarty was frightened of Worth and not of me, hence his rapid flight from Fonthill Abbey. Morgan, too, was a man petrified of being done away with. Remember the incident of the assassin who shot Morgan twice at his retreat at Glen Cove on Long Island, New York. No, Worth, having consolidated his criminal empire, was now in the business of removing all traces of its inception and all persons who had assisted him and could therefore identify him," so Holmes informed us.

"That would explain the arrogant behaviour of the butler when we paid Morgan a visit in New York?" I offered.

We all paused to consider what was being laid before us. Was there indeed a new Napoleon of crime more daring and more lethal than Moriarty? I shuddered to think. Notwithstanding this new concern, I replenished our guests' drinks, thinking we could probably use their beneficial effects. Even Sir James held out his empty glass for a refill of whisky and asked, "Could I possibly have the 'Coca~Cola' in my whisky too please?"

Holmes broke the stunned silence and said, "This is merely the overture. We have yet to experience the grand opera, as it were."

The basic plot was as simple as it is ingenious: to collect valuable art work from around England and Europe under the pretence of exhibiting it at the World's Columbian Exposition in a building designed deliberately, not as a picture gallery, but as the Transportation Building, housing transport machinery…"

"Because of the eleven-inch-thick concrete floors and the glazed wall structure," interjected Katherine, cutting Holmes off in mid-sentence, "we know that it is a long-standing plan, in which Adam Worth had no intention of exhibiting any paintings from anywhere."

"Which brings us to the point of the actual art work," Holmes said with an air of exasperation, looking sharply at Katherine.

"Ah Holmes, you need not entertain any fears or concerns there. The paintings are secured in the Naval Provost Yard at the Admiralty, under the guard of the Royal Navy," interrupted Sir James.

Holmes continued. "Moriarty, acting as Worth's lieutenant and under his strict orders, organises the collection of original works of art submitted by willing patrons, such as the Royal Academy, private collections and the National Portrait Gallery. These paintings were copied in order to create outstanding-quality fakes of original works of art. They were then put through the good offices of Christie & Manson Auction Rooms in St James' Square to be forwarded for shipment on the ill-fated 'Titanic'. The crucial characters lurking in the background to facilitate this endeavour were Arthur Staunton, John Clay, Lyon and the arch-fence and violin virtuoso, Charles Peace.

"We know that Lyon and Peace, not above cheating their paymaster, perpetrated a deception on Moriarty, unaware of his connection with Worth, the existence of whom they could not have known about."

"When you say cheat, Holmes, what precisely do you mean?" inquired Sir James.

"Simply, that it was Lyon's role to collect the original paintings and spirit them away to Moriarty, who in turn would send them on to Worth in America. What Lyon did, in conjunction with Charles Peace, was to have two fakes created. One produced by Arthur Staunton and the other by John Clay. One fake was scheduled for the Exhibition in Chicago via the

'*Titanic*', the other to be sent to Moriarty and onward to Worth instead of the originals. The original paintings were secreted in the mezzanine floor at No. 2 Harley Street."

"Go on," said Sir James.

"This ambitious plan by Lyon and Charles Peace failed because, as we know, Lyon was done away with in the same manner as Cadogan West, with strychnine poison administered through his fingers. We can be confident Moriarty was behind this killing, albeit at the instruction of Worth, who had discovered the fakes landed on him and who, at best, would brook no dissent or insubordination from members of his criminal fraternity."

"What is instructive, Holmes, is why did Peace make an effort to persuade you to go to Harley Street to investigate Lyon's death. Surely he was inviting his hoard of paintings to be discovered, as indeed it was, through my careful observation of the scratches on the floor," I said triumphantly, looking at Katherine, who returned a smile to me.

"The idea, Watson, was that Peace was now in fear of his own life, but wanted Moriarty to know that we had been to the house in Harley Street where there was nothing untoward. Peace would then think Moriarty had no further interest in Harley Street where the paintings were stored. He was using me as a foil to fool Moriarty."

"Really?" inquired Katherine.

"It was clearly the talented violin virtuoso Charles Peace's plan to leave the Metropolis, because he knew that Moriarty must suspect him. He feared for his very life because of his treachery, and fully expected to be done away with. What did he say?" said Holmes, referring to his green commonplace book in which he recorded any vital clue or witness remark. "Ah yes, here it is:

'...however, what I think is happening could make life difficult for a lot of us living in London for the foreseeable future! …and that would not suit my plans, since I have no desire to reside at Highgate or Kensal Green in lavender …Highgate or Kensal Green – cemeteries, Mr Holmes, cemeteries!'"

"You suspect Peace to be dead then?" asked Sir James.

"He is dead, of that fact we can at least be certain, hence the art remained in Harley Street undisturbed, and I would not have expected anything less."

"Are you sure, can you be that certain?" I questioned.

"Yes, and also that these killings as brutal reprisals were not in keeping with Moriarty's character, which was intelligent and subtle. What we are witnessing here is Worth's character re-acting with revenge."

"Moriarty sent what he thought was the original art aboard the *'Olympic'* to America for Adam Worth's personal enjoyment. It arrived, but Worth discovered the fakes and eventually revenged himself on Moriarty for that and other reasons. However, in the meantime, Moriarty still went ahead with loading the other fakes onto the *'Titanic'* so, no doubt, the world would learn of the tragic loss to the art world as a result of the catastrophe that overtook the ill-fated vessel."

Sir James, with an ashen face, started in slowly at first, as if trying to marshal his thoughts to answer Holmes' incredible proposition:

"But Holmes, what you are suggesting is incredible and even more monstrous than we thought before! Are you saying that Moriarty sank the wrong boat irrespective of the damaged state of the *'Olympic'* ship? That they effectively sank the perfectly good *'Titanic'* for the wrong reasons?"

"Yes," replied Holmes. "To make Worth think that the *real* original art was lost when the *'Titanic'* went down. Do not forget, the paintings were *seen, amid great publicity, to be loaded into the hold of the 'Titanic', and verified by the insurance clerks!*

How can anyone authenticate the art work now? It is beyond human ingenuity to do so, thanks to Moriarty."

"Good God, Holmes! Are you saying that they *sank* the wrong boat for no reason other than to fool Adam Worth? To deceive him into thinking the real paintings were actually aboard the *'Titanic'* and now of course lost forever and beyond inspection, in addition to depriving Worth of actually possessing the paintings?" asked an incredulous Sir James.

"Yes!" came the decisive answer.

"Did not Moriarty know that the paintings on the *'Olympic'*, destined for Worth, were in fact fakes?" I asked, in my attempt to make sense at least in my mind, which by now was reeling with improbabilities.

"I can not ascertain that fact after Moriarty's demise, but it is unlikely, since Moriarty himself was fooled by Lyon and Peace. It is more likely that Moriarty wished to revenge himself on Worth by depriving him of the works of art alone, by pretending it was sunk with the *'Titanic's'* foundering." replied Holmes.

"I beg all of you, Katherine, Hopkins, not to make public this dreadful fact. As for me, I have no intention of advising the Government of it, who in turn must inform Parliament and that means of course in the long run, the British public, who could never accept this monstrous crime upon the High Seas!"

We all of us tried to take in the enormity of this astounding, if tremendous, revelation.

"Clearly, Morgan knew nothing of the plan," offered Holmes.

"Ah, but Holmes, I remember Carnegie distinctly saying that he understood Morgan was in England at the time, and was booked on the maiden voyage of that *'Titanic'* ship, since he owned the boat, but cancelled at the last minute," I said.

"Possibly, but for any number of legitimate reasons. It is

unlikely that Morgan was going to sanction the sinking of a brand new capital ship of the line on its maiden voyage – for what reason?"

"I do not think Morgan had much of an option," I continued.

"The answers reside," said Holmes, "with both Adam Worth and with Moriarty before his death, for it was their combined malignant intelligence that worked out accurately a series of permutations to achieve their goal. Again, what Carnegie intimated at is instructive; remember he said something to the effect of:

"'…with this arrogance, do you honestly think sinking a boat in the middle of the Atlantic Ocean, fifteen-hundred miles away from these United States, is going to in any way cause anxiety?'"

"Though it seems to me that Moriarty was getting his own back on Worth by substituting the art, knowing his untimely demise was imminent," said Katherine.

"Just what are we talking about here? It seems to me that yet another criminal is free, despite his being implicated in this dreadful affair. And yet he appears more guilty than Moriarty, and definitely has something to answer for." Thus spoke Hopkins from Scotland Yard, who up until now had kept his own counsel.

It was Sir James who asked the question uppermost in the minds of the assembled group of persons.

"Where does this lead us now, and when will this nightmare end? Can we expect this Worth to begin a fresh campaign of atrocities involving ships of the line, or the illegal removal of works of art and people who cross him?"

"There is that to be considered. After all, Adam Worth has been frustrated in his grand design because the art work is still not in his possession and..." said Holmes.

"And never will be as far as I am concerned!" interjected Sir James.

"…something even more startling," continued Holmes, "which may account for why Moriarty met his supreme moment at Worth's hands at Reichenbach."

"Well do enlighten us, Holmes," demanded Katherine.

"Because Moriarty, although instructed to do so by Worth, did not substitute the *'Olympic'* boat for the *'Titanic'*."

"What!" exclaimed Sir James. "Are you now contradicting what we all thought? That the *'Titanic's'* sister ship, the *'Olympic'*, was substituted for the *'Titanic'* and sank in mid-Ocean? The reason being to destroy the damaged ship the *'Olympic'* for insurance, together with the physical removal of evidence of faked art work *en-route* to New York and the World's Columbian Exposition in Chicago? Accordingly, everybody would think a natural disaster at sea had occurred, with unfortunate loss of art as well as life?"

"But this is even worse," I said. "The perfectly good *'Titanic'*, the actual brand-new ship *'Titanic'*, was carrying faked art work destined for the World's Columbian Exposition? But, but this is incredible, why then sink the *'Titanic'* for no reason."

"More reason than you think, Watson. The only person who could have known that the art work sent to America on the *'Olympic'*, for the sole purpose of Worth's private enjoyment, was Moriarty. The *'Titanic'* had to be sunk with the faked art work to demonstrate that the so-called original paintings were sunk and out of circulation and lost forever," imparted Holmes, to his incredulous audience.

"However, Worth thought at the time that the art work sent over to America on the *'Olympic'* constituted the original paintings. That information was imparted by Miss Katherine's fiancé, who was not being threatened by Moriarty in the Crescent Hotel at Eureka Springs, but was done away with by Worth, having served his purpose," said Holmes, with a glint in his eye.

I noticed that quite clearly, and was about to admonish him for such insensitivity to Katherine's feelings, but the enormity of what was unfolding perforce took precedence.

"As far as I am concerned, everyone in this sorry tale appears to be a criminal, or in some way responsible or implicated for crimes both great and small. All of them seem to derive a perverse pleasure in organising the greatest amount of hurt against each other. Why do we not just let them deal with themselves, as they obviously deserve one another. This saga only vaguely makes sense to me after a couple of these," said Inspector Hopkins, rising to refill his glass with whisky.

"Why were the Robber Barons and Industrial Titans considerate and accommodating toward you both in Highland Avenue in Pittsburgh and at Rhode Island?" inquired Sir James.

"Because," I answered, "those Industrial Titans saw in us the ability to remove or at least incommode Moriarty, whom they thought was the *de facto eminence grise*, the harbinger of their woes, their Nemesis and the real foe bent on their destruction. Their manifest fear, they supposed, was his initiating their own *'Titandämmerung'*,* as it were. Little do they know that it is Worth, whose avowed wish is for their financial ruin! As this saga continues, so does Worth's financial and industrial strength increase."

"Thank God I have my faith to sustain me in these troubled times," informed Sir James.

"It is unlikely that the Titans will need our help in dealing with Morgan, acting as he has been for Adam Worth," said Katherine, decisively. "He is, after all, up to his neck in this sordid business and has also been tricked by Moriarty, for he has lost a perfectly good capital ship of the line. The sinking puts him and his beloved International Marine & Mercantile combine in jeopardy. Indeed, its stock value has begun to plummet almost immediately following the recent dismissal of Morgan by his own board for the spurious reasons surrounding the sinking."

"I agree with Katherine. Morgan is no real threat to the Titans, indeed his own collapse can only be imminent," I said

"What did the *New York Times* print some time ago?" asked Katherine.

"'Thoughtless disregard for life we can with equanimity accept, but a reckless disregard for capitalism we certainly cannot.'"

Sir James got up and, after shaking Katherine's hand warmly and then mine, turned to Holmes and said, "I remain perturbed by these events. It seems to me that we have substituted one venal individual for an even more vituperative criminal and, from all the accounts we have heard, an infinitely worse one. What can we expect from Worth, this, this 'Napoleon of Crime', what is he likely to do, Holmes?" implored Sir James.

There was a pause, and then a reply was formulated, but not one from Holmes.

"He is going to go for the art work," said Katherine, incisively.

"He will soon figure out the *apparent* double deception by the late Professor Moriarty, and the role of the boats," I said. "If we conclude the real reason for the fate of the '*Titanic*', then do you suppose Worth will not. He will realise the original art work is somewhere and, as Katherine has suggested, he will search for it."

Sir James regained his chair, sat down upon it again, and thought long and hard. At length, with the determination of one who has made up his mind, he said directly to Holmes, "What was the *status quo* regarding the art before this nightmare took real form?"

"It was owned by various people and organisations, not least the Jesuit College, and surely the correct and noble act would be to return the art work to them," answered Katherine.

"Quite right, Katherine, quite right. That is exactly what I intend to do. Worth will be in exactly the same situation as before and the art will be beyond him," said Sir James triumphantly.

Holmes looked visibly disturbed and rather annoyed at being robbed by Katherine of the opportunity of being able to suggest such noble a solution.

"I will speak with the Naval Provost and, through his office, arrange to have the art work returned to the rightful owner under navel guard," Sir James said.

"Some are going to be unpleasantly surprised when they learn of the fraud and loss perpetrated against them, but beyond measure relieved that the originals are to be returned to their keeping again," I said.

And with that remark, I escorted our distinguished visitor in the person of Sir James Walter down to his waiting Barouche. Sitting high on the bench was the liveried driver who had taken us on that mad dash to Paddington Station some days past.

"Evening, Doctor," he said touching his top hat with his whip.

I bade my farewells to Sir James as his Barouche swerved into Baker Street. By comparison, Inspector Hopkins, who had followed us out, staggered into a sturdy police wagon with bars on the window.

I ascended the stairs to our drawing room to rejoin Katherine and my drink. I confess to feeling severely tried mentally with the facts that had been laid before us. Holmes had gone off to his room, leaving Katherine and myself to reminisce over the astounding facts and actions we had recently experienced together. Whether it was the enormity of the startling facts we had heard or the whisky I could not be certain, but moments later I slipped off into a reverie.

"John! John!" said Katherine.

"Oh! Forgive me, I was just thinking."

"Thinking, about what?"

"I was thinking about Holst's music from the *Planets Suite*' and his treatment of the planets, in particular the one called Uranus, that has haunted me these last few days."

Katherine looked at me and very deliberately and slowly said, "Yes, John, what have you concluded?"

"Uranus, of course, is a Titan, as in the *'Titanic'* and the industrial and financial Titans we have been dealing with. This Titan Uranus is the son of Kronos and Rhea, who were from the race of Titans and who waged war on the classical Greek gods, and it is Uranus that features in Holst's *'Planets Suite'*. Likewise we have just witnessed the Titans of today doing battle with each other! " I said to Katherine, with evident delight in my voice.

Katherine thought for a moment and then said, "I have read so much about this London, this Metropolis, mighty and vast, that lies about us. I want to explore it in detail and in the sunlight. I should like to attend the Opera at Covent Garden. Ride in Brougham carriages, drawn by a four-in-hand in the Hyde Park with other ladies of refinement, just like me. Even ride in one of those new-fangled 'horse-less' carriages one sees now that is now all the rage. What I really want to do is experience riding a Rudge-Whitworth two-wheeler velocipede. Especially one with the new, improved, patented Dunlop pneumatic, vulcanised rubber tyres fitted to its metal wheel rims, allowing this *bi-cycle* to achieve smoothly, unimaginable speeds in excess of eight miles in a continuous period of one hour. Imagine that sensation!

"I would enjoy catching salmon from the River Thames at Charing Cross, go horse riding on Hampstead Heath, or see the new Tower Bridge in action and take afternoon tea in hotels. I could very happily experience great orchestras performing powerful, sonorous music in the various concert halls. Especially in that Royal Albert Hall of Arts and Sciences, and promenade around the upper sections of the auditorium, whilst sensuous music is being played. Hit the museums, the picture galleries, if there is any art left in London to look at, and music halls. Especially, the Hungerford Music Hall below Charing Cross Station which, according to the advertisements I have seen, seems to be a very entertaining and uplifting establishment."

"All this will but take months to do."

"Well John, have you anything better to do than show me around?" so asked Katherine, who *was* from Eureka Springs.

* Twilight of the Titan